THE WEIGHT OF GUILT

JON RIPSLINGER

RedAdept
Publishing
Unlocking New Worlds

Like the others, this book is dedicated to the love and light
of my life, my wife—Mary Colette Shannon Ripslinger. We
still have a lot of good times to come, Colette. Trust me.

ONE

JOHN HAWK

RILEY'S DRUNK, AND IT'S ALL my fault. Swaying near the blazing bonfire with a dozen other kids, she's guzzling beer from a red Solo cup. They laugh, jostle, and slop beer over themselves.

Damn! I should have been paying more attention to her. I should have kept better track of time. *You idiot, John!* I need to get her home and tuck her into bed—*now*—or we'll both be in deep crap. I step up behind her in the brilliant firelight. The heat feels good on my face and arms, but the smoke curls into my nostrils, and I cough. Someone must have piled wet logs onto the blaze.

I touch Riley's shoulder. "We better go."

She whirls. "Where have you been?"

"Checking out Brian's weightlifting equipment. I forgot the time. Sorry."

Flames leap and crackle into the crisp night air, casting flickering shadows across Riley's face. Her eyes glitter like stars in the inferno. A few kids rotate, trying to keep all sides warm. Earlier, we roasted hot dogs, bratwurst, and marshmallows over the oak blaze.

"What time is it?" she asks, her words slurred a little.

"Midnight." I'd promised her folks I'd have her home already. I don't need them yelling at me again. Or breaking us up. That thought jars me. I'd rather lose an arm and a leg than lose Riley. She's the only thing good in my life, except wrestling.

"They never come home before two or three," she says and gulps her beer.

"Let's throw that away. You've had enough to drink."

She smiles, her mouth crooked. "Look who's talking."

"I haven't had a sip." True statement. I never drink the night before a wrestling tournament. I dump Riley's beer but hang on to the cup—I don't litter. I also help little old ladies cross the street. "I can do without your folks being pissed at me. They already don't trust me."

"Yes, they do." Riley grabs my free hand and squeezes.

After planting a kiss on her forehead, I say, "C'mon, pretty lady. Home we go." I guide her by the elbow away from the fire.

The party was a spring break bash at Brian Holdorf's parents' farm pond. Dense woods block out half the sky, and a breeze ripples the treetops. My arm around her waist, I guide Riley across the pasture to my car, which is parked by the farmhouse. A squatty barn and a tall silo loom close by. Brilliant stars and a huge moon light our way. Laughter drifts up from the pond, and the scent of pigs floats in the air.

Opening the car's passenger door, I toss Riley's cup in the back. Then I slip her into the seat and close the door. After I climb in, I close my door and poke the lock button to make sure we're secured. "Buckle up."

Rather than take Interstate 80, I drive a ribbon of country blacktop that twists through hilly farmland. I think I can drive the blacktop faster than the highway—hardly any traffic and less chance of the cops picking me up for speeding. I don't need another face-off with them.

"I'll bet my parents aren't home," Riley says after we've been on the road a minute or two. She leans over and kisses my cheek. "Let's park somewhere. This road's dark." Her hair smells of wood smoke, her breath of stale beer.

I smile. I wouldn't mind parking for an hour or so and making out. "We need to get you home and into bed."

Wisps of fog curl in my headlights. I'm zooming downhill toward the Des Moines River, and the curtain of fog thickens quickly. I cut my speed from seventy to fifty, then to thirty. I don't want to be going too fast if a deer darts into the road. Fifteen…

The fog turns dense—a gray, billowing wall that reflects the glow of my headlights back into my eyes. I squint and dim the car lights. I swallow and slow the vehicle to a crawl: ten miles per hour. I glue my eyes to the yellow center line and guide the car's left fender along the line.

"Why are you slowing down?" Riley asks.

"Can't you see how soupy it is out there?"

I'm not sure when I cross the bridge over the river. The fog is too thick to see even the side rails. But when I head uphill, my grip on the wheel eases. I fill my lungs and exhale slowly. I've escaped the danger. The moment I can see ahead of me though—still going ten miles an hour—I spot headlights racing toward me. They blind me. I barely have time to swear.

This can't be!

Even Riley sees the headlights. She screams, and the next sound is the wail of my horn and the hideous grinding shriek of brakes as I try to swerve and evade the headlights.

TWO

CHARLOTTE COTTON

J OHN *HAWK!* THE NEW GUY in school is nothing but trouble. I can feel it. Even his name gives me shivers. *Hawk. A bird of prey.* The minute Megan mentions his name, I know she'll find herself in a jam because of him. When it comes to guys, she never makes smart decisions.

She says, "You cannot *believe* what a hottie he is. From Des Moines. Just arrived."

We're standing by Megan's locker at River Valley High. It's January, the first day of our last semester of high school. First period starts in five minutes, so she's hurling books into her locker and dragging out others. Hundreds of kids stampede by, the chatter and locker-door slamming deafening.

"Every new guy you meet is a hunk," I say and shift my books in my arms.

"I was in the weight room early this morning lifting," Megan says, bubbling with excitement. Since she had her stomach pumped, Megan's been on this health kick—running, lifting weights, eating right, and staying off the booze. "So was he. I strolled up and introduced myself—I couldn't help it. He's a senior. Like us."

"Got your World Cultures book? You need your chemistry book too."

"He's going to finish his final semester here. When I talked to him, he was barbell-powerlifting. All rippling muscles and gleaming sweat."

"Good for him."

"My God, you should've seen him. I'm telling you, John Hawk rocks!"

"We're going to be late," I say.

"He's got this jagged scar on his left cheek that makes him look mysterious. I'm sure he doesn't have a girlfriend here. He doesn't know anyone yet. He's your perfect chance. Hit on him."

My eyebrows bunch up. That Megan would offer me first shot at a new guy surprises me. "What? You're giving him to me as what, a pity present? No, thanks."

"I've got enough on my plate—and Cole's convenient. I think we can last at least until the prom. Maybe till we graduate. Then he's history."

"I'd dump him now. He's a scum-sucker. Your chemistry book."

Megan throws her American Lit book back into the bottom of her locker and grabs her chemistry book from the shelf. "Go after John Hawk, Charley. You can do it! Add some spice to your last semester of high school."

"I'm not you. I can't snare guys. I don't have the equipment."

Megan Jones can snag any guy she wants. She's a spider, and they're flies. Long midnight-black hair, mysterious-looking olive-shaped dark eyes, perfect body—that's the stuff her silky web is made from. Her mom is part Filipino—thus the eyes and hair. Me, I'm not so lucky: barely five foot, skinny, freckles, A-cups that make me almost boobless. And I'm going to be eighteen in a month. How disappointing. Disgusting, even.

Megan stacks her books in her right arm. "You have what you *think* you have. It's all in your mind. You're a fox, and you don't even know it. Don't be a wuss." Peering into the mirror stuck to the inside of her locker door, she runs her tongue around her red lips and fluffs her hair.

"I know *exactly* what I have and don't have."

"You look great." Megan slams her locker door and spins the dial on her lock. She turns and smiles at me. "That curly auburn hair and killer green eyes? Think positive." She glances at the hall clock. "We better jet!"

John Hawk is in my seventh-period American lit class. Though he sits close by, I wouldn't have paid much attention to him if Megan hadn't mentioned him. *Oh my!* He is hot for sure: reddish-brown hair like the tail of a red-tailed hawk, built. He's very quiet. He never volunteers to answer questions, but when called upon, he always knows what he's talking about.

Over the next few weeks, Megan keeps telling me I should wait in the hall for him, walk into the classroom with him, and say something like, "Hi. Did you understand that story we read for today?" She wants me to flirt with him and bat my eyelashes, but I can't make myself do it. My knees shake every time I think about it.

Besides, I never see him gabbing with anyone. He just slips into the classroom, eases into his seat, and keeps to himself. I get the impression he wants to be left alone. He's hiding. Probably keeping some dark secret buried inside himself.

Megan says the scar on his cheek makes him look mysterious. I think it makes him look sinister. Still, he's—well, smokin' hot. My heart pinballs whenever I picture him clutching me, my arms flung around his neck, and his lips smashed against mine, like on the cover of a steamy romance novel. As if that would ever happen. Besides, I'm convinced John Hawk's a guy a girl should stay away from. He's probably carrying enough baggage for a lifetime.

Then one March afternoon, Megan is driving me home from school because my truck isn't running. We spot John walking on the sidewalk on the opposite side of the street.

"That's him!" Megan cries.

"Don't get excited."

She veers her red Mustang across the street and stops alongside him. She punches the button to lower her window and sticks out her head. "Want a ride? You're going to freeze your buns off!"

He halts. He's wearing a denim jacket, hands stuffed into his front pockets. No hat. He bends a little, squints, recognizes Megan, and smiles. "You're going to get yours *knocked* off. You're on the wrong side of the street."

All the while this is happening, I'm scrunching down in my seat.

"Your car break down?" Megan asks.

He shakes his head. "Just walking."

"Hurry up, get in! I'll give you a ride." Then she says, "My friend Charley Cotton is dying to meet you."

I gasp. *This girl is crazy!* But I've known that for years.

"Where are you going? Get in!" Megan insists.

"No, thanks!"

Megan shrugs. "You don't know what you're missing! Charley Cotton's hot!"

Crap! I roll my eyes. I'm ready to pull Megan's hair out by the roots.

She guns the engine, cuts across to the proper side of the street, zips by an oncoming car, and speeds away. "Damn, he's stubborn!"

"Why did you say that about me? I'm not dying to meet him! I'm not hot!"

"Sorry," she says and chews her bottom lip. "He is a specimen though, isn't he?" She glances at me. "Well, isn't he?"

I shrug. "He's all right." I spy a familiar glint in Megan's eyes. *The lusty one.*

Megan loves the challenge of meeting a new male. Her on-again, off-again relationship with her scum-sucking boyfriend, Cole Wainwright, has been crumbling fast. They've been fighting more than usual. I get an eerie feeling Megan's going to spin a web for John Hawk.

"Look," I tell her, "this guy might be trouble."

"You don't know that."

"Why does a guy start the last semester of his senior year at a new school unless he screwed up at his old one?"

"His parents moved."

"Why is he walking and not driving? No senior guy walks back and forth to school unless he has to for some reason. How'd he get that ugly scar? A fight? Must've been a bad one."

Megan shakes her head. "I'm going to seriously check out John Hawk. Cole and I are slipping fast."

"Good luck." I mutter, "You're going to need it."

THREE

JOHN HAWK

I N April, when the weather turns balmy, I ride my ten-speed to school.

I live with my sister, Anne, and her four-year-old son, Donnie, in River Valley, a little one-high-school town located on the banks of the Mississippi River in eastern Iowa. A drab white bungalow in a neighborhood with lots of other shabby-looking houses, Anne's place is about three miles from River Valley High. That isn't a bad walk twice a day during the winter, but the distance is hardly worth the effort of biking. So after school, I ride straight out Locust Street, a hilly blacktop leading into the country. After four or five miles, I turn around and come back, making a thirteen- to fifteen-mile trip out of my ride home. I pedal past a Pony League diamond, a small cemetery, cornfields, and a few nice-looking brick homes, their rolling lawns green from the spring sun and rain. There's seldom any traffic, making my ride peaceful.

One afternoon, I pump along under the bluest sky I've seen all spring, and a gentle sun spreads its warmth through my body. A breeze blows in my face. My legs feel strong, my muscles loose. Thinking of nothing, not even of Riley, I keep pedaling.

Dropping out of school in Des Moines and enrolling at River Valley High during the last semester of my senior year was a monster change for me, but it gives me a chance to leave the trouble I created back home and flee my reputation. Thank God I no longer have to listen to my dad yell that I'm as worthless as my mom. No more black roses sent to me in the mail either. Really, my switch from Des Moines to River Valley has given me a chance to hit the restart button.

To breathe again.

To discover my real self.

At age eighteen, maybe a *new* self.

If I stay cool and avoid trouble.

I have no idea another cyclist is following me until a car passes, then the rider pulls up on my left.

"Slow down, will you?" a female calls.

I jerk my head to glance at the cyclist. Megan Jones is pedaling alongside me, breathing hard, sweat running down her face.

"What are you doing?" I yell.

"Riding with you! What does it look like? Slow the hell down!"

I slow down. "How long have you been following me?"

"Forever." She gulps a breath and exhales. "You've been riding by my house all week."

"Your house? Where?"

"On this street—Locust Street."

"Oh."

"This is the first time I've had a chance to hop on my bike and catch you. Sloooooow dooooown!"

"What the hell! I might as well be walking."

"I should've used my car." Megan glances at the road behind her then at me. "Let's turn around."

"Why?"

"So we can go back to my house. Give me a break!"

Five o'clock.

We sit on the top step of her front porch, which runs along the entire front of the house, and drink iced strawberry pop from tall glasses. Megan has already gulped her drink, but I'm taking my time. The sun slipping behind the treetops paints cool shadows across the grass. She lives in one of those nice-looking brick homes on Locust that I've been riding by all month. Red, yellow, and lavender tulips bloom brightly along the drive.

"Sure you don't want a beer instead of pop?" she asks.

She wears cutoff jeans that show off her long, tanned legs and a pink T-shirt that clings to her breasts. Riding has left her flushed. Her tiny diamond earrings wink at me as if they're flirting.

"Thanks. No beer."

After she offered me a ride a month ago, I seemed to see her everywhere in school—halls, cafeteria, gym, and weight room. Whenever she spots me, she waves and flashes a smile—perfect white teeth surrounded by full red lips. But I steer clear of her. A tall rawboned guy with long brown hair and dark, brooding eyes sometimes hangs around her, bugging her and looking hurt and angry. Her always-pissed-off boyfriend, I guess.

"Beer's cold," she says.

"Don't drink."

"Me either. Not anymore. But I can get you one. You probably know my dad's the principal at River Valley High, but he won't be home for an hour or more. My stepmother's working. They won't catch you sucking on a brew."

I tell her again I don't drink and sit straight. That news about her dad being the school principal unnerves me a bit. Principals and I have never gotten along. "Seriously, your dad's the principal?"

"That's right," she says and smiles. "You probably didn't guess because there are so many Joneses in the world. You didn't make the connection."

"I didn't think about it."

"I don't look like him. I look like my mom, but she's dead." Shuddering, Megan adds, "Stephanie, my stepmother, is a witch."

Why is she telling me this?

"How you been getting along?" she asks, sliding a bit closer to me.

"Fine." I set my glass—sort of a barrier—between us on the porch. I mean, I'm sure she's not going to attack me, but I'm not ready to be close to a girl again. Not right now.

"You never say much. Everybody says I can't keep my mouth shut."

Truthfully, I'm glad she's talking a lot—it means I don't have to. "I don't have much I want to talk about." I smooth my jeans over my thighs with my palms. I expect her to tell me people like that are usually hiding something.

Instead she says, "Teachers hate to have me in class. In junior high, they called me Motor-Mouth Megan because I talk too much and too fast. I don't talk quite as much now. You like it here?"

"It's all right."

"You seem so... so different."

"Probably because I'm new."

She leans her elbows back on the porch. "I've spent all spring trying to figure out what you're doing at River Valley High. Nobody knows."

I shift my butt on the hard wooden step so I can see her better. Beautiful, silky-black hair. Dark eyes. A luscious red mouth—heart-shaped. Any guy would die to be with this girl. The thought makes me a little nervous, so I tap my foot. Besides, I don't like anyone poking into my background. "What am I doing here? I'm going to school—like you."

"I mean, why did you come to River Valley in the first place? Charley and I have been trying to guess."

I tilt my head, my lips curving upward. "What's your best guess?"

"That's the first time I've seen you smile. You've got an awesome smile." She narrows her eyes and sizes me up. "Let me see... you're an undercover drug agent like in that *21 Jump Street* movie."

I laugh. Despite all her questioning, I like Megan Jones. "Yeah? Then why aren't I hanging out with the worst druggies at school so I can make a bust?"

"That's exactly what I told Charley. Your being a drug agent doesn't make sense. Besides, our principal's got a tight lid on drugs at school." She sighs. "Nothing exciting ever happens on his watch."

"He's really your dad?"

She nods. "Haven't you been called into his office so he can read you the riot act about self-control and following rules, being a good school citizen?"

"Not yet."

"He's got a million speeches like that. He thinks he's such a great leader, such a great organizer. But he doesn't have his own life together—don't get me started. You know Charley Cotton?"

I think a moment. "Charley Cotton?" I recall the thin girl with frizzy, rust-colored hair in my lit class. "I'm in lit with her. Don't know her personally. She's your friend, isn't she?"

"She was in the car with me when I tried to pick you up a month ago."

"Ah! I remember that."

"She says you're smart. Will you go to the prom with me?"

I stare at Megan Jones. Her eyes lock on mine. *Where* is *this girl coming from?*

"Will you?" she says, sitting up straight.

I frown. "You're crazy. You don't even know me. If you did, you probably wouldn't ask me for a date."

"I don't care why you're at River Valley. So you've got a couple of secrets. So do I." Her face lights up with a huge smile. "We still could have lots of fun."

I shake my head. Fun with a girl hasn't been on my mind in a long while.

"C'mon! I'm not going to bite. I'll bet you've dated lots of girls."

I shift on the step again. *Not since Riley.*

"Haven't you?" Megan insists, lifting her chin.

"Some."

"Well, I'm not going to cling to you, if that's what you're afraid of. As soon as I graduate from high school, I'm out of River Valley and off to college. I hate it here."

That last statement gives me a great chance to steer this conversation in a different direction. "Seems to be a nice, quiet town. How long have you lived here?"

Cheeks puffed, Megan blows out a breath. "All my life. I'm stuck here till I graduate. I'll be eighteen, and then I'm taking off. But I want to have some fun first. What do you say?"

I reach for my glass of pop. I slosh the ice around then knock back a big gulp. I set the glass carefully on the porch. "Bad plan."

"I've never seen you talk to a single person at school. You've got to be freaking bored. One dance won't kill you."

"What about your boyfriend, the guy I see you with sometimes?"

Megan laughs. "Cole Wainwright? Don't worry about him. Our relationship is all but fried."

Maybe one confession will be enough to change her mind about me and make her back off. Leaning toward her, as if I'm going to reveal classified information, I say, "I don't have a driver's license. Or a car."

She nods. "Trouble with the cops?"

"More than once." I wait for her to dismiss me as a prom date.

"I'll drive," she says with a wave. "I won't drag you to any parties before the dance to meet my friends. Nothing like that. Just you and me, one-on-one." She raises an eyebrow and smiles. "All night."

Rubbing my palms on my thighs once again, I glance at my bike leaning against an oak tree in her front yard. A voice in my head whispers, *Grab that bike, John, and ride away into the sunset.*

A guy zips by on a motorcycle and waves. Megan scowls and doesn't wave back. Her attention lands back on me.

"A friend?" I ask.

"No one important," she says. "I won't drag you to the After-Prom Party either. I promise. And you don't have to be afraid of my dad, because he's the principal and anything you do is likely to end up on your permanent record."

"He might have me checked out."

"No, he won't."

"He won't like what he finds."

"What?" Megan cocks her head. "You pulled the smoke alarm at your old school? You're a serial rapist?"

"Not quite."

She leans even closer, her lips right in front of mine. "Just you and me, all evening. Nothing permanent. How about it? The dance is only ten days from now."

My heart jumps. I don't know what the hell to say. I like Megan Jones, the way she comes straight out and says what's on her mind. She looks great, and I'll bet she's fun to be with. But one thing I told myself when I came to live with my sister was that I could stay out of trouble by staying out of sight. Sort of make myself invisible. Dating the principal's daughter will certainly put me in a spotlight—especially if I take her to the prom. Headlines in the school newspaper flash in my brain:

NEW GUY DATES PRINCIPAL'S DAUGHTER; EX-BOYFRIEND PROMISES REVENGE

"Last chance." Megan crosses her arms. "I'm not going to beg anymore." Her wide mouth turns pouty.

I slam my eyes shut for a second. That voice in my head screams, *You'll blow your anonymity. Trouble stalks you. You know that for a fact.* Another voice fires back, *You can't hide forever. You've got to start living again.*

I suck in a deep breath, blow it out, and reach for my pop. I drain the glass, the ice cubes melting against my lips, and hand the glass to Megan. "I don't know. I don't think so." I rub the back of my neck. "Let me think about it, okay?"

She looks into the empty glass then at me. "We don't have much time."

I nod. "I know. Give me a day or two."

"A girl needs time to get ready," she says and sets the glass behind her.

This girl isn't going to give up. "Umm… maybe on one condition."

"What?"

"I don't think so… never mind."

"On what condition?"

Big sigh as if my lungs have developed a slow leak. *Here goes.* "That you don't tell anyone at school ahead of time."

"Is that all?" Megan's eyes light up. "I won't, I swear."

"Forget it," I say, slicing a hand through the air. "It's a bad plan."

"No, it's not!"

"I don't want more kids staring at me, pointing at me, wondering what's up with me."

"It's a deal!" Her face beams. "I won't tell anyone. Not even Charley."

I shake my head again. *Oh, man! Why am I doing this?* "A deal."

I thrust out my hand to shake on it, but Megan leans forward, moistens her lips with her tongue, and kisses me softly. My heart rate jumps, like, a million beats. I haven't been kissed in a long while. Not since Riley.

I stand, smooth out my jeans for a final time, and clear my throat. "I should go."

Megan stands too. "You have a computer? We can email."

"No computer."

"Give me your cell phone number. We'll talk. Text."

I think about lying and telling her I don't have a cell, but instead I surrender the number.

She says, "I'll let you know what I'm going to wear, what time to pick me up."

"I don't drive. Or have a car."

"Right, I forgot that." She nods. "I'll pick *you* up. We have to decide on a place to eat, what we want to do after the dance."

"No big parties, before or after."

"All right. I promise, I told you that."

"What about your boyfriend?"

"I'll take care of him." She squares her shoulders, military style. "I'll take care of everything. Don't worry."

A shiver skips through me. I swallow. This is an unexpected move, a gigantic move. I'm already regretting it, but I can't back down.

"We're good to go." Megan's dark eyes narrow. "Right?"

"Right." Feeling a little shaky, I scoot down the steps and hustle across the lawn to grab my bike. I hop on and pedal away into the late-afternoon sunshine without looking back.

What kind of trouble can I get into dating the principal's daughter? None, probably.

But trouble stalks you, John.

Your life is cursed, remember?

FOUR

CHARLOTTE COTTON

MEGAN SAYS, "WOOHOO, CHARLEY! JOHN HAWK and I are going to the prom. I can't believe it."

"I can."

"But you can't tell anyone. Swear?"

I offer her a wry smile as she plops down across from me. Our table is located in a corner of the noisy, smelly, overcrowded cafeteria. "What are you going to do about Cole?"

"Just swear you won't blab this around, okay?"

"I swear. But what about Cole?"

"You pissed at me?"

I stare at my sloppy joe, french fries, and piece of apple pie and make a face. None of it looks edible, but other kids are eating like hogs slopping at a trough.

"Tell me you're not pissed at me," Megan says.

I sigh. "I knew he was yours the minute you told me about him."

She plunks her elbows on the table, spoon in one hand. All she's got in front of her is a bowl of chili and two cellophane packets of crackers. She eats like a bird. "I think he was happy to make friends with someone. I know he's been lonely, and he seems—I don't know—spooked. Like he's afraid."

I tear open my packet of ketchup with my teeth and squirt it on my plate. "Cole won't like this."

"No point in telling him anything. I'll simply dump him. He'll get over it. He *always* does."

Last year, Megan dumped Cole for a new guy—Tim O'Brien, a kid from Boston with red hair and an eastern accent. His dad had been transferred to the nearby Rock Island Arsenal, a government installation where they make artillery for the Army. Megan's hookup with Tim lasted only three months though. The school board expelled him after a janitor caught him trying to hide a tiny camera in a stall in the girls' bathroom. I think the kid ended up in a military school, no charges filed.

Megan says, "I'm really tired of Cole. I mean, like I told you, I thought we'd last until the end of the school year. But lately he's so moody I can't stand it. His friends are becoming even bigger assholes. Worst of all, he thinks he needs to get laid every night."

"He's a ticking time bomb. Dump him for good and stay out of his life."

The last time she cut Cole loose, he harassed her with threatening phone calls, texts, emails, and notes left in her locker. In gym class, I spotted finger-shaped bruises on her arms where he'd probably grabbed her and shaken the hell out of her. But she wouldn't admit that. She wore long-sleeved blouses for a month.

She stirs her chili with her spoon, takes a taste, and mutters, "Cold."

I dip two french fries in the ketchup and pop them in my mouth. "Cole might get a few of his buddies together and go after John Hawk. Ever think of that?"

"Have you taken a good look at him? He can take care of himself."

"It's you I really worry about."

"Cole is a spineless coward," Megan says and shoves her chili aside. "Everyone knows that. He talks big, makes threats. That's all."

"Cowards are the ones you have to watch. Sometimes they sneak up on you in the dark."

Dismissing my warning with a shake of her head, she says, "I already have a dress. I'm not sure about what kind of shoes I want."

"Spiked heels, of course."

"Probably. My dress is black with a full skirt and sequins and bows and lace. It's off the shoulder. I hope he'll love it."

I dip another french fry. I've seen Megan dressed for a party. Smile, boobs, butt, legs—no guy can take his eyes off her.

"Can't you imagine," she says, "how handsome he'll be all dressed up? How every girl will stare at him and be jealous of me? We'll be awesome together. I'll even bet—"

I shake my head, signaling Megan to shut up, because Cole Wainwright, the supreme scum-sucker of all scum-suckers, is stepping up behind her. *Crap!* He grips her shoulders close to her neck and squeezes.

Wincing and scrunching, Megan knows who it is without turning around. She twists her shoulders out of his grasp and growls through clenched teeth, "Knock it off, Cole!"

"A little love squeeze, baby. We need to talk." Standing aside, he hooks his thumbs in his belt loops. His narrow chin is stubbled with bristly whiskers, and his brown hair hangs down his back in a single braid.

Cole is a weird one. His dad's a banker, so Cole always has plenty of money. I'd expect him to dress like a preppie and hang with the preppies, but he's into Harley Davidsons, black Harley T-shirts, black jeans, black leather jackets and boots, and black studded belts with big silver buckles. Stuff he thinks makes him look tough. I think he looks stupid. I don't know what Megan sees in him, except that he likes to party. She loves to ride on his Harley. Maybe his you-know-what is longer than his ponytail. I doubt it.

"Can't you see I'm eating lunch?" Megan drags her chili bowl back in front of her, pulls out a big spoonful, dumps it into her mouth, and swallows. She still hasn't turned around to look at him.

"Leave her alone," I say.

"Screw you." Cole grins and adds, "You'd like that, wouldn't you, Bones?"

I resist the urge to flip him off. "Bite me!"

He bends close to Megan, his thin lips pressing against her left ear. She scrunches her shoulders again.

"Dwight says he saw you and a guy hanging out on your porch steps yesterday. Saw him when he drove by."

"So what?"

"Said it might be that new guy, that creep who doesn't talk. What's his name? Big Bird? Something like that." Cole smirks. "Tweety Bird? Monkey-butt ugly scar on his cheek."

"Try saying that to his face."

"Stay away from him."

Megan's expression is blank. "Tell you what." She sighs, staring at the table. "I'll meet you tonight after school. Parking lot, by your bike. Okay?"

Cole strokes her long black hair, and Megan jerks her head away.

"Sure, baby," he says. "Like I said, we got things to talk about."

He sticks out his gross tongue at me and waggles it. I'd like to hurl in his face.

When he strolls away, I say, "You're in trouble, Megan."

"Like Cole's never been dumped before," she says. "I'll give his ring back. He won't die."

"You should've given his ring back a long time ago. Especially if you want to stay clean and sober."

When school started this year, Megan developed a reputation as a serious binge drinker. She was drunk out of her gourd every Saturday night and bitching to me every Sunday about her monster hangover. I think she figured this was her last year of high school—what the hell, live it up!

"You're on the right track now—working out, staying away from the booze," I say. "You don't want to relapse. Remember how you liked having your stomach pumped."

"Ugh! I know."

"But I'm still afraid for you."

"Cole's sneaky," Megan says. "He won't do anything in the daylight in the parking lot. Not with hundreds of kids around."

"You hope."

Megan's dark eyes light up. "Besides, maybe John Hawk will come strutting by, a club in his hand. Cole will plead for mercy, speed away on his bike, and disappear forever."

"Dreamer."

That night, I stumble onto some startling information. I'm in my room, doing research for a class term paper. Mr. Williams, my social studies teacher, assigned the topic Teen Drivers, and students have to narrow the topic for their papers. I'm searching through issues of last year's *Des Moines Register*, looking for an article with a bunch of statistics about Iowa teens driving drunk, when I spot a related story with pictures of John Hawk, a pretty blond girl, and a mangled car in a ditch. The last picture shows a turned-over semi.

Holy crap!

As soon as I finish my research, I lie on my bed in the dark, call Megan, and spill everything. "It was a terrible accident. It happened on a back road way out in the middle of nowhere. No one found the wreck till hours later. It wasn't John's fault—and he hadn't been drinking. The semi driver admitted he fell asleep at the wheel. The girl was drunk though. She died. Sounds like she was popular. She was homecoming queen."

"God," Megan says, "he must still feel terrible."

"The article said he'd already had a long list of scrapes with the police. Chances are he lost his driver's license after the wreck. I bet that's why he always rides a bike."

"When I asked him to prom, he said he didn't have a license. I didn't ask him why. He didn't offer any details."

"He was an undefeated state wrestling champion as a sophomore and junior."

"Uh-huh! That's why he's got all those gorgeous muscles. The accident explains the scar on his cheek."

"Wrestling's a violent sport, Megan. He's probably meaner than Cole."

"You don't know that."

She's right, but I still have this eerie feeling about John Hawk. He's trouble. I roll onto my side and switch the phone to my other ear. "What happened between you and Cole this afternoon?"

"It's officially over. I threw his ring at him. It hit him in the forehead. There's no coming back from that."

Finally Megan might be rid of this guy. I couldn't be happier for her, but I still think she's in over her head. "How pissed was he?"

"He didn't raise a finger. Except his middle one. He got in my face and called me every name he could think of though. Yeah, even that one. I didn't tell him about John and me or the prom or anything. I just told him we were history. Finished forever."

"Did he threaten you?"

After a long pause, Megan says, "Look, I've got to go. Loads of homework."

I prop myself up on an elbow. "He threatened you, didn't he? What did he say?"

"He's a coward, I'm telling you. Don't worry about it."

With that, Megan hangs up. I stare at the cell phone in my hand and fall back on my bed. Megan is in trouble at every turn. John Hawk is a questionable guy with a questionable reputation, and no one knows what that scum-sucker Cole Wainwright is capable of.

FIVE

JOHN HAWK

WHEN I OPEN MY LOCKER door before lunch, a folded note tumbles out and onto the floor. Someone must have stuffed it through the air vents at the top. I know it can't be from Megan. She always texts me. When I read it, a chill shoots up my spine. "IF YOU GO TO THE PROM WITH M. J. YOU'RE DEAD MEAT!"

I swing around and search for someone leaning against a locker or a wall, watching to see my reaction. Cole Wainwright, maybe.

I read the note again. The back of my neck prickles. Someone scrawled the note in capital letters. The handwriting looks like that of a right-hander who decided to write left-handed. That's the way my handwriting looked when I broke my right arm wrestling in ninth grade and wrote left-handed for a time. I should have guessed I'd get a note like this.

Nearly every day this week, Megan's been texting me like crazy about little stuff: *Lots of homework last night. What did you have for breakfast this morning? Don't you just love this weather we're having?* But last night she called because she had "a million things on her mind." She seemed so happy about our date that she couldn't stop talking. She described her dress and shoes—I'd thought she might try to surprise me on prom night. She said she'd like a gardenia for her wrist. She said I don't have to go through the bother and expense of renting a tuxedo though. I could wear jeans, a flannel shirt, and sneakers, and she'd still be thrilled to go to the dance with me. I told her it's her senior prom; I'll wear a tux.

Then I asked, "You haven't told anyone, have you?"

She hesitated. I heard her breathing.

"Have you?" I asked.

"Um… just Charley. She won't tell anyone, I know she won't."

Shit! "Megan, we had a deal."

"I couldn't keep a secret like that from her. She's my best friend!"

"We had a deal," I said again. "Did you tell Cole?"

"Absolutely not. I broke up with him. I threw his ring at him."

"He's pissed, isn't he? He's got to be."

"You worry too much, John. Go to sleep. Dream about me. I'll dream about you."

"Look, Megan…"

"Sweet dreams, sweetie." She hung up.

Note in hand now, I swing my head back and forth again. No one. I read the note one more time. "IF YOU GO TO THE PROM WITH M. J. YOU'RE DEAD MEAT!"

"Says you," I mumble. After crumpling the note, I pitch it into a trash barrel in the cafeteria.

My night-table light is on, and I'm sitting in bed reading *Death of a Salesman* for my American Lit class. Besides promising myself I'll stay out of trouble during my senior year of high school, I've also promised myself—for the first time in my life—that I'll earn good grades.

My sister's at work. Donnie is asleep under his Spider-Man sheets down the hallway. My cell phone's ring—a freight-train whistle—jolts me. I snatch the phone from the table and glance at the digital clock as I answer. Eleven p.m.

"Were you dreaming of me?" Megan asks in her whispery phone voice.

I close the book and rub my eyes. "I was dreaming Charley told Cole about us, and he left a note in my locker today that said I was dead meat if I take you to the prom."

"You're kidding, right? You didn't get a note like that."

"The hell I didn't."

We're silent for a second.

"Couldn't be Charley," Megan says. "She'd never tell Cole anything. She hates him. Had to be a friend of Cole's. Want to know how I know?"

"Enlighten me."

Megan explains that the guy who rode by her house the day we sat on her front porch talking was one of Cole's buddies. He spotted us and squealed to Cole, who probably guessed Megan and I might go to the prom together.

"Doesn't make any difference," Megan says. "Cole won't bother us. He won't be at the dance. Besides, he's a coward. Relax."

"He didn't leave that note for giggles."

"You're not going to weenie out, are you?"

I detect a definite note of panic in her voice.

"John, tell me you're not."

"I wouldn't do that."

"Please don't."

"I wouldn't," I say.

"All right." Big sigh. "What I wanted to tell you is I've made reservations for us at the Rusty Pelican. Awesome food. You'll love it. I'll pick you up at five."

"I can get a ride to your place."

"How?"

"My sister."

"She doesn't have to bother," Megan says.

"It's bad enough I can't drive. You don't have to pick me up too."

"All right. I understand. It's a male thing." She smacks a wet-sounding kiss over the phone. "Sweet dreams, sweetie."

"You too."

SIX

JOHN HAWK

THE NIGHT OF THE PROM, my sister drops me off at Megan's house at exactly five p.m. I stand on her front porch, ring the doorbell, and clutch a box with her white gardenia corsage in it. I wear a white carnation for a boutonniere. I tap my toe on the porch and inspect my fingernails. I blow out hard little puffs.

My last date was with Riley. These past couple of days, especially while I was getting ready tonight, guilt weighed on me like a giant hunk of granite. I'm alive. I have an opportunity to attend a senior prom. This is another step toward getting a new life. But because of me, Riley's dead; she has no chance at anything.

When we started dating, I was the one who coaxed Riley into taking her first sip of beer. I was the one who didn't keep track of how much she'd been drinking that night around the bonfire. I was the one who forgot her midnight curfew and raced home along back roads so I could avoid the cops. I was the one who didn't check her seat belt.

Is she watching me now from her place in heaven? Is she crying? Jealous of me? *You bastard!* Or is she smiling, happy for me? *Have a good time!*

Do I have a right to have a good time? Will I be screwed up like this for the rest of my life—forever?

Low gray clouds hang over Megan's house. I breathe deeply, slowly. I ring the doorbell again. I shift the flower box from one hand to the other. I reach to poke the doorbell once more, but Megan opens the door. The sight of her sweeps my breath away. She looks awesome—silky black hair pulled back tight and curling down her back, bare shoulders glistening, sequined black dress hugging her waist and flaring to her ankles. I smile, and my heart flip-flops.

"Hey." She flashes a smile, a bit flushed and nervous too.

As my eyes continue to roam her body, the scent of her lilac perfume swarms me, and my knees feel weak. "Hey! You look great!"

A silver necklace sparkles on her tanned neck. Silver cross earrings dangle from her ears. "You too! Tux. Red bow tie. Red cummerbund. You're the hotness, sweetie."

She kisses my cheek, her lips soft and wet with red lipstick. My heart performs that flip-flop trick again.

She leads me into a huge living room with a stone fireplace at one end. I catch the scent of vanilla—it gives me a start. My eyes dart to lit candles stuck in solid, bronze-looking candleholders on each end of the fireplace mantel. I recognize the smell because when Mom knew Dad would be gone for a day or two, she'd light candles like that in her room at night, drink, and listen to music.

A huge framed painting of River Valley High School hangs above the fireplace. All the shrubs and trees are in the right places, the tennis courts off to the left. *Pretty cool.*

Megan's parents rise from their oak-and-leather furniture.

"I'm Doctor Jones." He removes his horn-rimmed glasses with his left hand and holds out his right hand.

Megan's dad is a big man, tall and bulky but not fat. His salt-and-pepper hair is cropped into a butch cut. I've seen him in the halls and heard him fire up the student body with fist-pumping speeches at pep rallies for the basketball, volleyball, and wrestling teams.

Stepping forward, I force a big smile. My hand spews moisture. "I'm John Hawk."

Dr. Jones gives me a firm handshake, three quick pumps. "Glad to meet you, John."

When we step back, he slides his glasses into place, and Megan approaches, glancing at the florist box in my left hand.

"Your corsage," I say quickly and hand it to her.

"Thanks!" She beams, her red lipstick shimmering.

"For your wrist. Like you wanted. A gardenia."

Dr. Jones says, "John, this is my wife."

Tall, beautiful, and blond, maybe thirty—probably twenty years younger than Dr. Jones—Stephanie Jones wears a maroon silk outfit with tapered pants and white sandals. *Different.*

"Hi," I say. "Glad to meet you."

"How are you, John?" she says.

"Great. Just great."

"I'll help you with your flower," Stephanie says to Megan.

"I'll do it myself." Megan waves her away and backs up.

Clearing his throat, Dr. Jones says, "I understand you're new at River Valley." He indicates a plush lounge chair behind me. "Won't you sit down?"

Stephanie says, "I'll get us something to drink."

"We don't have time," Megan says. "We have reservations for five thirty. I told you that. We're leaving."

"Don't be rude, sweetheart." Dr. Jones gives his daughter a sharp look. "John and I would like to talk a moment, wouldn't we?" His gaze swings my way.

My neck burns. *Here it comes. The lecture about behaving, not drinking, respecting his daughter, getting her home on time. The same lecture Riley's parents delivered to me over and over.*

"I'll get my things." Megan darts away.

Dr. Jones sits in a leather couch across from me and leans back. He appears casual in his jeans and white polo shirt. Because he's the school principal, I figure he'll help chaperone the dance. Maybe his wife will be there too, but they don't have to dress until later. Stephanie eases into a rocking chair by the fireplace.

"Well, John," Dr. Jones says, "what do you think of our school?"

"It's fine."

"One of my missions is to provide a safe educational environment for our young people. Smoke-free, gang-free, drug-free, gun-free— that's the kind of campus I maintain."

"It's a great school."

Dr. Jones sits a little straighter. "I like to hear that. The staff and I have worked hard to make River Valley High the best it can be."

When Megan returns with a knee-length black cape buttoned around her bare shoulders, I grab a second look. I mean, I'd never seen a girl wear a cape before. It's different but cool. Just what I'd expect from Megan. I stand quickly, and she slips her clammy hand into mine.

"Let's go," she says.

Dr. Jones eyes us both. "I understand Megan's driving." His gaze settles on me again.

"Yes, sir." I tug at my collar. It seems much tighter than it did seconds ago.

"You don't have a license?"

"It's been suspended," I say evenly. I've made this explanation many times, and though it's never easy, at least I can explain now without getting tongue-tied.

"Care to tell me why?"

"Daddy, that's John's business," Megan says flatly.

"I don't mind," I say.

Dr. Jones's eyes remain on me.

"Traffic violations," I say. "Habitual offender. And I was in a bad accident. They took my license."

"Alcohol related?"

"No, sir. I hadn't been drinking. The other driver was at fault. It's all public record and probably in my school file. You can check it out."

"What do you use for transportation these days?" he asks.

"I ride a bike."

Megan says, "Daddy! Stop with the questions."

Dr. Jones nods, his lips pursed. I can't tell if he believes me or not. I hope he does check me out. He'll find I'm telling the truth.

He turns to Megan. "Then I assume it's your responsibility to get yourself and John home at a reasonable hour."

"Whatever," Megan says, staring at him.

I blink and step back. Her rudeness surprises me. "We won't be late."

Dr. Jones glares at Megan for a moment, then his eyes land on me again. "Nice to see you're a sensible young man."

"Thank you, sir."

"I worry about young people on prom night. Any night, actually. But more so on prom night because—"

Megan cuts in. "Daddy, please! No lectures tonight."

"Because no matter how much you caution young people, no matter how much you preach about self-control, about alcohol, drugs, and driving, you can never be sure they'll listen and use common sense."

Megan rolls her eyes. "We're out of here." She squeezes my hand, pulling me toward the door.

"Have a good time," Stephanie says, rising from the rocker.

"Like you care," Megan snaps.

"We will," I say. That final shot Megan aimed at her stepmother nearly floored me. I try not to gape, but I wonder what the problem is between them.

With that, Megan drops my hand and flounces out of the room. I scurry down the hallway to catch her. She yanks the front door open, waits for me to step outside, then slams the door behind her. Her spiked heels click sharply across the wooden porch. She marches down the steps and across the drive, where she jumps into her sporty red Mustang.

The clouds pressing down on us look like gray, wet blankets. A steady drizzle spills, and a chill pierces me. I climb into Megan's car and shut the door.

After I settle in, seat belt buckled, I say, "You came down hard on your folks, especially your stepmom."

Jabbing the key into the ignition, Megan says, "Look, you don't know anything about my dad or me. Or about my bitch of a stepmother." Megan twists the key, and the car roars to life. "Or how dysfunctional my family is. You don't even *want* to know what's going on. Let's have some fun."

"Right."

She backs into the street, slams the gearshift into drive, and we take off, the tires spinning on the slick blacktop.

What the hell have I gotten myself into?

SEVEN

JOHN HAWK

THE RUSTY PELICAN IS A fancy restaurant on the Mississippi River levee. From our vantage point in the restaurant's parking lot, I spot the giant paddlewheel gambling boat, *Rhythm City*, docked about fifty yards away. Climbing out of Megan's car, I gawk at the scene in front of the boat. Tour buses and stretch limos, along with fancy luxury cars and SUVs, crowd the levee parking lot. Lots of clunky pickups and sedans are scattered around too. Nearly everyone likes to gamble, I guess. In the gray twilight, rows of bright lights on all the decks light the ship from bow to stern. Calliope music floats from the boat as hundreds of umbrella-carrying tourists and locals jostle aboard to have fun losing money.

"Look at the size of that boat," I say. "It's, like, a block long and three decks high." As we scamper toward the Pelican, I hold Megan's hand. We dodge puddles, and I keep glancing at the boat. "Look at those giant stacks and that awesome paddle wheel."

"Stay away from that boat," Megan says. "Gambling's a disease. It ruins lives, just like drugs and alcohol."

We halt in front of the Pelican under an awning that protects us from the rain. I look at her. *Where did that come from?*

Inside, the hostess seats us by a window. I gaze out over the river, through the rain, to the misty city lights of Rock Island, Illinois. Old fishing nets, ropes, anchors, chains, and oars decorate the restaurant walls, giving it a river atmosphere. I'm impressed.

The place is crowded with adults, but two other couples wearing tuxes and cocktail dresses sit at a different table. They're laughing and giggling a lot. Maybe they've been drinking. Megan apparently doesn't know them, so we all smile at each other when our eyes meet but say nothing.

Halfway through our meal, Megan sets her fork down next to her plate, takes a sip of her ice water, and pats her gleaming lips with her napkin. "You've said hardly a word. Are you pissed?"

"Not at all."

"Is it the way I treated my dad? My stepmother?"

"You're the one who seems pissed. Back at your house, I felt hostility oozing out of you."

"Look, my life is a total wreck, and today it got worse. Of all days." She taps the fingers of her right hand on the table and puffs out a big breath. "All right. Listen, let me tell you a couple of things."

"You don't owe me any explanations."

"Listen, okay?"

"I'm listening."

Megan's face tightens. "My mother died of cancer when I was in eighth grade. I was thirteen. She was hardly in the ground six months before my dad married Stephanie. I freaked. I loved my mother. I thought my dad did too, but he got married *six months* after she died. Can you believe that? I found out Stephanie and my dad had been having an affair for over a year. So I ran away from home. I wanted to hurt him like he hurt me. Like he must've hurt Mom. I wanted to punish him."

"I can relate to that, parents having affairs. Nothing hurts more."

"You've got that right."

But I don't say anything about my mom. I want Megan to keep talking about herself.

"Well, like, if that's not bad enough," she says, "listen to this. All the time my dad's been a high school principal, he's preached his favorite gospel—self-control, say no to drugs, say no to alcohol. He's on my case all the time. But listen to this! Just listen to this!" She stops and draws a breath.

"I'm still listening."

"He's addicted to gambling." She thumps a fist on the table. Our silverware jumps.

I sit back, my mouth falling open.

"Dogs, horses, riverboats," Megan says. "He does it all. He throws his money away everywhere."

"Are you kidding?"

"Hell no! He's got a major problem, but he doesn't think so, and you'd never in a million years guess. When he was in the Navy stationed in Hawaii—where he met my mom—he started with poker and blackjack with his sailor buddies. But it escalated. He admits that."

"You're serious, aren't you?"

"Dr. Franklin W. Jones, principal of River Valley High, is out of control. You don't believe it, do you? *But he is!* You want to hear the worst of it?"

"I thought I already had."

"Oh, there's more." Megan pauses as though she's gathering her courage. "Stephanie's a blackjack dealer. They met on the *Rhythm City.*"

"A blackjack dealer? He's addicted to gambling and he marries a blackjack dealer? That doesn't seem smart."

"That's the point. He's misplaced his brain. And then what happened today pisses me off so bad—" She stops, huge tears bubbling in her eyes.

"What about today?" I ask. Maybe her dad took a mortgage out on the house and gambled the money away. Something bad like that.

Megan shakes her head and swears softly. "Sometimes I feel like running away forever." Her face crumbles.

I expect tears to gush out of her eyes. "What happened today?"

She shakes her head again. "I talk too much." She pulls her face together, grabs the napkin, and dabs at her glassy eyes, careful not to destroy her makeup. She sniffles. She squares her shoulders, stiff and awkward. Her bottom lip quivers. "I don't want to cry. I don't know why I even care about my dad."

"Megan…"

"When I said my dad and Stephanie were having an affair, you said you could relate. Your dad too?"

"My mom left town with a drummer in this band she liked—Night Stalkers. She always wanted to be a pop singer. She married my dad, but she never gave up the dream."

Megan grips my hand. "I asked you to the prom so we could have a good time, and now I've got us talking about all this shitty stuff in our lives."

"It's all right."

"Motor-Mouth Megan, I always talk too much." She turns on her brightest smile, highlighting her white teeth and wide red lips. "Let's finish eating—then let's go dancing!"

As we finish eating, I think, *Megan's dad is addicted to gambling and his new wife is a blackjack dealer—what a stupid combination. How can such a smart guy—a principal of a high school—be such an idiot?*

The more I know about Megan, the more I realize her life is in shambles too. Maybe worse than mine.

The prom is at the Starlight Ballroom at the fairgrounds. With its hardwood floor and high ceiling, a bar at one end and restrooms at the other, the place looks like an old gymnasium. But it doesn't smell of sweat-raunchy towels and jockstraps; it smells of fresh paint and varnish. Decorated with balloons, streamers, and whirling, pulsating lights, it's a great ballroom. The music is loud enough to rip your ears off and blow your mind.

I'm not a dancer, but when I'm in the right mood, the music is right, and the girl is right, I can let myself go. I can shake, jump, spin, twirl, leap—arms and legs flying everywhere. I dance with Megan until we're sweaty and breathless and can hardly hang on to each other's hands as we send each other flying across the floor. She's spectacular in her black dress, ebony hair flouncing, silver earrings twisting and glittering.

I feel eyes on us from the kids and chaperones alike. Several times Megan scurries off to the restroom with girlfriends, leaving me alone. I spot Dr. Jones in a shadowy corner watching me. Stephanie's watching too. I don't care.

Two off-duty cops roam the edges of the dance floor, mentally frisking everyone. I'm sure Dr. Jones feels their presence will make kids think twice about causing any trouble—like sneaking in a bottle or lighting up a roach. Again, I don't care. I'm not into alcohol and drugs.

Megan is fun to be with. Going to the prom with her has been awesome. All my fears and doubts have vanished like sunshine burning away a fog. Worn out by ten thirty, I dance a slow one with Megan, holding her tightly. Her fingers creep through the hair at the back of my neck. She kisses my throat, sending a shiver through me, then kisses my scar.

I stiffen a little and say, "Don't. Please."

"Sorry," she whispers.

We nuzzle closer, dancing slowly.

"What are we going to do now?" she asks. "The prom's nearly over."

"What do you want to do?"

"The after-prom party at the mall is out. My dad and Stephanie will be chaperoning that. It's enough having them watching us now."

"Right. No parties. We agreed, remember?"

Megan cocks her head back. "I'm driving…"

"So?"

"You'll have to do whatever I want."

"Depends."

"Don't argue," she says, and kisses me again on the throat. "Let's go. I want to get out of here before my dad grabs me and lectures me in front of everyone about behaving and getting home early. No drinking."

Holding hands, we stroll off the dance floor toward the coat booth. Lots of other couples are leaving too. Many of them stop to talk to Megan, eyebrows tilted as they survey me. I linger in the background, saying hello when I have to and trying to smile. I'm sure they're all thinking, *Who is this guy dancing like crazy with the principal's daughter?*

I fetch Megan's cape from a redheaded girl working the coatroom. What does Megan have in mind for us after the dance?

We could rent a movie and watch it at Anne's house. That would be safe. She won't care if Megan stays a while. Watching a chick flick with Megan will be fine with me, if that's what she wants.

I head toward where she's been gossiping with a bunch of friends, and I freeze in my tracks. My stomach drops, and my heart kicks into high gear. Squared off at the ballroom exit like two prizefighters, Cole and Megan face each other, their faces flaming red.

EIGHT

JOHN HAWK

"You're an asshole!" Megan screams at Cole.

"You're a whore!" he hurls at her.

Elbowing between them, I grab Megan's arm and pull her aside. She jerks out of my grasp. She's totally pissed, her face flushed and scrunched.

"We don't need any trouble," I tell her. "Put this on. We're leaving. Now."

"Good!" Megan says and shuffles farther back, cape in hand.

I turn to Cole. I smell booze on his breath.

"Get out of my face!" he yells. "She's not going with you!"

My arms hanging loosely at my sides, I step up to Cole. That voice in my head yells, *Don't do this. Walk away… walk away… walk away…*

As tall as me—I'm six-one—Cole is lean, sinewy, and quick-looking. He licks his lips and stiffens his jaw. "Back off!"

My first response is to stare. "Don't start anything you can't finish."

His jaw rises. A scowl leaps across his face. "You're an asswipe."

He wears a black leather jacket, black jeans, and pointed black leather boots. A red do-rag snuggles his head. Two guys dressed like Cole stand beside him. They could be triplets. I didn't see Cole at the dance earlier. He and his buddies must have straggled in.

"Megan's with me," I tell him, struggling to keep my voice calm. "I'd appreciate your not yelling at her or calling her names."

Kids gather around Cole and me. Faces bright and shiny, they thirst for a fight. *Let's see what the new kid's got.*

Cole's Adam's apple bobs. "You got no right to be here. An out-of-town killer like you."

Killer! I feel as if he's body-slammed me to the floor, the wind knocked out of me. I shove Cole into the circle of kids. He would have toppled backward if his buddies hadn't caught him. He shakes himself free of their grasps but doesn't advance toward me.

My hands ball into fists. "Killer? Did you say *killer*?"

"You killed a girl! Everybody knows that."

The dance hall walls crowd in on me. For a moment, I can't breathe. Sweat pops out on my forehead. This is exactly the situation I wanted to avoid. *Walk away. Walk away...*

Cole lifts his chin again. "Megan's going home with me, so back off."

"I'm not!" Megan cries.

I capture a deep breath, and my wrestling reflexes kick in. A shot of adrenaline shoots through my body, popping my veins. Crouching low and sucking air though my teeth, I'm ready to launch an attack on Cole. I intend to arm-drag him to the floor and tie him up in a cradle until he can't breathe, but two broad-shouldered figures step in front of me. One is a cop. The other is Dr. Jones. Both grab my arms, hold on tight, and wrench me back.

The cop keeps saying, "Cool it, okay? Cool it!"

"Settle down," Dr. Jones says. "We won't tolerate fighting. Settle down..."

"Throw those guys out!" Megan yells. "They don't belong here."

I'm shaking now, breathing hard.

"Relax!" The cop clutches my arm tighter.

"Let him go!" Megan cries. "And *we'll* get out, John and me!"

Teachers start breaking up the disappointed onlookers. "C'mon, folks, keep moving. Don't crowd around. Nothing to see. Time to leave, anyway."

The cop and Dr. Jones still grip me.

"Where's Cole?" I say.

"We don't want any trouble," Dr. Jones says.

I stop resisting and stand with my arms limp at my sides again. My breathing slows down and evens out. "I just want to know where he is. I don't want to get blindsided."

"A policeman has him," Dr. Jones says.

"Let's go," Megan says.

"Good idea," the cop says. "You guys get out of here."

Dr. Jones looks at Megan, shaking his head as if he's thoroughly disgusted. "Perhaps you should take this young man home then go home yourself."

"You're not planning my evening, and Cole's not going to ruin it."

My fingers fumbling, I help Megan button her cape. "Let's take a hike." I glance back, searching for Cole. My throat feels dry.

A cop and another guy, probably a teacher, hold Cole in a chair at a table thirty feet away. His buddies still flank him. I don't intend to do or say anything. I just want to walk away quietly. I hate what happened. That's not the person I want to be again: John Hawk, brawler. *Killer.*

It's Megan who ignites a final exchange. She flips Cole off and shouts, "You're the *asswipe!*"

He struggles to jump up, but the cop and the other guy clutch his shoulders and stuff him back into the chair.

"You're dead meat!" Cole screams, his face blotchy red. "*Both* of you!"

NINE

CHARLOTTE COTTON

W HAT DOES A GIRL DO on prom night when all the popular people are partying? She works her already non-existent ass off at her folks' restaurant, the Catfish Hut, as a fry cook. She finishes the night smelling like fried fish then darts up the stairs to the apartment she shares with her folks above the restaurant. She takes a hot shower, throws on an oversized T-shirt, flops into bed, and snaps out the light on her night table.

All this week before the prom, Megan kept saying, "Pick someone, Charley. You're a hottie. What have you got to lose?"

"My pride."

I could easily imagine Megan and John making out after the prom—no guy ever resisted her—but I sure as hell don't want X-rated pictures streaking though my mind.

My not having a date to prom was better than last year though, when a guy I knew from science class asked me. I'd rushed out and bought a dress and shoes. I planned to do something with my renegade hair, twisting it into a chignon, maybe. Then the guy called me the night before the dance and said he couldn't make it. He didn't give an excuse. He just mumbled that he couldn't make it. *Couldn't make it!* I'd wanted to kill him.

For six months after that, every time I saw him in the school parking lot, I gritted my teeth and stopped myself from running him over with my truck. One day, I marched up to him when I saw him standing alone by his locker.

I said, "I'm glad you stood me up. I learned something."

At first he looked confused, as if he'd forgotten about me. "I'm sorry about that."

"Like hell you are. You were glad to ditch me. Why ask me in the first place? You lost a bet, didn't you?"

He looked sheepish, his eyes darting away from mine. Then he looked at the floor. "I've been meaning to explain."

I didn't give him a chance. "A girl is more than the way her hair looks or the size of her boobs. What you *see* is not the whole reality. Like how your eyes are a little close together, but I said yes because of the great conversation we had that one time about Marvel vs. DC characters. I thought maybe you were into me, and we could've had fun."

He looked more confused than ever, his face twisted. Obviously I was an alien speaking gibberish—he didn't get it or me. Why waste any more time with him? I whirled and stomped away. I knew he thought I was just another wacko female who was probably getting her period.

What I really learned was that this is the way it'll be. I'm me— Charley Cotton. I have to accept myself. I'll never be a Megan Jones, popular and beautiful. I'm going to be happy the way I am. *Quit crying.*

Even if I am dateless. No Greek gods and football heroes in my life. Maybe nobody at all. A-cup boobs. Hardly any butt. Hair like I'd jabbed a fork in a light socket. *Shut up!*

TEN

JOHN HAWK

O N THE WAY TO ANNE's house, driving through a pounding rain, Megan pats my leg and says, "I'm sorry."

"It was my fault."

"I knew Cole didn't have a date. I didn't think he'd be there, I swear. I'm so sorry."

"Not your fault. I knew better. I should've grabbed your hand and walked away."

"He would've followed us outside. His asshole buddies too."

"Probably." I tilt my head back on the headrest, imagining a bloody fight in the parking lot, the cops swarming and dragging me off to jail. Or the paramedics throwing me into an ambulance. Been there. Done that.

Megan says, "You did the right thing, facing him, so Daddy and the cops could stop him and send him home. I'm sure he showed up and started trouble because he wanted attention. He knew someone would stop a fight inside the dance. He wouldn't get beat up—he's a coward."

Rain pelts the car, and the windshield wipers clack to keep up. A jagged streak of lightning cracks across the sky.

"Maybe we should call it a night," I say.

"Are you kidding? A fight with Cole Wainwright is not how I want to remember my senior prom. We're going to have our own party and make an awesome memory."

I smile. "Where did you say we're going?"

"After we change out of these clothes, I'm taking you to a famous historical site."

Looking straight ahead, keeping her eyes on the road, Megan can't see me rolling my eyes.

"At this time of night?" I ask. "A historical site? Are you kidding?"

"You'll see."

Megan drops me off at my house. Before she dashes home to change, she kisses me and says, "I'll be back in no time."

The house is silent but not dark. Anne left a table light on for me when she left for her shitty cocktail hostess job. I couldn't ask for a better sister. She's twenty-two, four years older than me, but she's like a mom. Donnie's at the babysitter's. His dad lives in town; that's one good thing because they can see each other often. I don't know where my mom is. Last I heard, over a year ago, she was in Nashville. She never writes or texts or calls. Not even on birthdays or holidays.

I change from my tux into my jeans, T-shirt, and hooded sweatshirt. I'm a lot more comfortable; a tux really isn't my thing. I wear my new black-and-white Nikes. I hate wearing my new sneakers in the rain, but I left my old ones in my locker at school.

Every other minute, I pull the curtains away from the front window and peer outside, looking for Megan's car parked under the streetlight at the curb. Voices quarrel inside my head again. One says: *Stay home. You could be headed for even more trouble.* Another voice counters: *What trouble? Wainwright's out of the way. When's the last time you spent an evening like this with a girl? Go for it, man.*

When I climb out of the rain into Megan's car and close the door, I ask, "Okay, what historical site?"

"An island in the Mississippi River. The British fought us there in the War of 1812. You and I are going to have a long talk. You're going to tell me more about yourself."

Frowning, I wonder if she thinks she's going to turn tonight into a therapy session. Also been there and done that. "You already know everything."

"Not hardly. You're going to explain that scar. Then we'll make out."

"The scar's a souvenir. You'll have to find someone else to make out with."

Her face swivels toward me. "Don't bet on it."

"Besides, how are we going to get there, an island in the river? Swim? I can't swim."

"There's a causeway leading to the island. Indians and settlers used to do their trading there. That's how the island got its name, Credit Island. Now there are tennis courts, softball diamonds, stuff like that. At the far end is woods."

Megan zips into the left-hand lane, stops, waits for traffic, then makes a turn. Black and rainy as the night is, I see in the headlights' glare that we're crossing a blacktop causeway about a hundred yards long to get onto the island. On both sides of the causeway, the water has risen almost to the road.

I eye the black water practically lapping at our car's tires. "We might get stranded here."

She smirks at me. "Scared?"

"It's been raining practically all day and night, and the river's already up to this road."

"Parts of the island go underwater in the spring, but real flooding takes a lot more rain." When we reach the island, Megan makes a right-hand turn onto a road that follows the island's outer edge.

"Is that the river on my right?" I ask.

"Credit Island Harbor. The actual river channel is on the other side of the island."

In the headlights' glare, I see a dozen or so picnic tables under a metal pavilion on my left. I glimpse monkey bars, swing sets, slides, and a big old antique army tank. The road gradually narrows, cutting through woods. Branches bend over us, creating a tunnel to drive through.

Even in the car with the windows closed, the night air smells musty and fishy. An eerie chill creeps up my spine. With the rain, trees, river, and blackness, I think this is a scene out of a chainsaw murder movie. My breath comes in raspy little gulps.

All right! Here's something I have to admit—I mean, I hate to admit it, but I have to—since the accident and Riley's death, I've feared darkness. I lay seat-belted in my upside-down car for four hours before a passing motorist discovered the wreck, my car in a ditch, a semi across the road in another ditch. Since I can't shake the fear, I've tried to keep the secret buried deep inside me. No one knows but my sister. I can't sleep in the dark at night. I need a light turned on. *How stupid is that?* Not even my four-year-old nephew needs a nightlight.

My knees jiggle. I force them to quit. I glance at Megan, hoping she hasn't sensed something is wrong with me. A guy like me: a two-time state wrestling champion, a brawler—a *killer*—isn't supposed to be afraid of anything. *Wimps are afraid of the dark. Not John Hawk.*

In the side mirror, I catch a flash of lights behind us. "A car's following." I turn around to stare out the back window.

"They're looking for the same thing we are, a place to park."

I turn back around and peer through the windshield. Megan makes a sharp right turn to cut down a weedy path. I can't see the black river through the dense undergrowth, but I know it can't be more than ten yards ahead.

I lick my lips. "You know where you're going?"

"Right here." She stops the car, killing the lights and engine.

We're alone in the black, trees creating a canopy overhead. I can't see a thing. My heart rate spikes. I swallow and swing my head around, thinking that the car following ours might pull in behind us. We're trapped.

Maybe the driver is Cole Wainwright. With friends. *You're dead meat! Both of you!*

Tightness grips my chest. Cole and his friends I might handle. *But not this darkness. I hate darkness.* I swallow again.

The car rolls slowly by, its taillights flickering and disappearing in the darkness.

"Satisfied?" Megan says.

I can't see her. I can only guess that she's settled back against her door, facing me. I tug at the neck of my sweatshirt with shaky fingers. "Turn the dome light on. Please."

"Why? Afraid of what I might try under the cover of night?" She pushes a button somewhere, and the dome light casts a soft glow behind our heads. Half her face is draped in a shadow as though she's wearing part of a dark mask. "How's that?"

I concentrate on breathing slowly, deeply, evenly. "Better."

"You look pale."

"Must be the light. You come here often?"

"Not recently." She smiles. "Relax."

I rub my palms across my thighs, hoping my jeans will soak up the sweat. Sliding down in my seat, I ease my head back and try to take Megan's advice to relax. The dome light helps. The wind blows, and fat raindrops thump off the car's roof and splatter off the windshield.

Megan leans across the gearshift between our seats. "I like the sound of rain."

Her head drifts toward mine, and I inhale her lingering lilac scent. She kisses me, her lips soft and moist. Her palm is warm on my scar. My heart swells, but I keep my lips tightly together, my hands to myself.

"Kissing works better if both people participate," she says.

"I know."

"Then try harder."

I smile. I totally like Megan Jones. But I don't try harder. I look back over my shoulder to see if the car that followed us is coming back. I expect to see its headlights any second and hear its engine. But I see and hear nothing. I drag my hand through my hair.

Megan leans back into her seat. "Cole really got to you, didn't he?"

"A little."

"When you went for him, I saw murder in your eyes."

"I don't need anybody else telling me I killed a girl. Is that what kids are saying about me?"

She nods. "That's the rumor around school. Kids say you were in a bad accident, and a girl got killed."

"Where did that information come from?"

"The *Des Moines Register*." Megan tells me about Charley's English assignment and what she had found out about me by searching the

Internet. "Other kids read the same article. That's how the word spread."

I stare through the windshield at the blackness.

"Your scar is from the accident?" Megan asks.

Hell, admit it. I nod and touch the scar. I measured it once. It's three jagged inches long. Someday I might hide it with a beard. But— why hide it? It's part of who I am.

Megan sits up, inches closer to me again, and slings her arm around my shoulders. "Want to talk?"

I haven't talked to anyone about what happened or how I feel, about the accident or anything else, for over a year. I'm not sure I know how to express myself anymore. For the last three years, I haven't spoken much to my dad—he's pissed at the way I turned out. I can't blame him. So we ignore each other, except when I get into trouble. Then we're in each other's face.

I hate bothering my sister with my problems. She has enough of her own: no husband, raising her kid by herself, her shitty job. Then she's responsible for me—her little brother, a big-time loser—because she agreed to take me in for my final semester of high school.

I take a breath, wait a moment, and blow it out. I take another.

"I talk a lot," Megan says, "but I'm a good listener. Seriously."

I pinch my eyes closed for a second. "Like I told you earlier, my mom ran off with a drummer in a band. She was into theatre and drama when she was in college. After, she sang with a couple of groups and cut a record. I have a copy, but I don't listen to it anymore. Anyway, she gave it all up to marry my dad, a lawyer. She always bought Night Stalker's CDs, played their music all the time, and went to their concerts when they had a gig in Des Moines."

"Sounds like something a college freshman would do, running away with a musician. Not a mom with two kids."

"I guess she decided music was more important, or that she'd miss out if she stayed. I'm pissed at her, but I love her. She drank a little. I smelled it on her, but I never felt neglected." I take a big breath and let the air slide out slowly. "After my parents divorced, I got into so much trouble you wouldn't believe it."

"It's called acting out. I know all about it."

"Fights. Drinking. Traffic violations. Lots of stuff. My dad's a lawyer, a county prosecutor in Des Moines. He's in good with all the cops, so he always made sure they 'treated me right.' But that means he'll never stop reading me the riot act."

"Sounds like my dad."

"Kicked off the wrestling team. I got suspended from school a couple of times. All stupid stuff."

"You were looking for attention."

"I got a lot of it—the wrong kind. You don't know how totally worthless my mom's leaving made me feel."

"Yes, I do. How old were you?"

"Fourteen." I massage my eyebrows with my thumb and forefinger. "And then Riley..."

"She died in the accident?"

"My girlfriend. She didn't drink till she met me. She was going to reform me, but I convinced her to try a bottle of beer before she had a chance to do any reforming. 'One bottle of beer—what harm can that do?' I asked her." Words pour out of me. I mean, like, I tell Megan the whole damn story of the accident.

When I reach the end, she says, "Doesn't sound like the accident was your fault."

"But if I hadn't forgotten the time, we would've been on the road at a different hour, long before the truck got there."

"Forget the *ifs*."

"If I'd have taken the Interstate, I would've never met that truck on a country road."

"Stop!"

"Or if Riley hadn't been drinking so much, she might've buckled her seat belt—I told her to. She wouldn't have been thrown from the car."

"That's how she died?" she asks.

"She smashed her head against a telephone pole."

"Oh wow."

"I buckled my seat belt. Why didn't I check hers? I helped her into the car. I threw her beer away. I locked her door. Why didn't I check her seat belt?" My heart's pounding. My palms turn sweaty again, and tears burn my eyes. *Christ, don't cry in front of Megan.* I swipe my eyes with my fingertips.

"You've got to stop blaming yourself."

"I try, I try, I try. Believe me, I keep trying."

"You know what you're dealing with here?"

"What?" I ask.

"Survivor's guilt. Happens to soldiers all the time. A guy's buddy dies, the guy survives, and he can't figure out why he's still alive. He doesn't feel right because he's not dead too. He feels guilty."

"But a soldier doesn't cause his buddy's death. An enemy roadside bomb kills him. Or a mortar round. A sniper's bullet."

"You've got to shed that blame."

I grab another breath and exhale. "You want to hear something else?"

"What?"

"The seventeenth of every month—Riley died on May seventeenth—her brother sent me a rose spray-painted black."

Megan makes a face. "That's terrible."

"I got eight black roses till I finally decided to quit school in Des Moines and come here to live with my sister and her kid."

Megan tunnels her hands through my hair. "Well, finally. Finally the truth about why you're here. Kids were bullying you in a really shitty way."

I stare through the windshield at the darkness. "I couldn't handle the bullying any longer, kids calling me killer. The black roses sent me over the edge. I wanted to curl up inside myself and disappear."

Silence descends on us except for the rain pounding the car, rattling off the roof.

I breathe slowly, deeply, evenly. "I came to River Valley so I could start my life over where no one knows me." I rest my head back on the seat. "So now you *do* know everything about my screwed-up life."

"Your mom's ditching and Riley's death were not your fault, I'm telling you."

"Still, I've made a lot of stupid choices. Everything I touch turns to... you know what."

"Does that include me?"

I smile. "No."

Megan leans over and kisses me. Once more, I inhale her scent. Her sweet lips tease my mouth open this time, and her tongue begs mine to come out and play. Maybe because she's beautiful and bold and I haven't been close to a girl for over a year, I respond. My arms capture her. Closing my eyes, I press her close and return her kiss, the first kiss I've given a girl since Riley.

Riley's blue-eyed smiling face flashes behind my eyelids, and I jerk back, hitting my head on the door window. "Megan, please. Let's not do this right now."

She presses a silencing finger to my lips. Surprising me, she hoists herself over the shifting lever, wiggles onto my lap, and circles her arms around my neck.

I groan. "We can't do this."

She wiggles again.

"Please…" I twitch.

Nodding at the glove box, Megan says, "Condoms in there. The backseat in this thing isn't very big, but we can adjust the front seats forward."

She reaches to open the glove box, but I grab her wrist. "No," I whisper.

She snaps her wrist free, opens the glove box, and pulls out a condom. "You're still in love with Riley, aren't you?" Megan tosses her black hair and slams the glove box closed. "I'll cure that."

Maybe it's true that I'm still in love with Riley, but I say, "I'm not in love with anyone."

Megan grabs my hand. "It's been a year, John."

I try to back away from her, but there's nowhere to go. "Look, I really like you."

Pressing the condom into my palm, she says, "Prove it."

Oh wow! I stare at the foil packet, gleaming like a silver dollar under the dome light. Then I look at Megan. "I wouldn't have gone to the prom with you if I didn't like you."

Her eyes drill me. "I want more proof."

"I need to be cautious." I swallow and drop the condom on the dashboard. "I don't need more complications in my life."

Megan's head tilts. "I'm a complication?"

"What I'm saying is I've already screwed up enough for one lifetime. I can't afford to make another mistake."

She kisses me again, a soft lip-to-lip kiss with no tongues, a kiss that makes my heart quiver.

"All right," she says. "I understand."

"You're not pissed?"

"It's like you think no matter what you do, it'll turn out bad. Like you're cursed or jinxed. Or deeply flawed."

"That's it. Exactly. I don't trust myself. Just going to the dance with you tonight was a big chance, one I thought I'd never take. I don't want anything bad to happen to me again. Or especially to anybody I hang with."

"But you can't live your life in a bubble." Megan curls herself around me.

I hold her a long while, hearing our breathing, feeling her chest swell against mine. She delivers another kiss, and another. Soon my breathing matches the pace of my pounding heart.

"You've got to stop kissing me like that," I say.

"A guy who's thoughtful, sensitive, and handsome—I can't believe I found you."

"A guy who's been mostly in trouble and is carrying more baggage than anyone would believe."

She lifts my chin with her forefinger and looks me straight in the eye. "I've changed my mind about you, John Hawk."

"What about me?"

"I *am* going to cling to you."

"You think so?"

"You're my project this semester," she announces, releasing my chin and snuggling closer. "I'm going to help you bury all that baggage. And when you do, I'll be right here, sitting on your lap, hugging and kissing you like this." She squeezes me harder. "Now I'm going to climb off your lap…"

"Good. It's probably time we leave."

"But first, I'm going to do you a quick favor so you won't go home tonight hurting."

With that, Megan hikes herself back over the gearshift, lands in her seat, and unzips my jeans.

ELEVEN

CHARLOTTE COTTON

S LEEPY-EYED, HER HAIR ALWAYS A mess—just like mine—my mom wakes me up and hands me the cordless from her bedroom. I'm still struggling to sit up in bed. I can't imagine who's calling me at five in the morning. It can't be Megan. She'd have texted me or called my cell to tell me about her date with John Hawk. Maybe bubbling with excitement. Maybe crying with disappointment.

Turns out it's Dr. Jones. His voice vibrates with panic. He's looking for Megan. She hasn't come home. Have I heard from her?

I rub my eyes. "No."

I know why he's calling me. When Megan ran away from home after her dad married Stephanie, Megan ended up in a shelter in Chicago. She went there because she was tired, cold, and hungry. She called me, not her dad.

"Did she tell you what she might be doing after the dance?" Dr. Jones asks.

"Didn't she go to the after-prom party?"

He says Megan wasn't at the party then tells me about the shoving match between John and Cole. He's worried that maybe Cole started something with Megan and John after they all left the dance.

That's a distinct possibility, but I don't tell him that since I don't want to freak him more than he already is. "Maybe Megan and John went to one of those all-night breakfast places and they're just talking. You know how Megan talks."

"I don't think so," he says. "It's been seven hours since John and Megan left the dance."

I have to agree. No one could talk that long, not even Megan. Not John Hawk for sure. *Maybe they're shacked up in a motel.* But I don't want to say that to Dr. Jones either.

He says, "I've got the boy's landline number—I can get into the school computer from home. I've called but get nothing but a busy signal. Call me immediately if you hear from her."

"I will. I promise."

We hang up, and I flop back in bed. Megan's not home. *Crap!* It could be nothing. Megan's pretty unpredictable. Or it could be something really, really terrible, and now I feel totally sorry for Dr. Jones because has no idea how much trouble is piling up on him.

Megan called yesterday afternoon and told me something horrible about his wife. His knowing about her wouldn't help find Megan, so I didn't say anything. Besides, I promised Megan I'd keep my mouth shut.

I work weekends at the Hut. About two o'clock yesterday afternoon, I was on break. I was sitting outside at a picnic table in a grassy, tree-shaded spot behind the place. Cloudy skies. Looked like rain for prom night. Did I care? Hell, no.

Megan called, muttering so fast that I could hardly make sense out of what she was saying. She was on her way to the mall.

"Pull over and park someplace," I told her. "Driving when you're upset, talking on a phone—you'll kill yourself."

I didn't hear anything for a second or two, maybe longer. I hoped she'd pulled into a parking lot. Then in a shaky voice, she told me she was going to the mall to buy black nylons and different shoes for the prom. Dr. Jones was already at the mall helping kids set up for the after-prom party.

"I was, like, nearly all the way there," she said, still talking fast as hell, "when I realized I forgot my purse. No purse, no credit card. So I quick drive back home, stomp into the house steaming mad, and guess what I hear from my dad's bedroom? You won't believe it."

"What?"

"Stephanie and a guy!" Megan screeched. "In my dad's bedroom!

I'd know her voice anywhere. *I cannot believe it!* But why not? She *is* the stepmother from hell."

"What? What did you hear?"

"All the crazy noises they were making," Megan said. "All the groaning and shrieking! They're fucking doing it in my dad's bedroom. It's why they didn't hear me come in—all that noise! And the door was closed."

That news was so astounding, I nearly fell backward off the picnic table. Rudy, my pet squirrel who always shows up when I take a break, scampered down a hickory tree, hopped across a grassy clearing, and sat up twenty yards away from me.

"You know who the guy is?" I dug in my apron pocket then tossed Rudy a couple of peanuts in the shell.

"Don't ask me."

"Why the hell not?"

"It's too unbelievable," she said.

"Did you open the door?"

"I recognized his voice before that."

I jammed the phone to my other ear. "Who? Whose voice?" *Tell me! Tell me who!*

"I can't believe it, I'm telling you. It's way too weird. You're better off not knowing."

"Who?" I stomped the ground, dying to know.

My quick movement frightened Rudy. He hustled back to the hickory tree, a peanut in his mouth, and scurried up the trunk to a branch, brandishing his fluffy red tail.

"I'm going to get in his face at school Monday," Megan said. "Before I say anything to anybody."

Oh. My. God. It's a teacher. It's got to be! I slid off the picnic table bench and stood up. "Was there a car in your drive? One you recognized?"

"No car."

"That's strange."

"I know," she said.

I was so nervous about what she was telling me that I started circling the picnic table. "You going to tell your dad?"

"I don't know what to do. He's got enough problems already."

"He's still gambling?"

"More than ever." Megan sounded as though she was going to cry. "He is so *stupid*! I snatched my purse from my room, ran out of the house, jumped into the car, and got the hell out of there." She went on cussing Stephanie out and complaining about her dad. "You can't tell anyone, promise!"

"I won't, I promise."

"Sometimes I wish I could run away and never come back. I wish I'd die."

Crap!

As I lie in bed, my head spinning with Megan's words, a terrible sinking feeling lodges in my stomach.

When she said it, I didn't take that line seriously, though I know I'm supposed to listen when kids talk like that. *I wish I'd die.* Lots of times a kid who says he or she wants to die becomes a statistic. I wonder if Megan really meant it. *I wish I'd die.* She's not home from the prom. Did she have a bad experience with John Hawk? Did he get her drunk? *I'll bet he did!* Did she finish the evening feeling used and ashamed? Abused? Hating her dad? Stephanie? John? Everyone? Feeling totally depressed?

I wish I could run away and never come back.

I stare at the ceiling. I hope Megan's shacked up somewhere with John. Even if her dad finds them together, at least she'd be alive. *But where is she?*

TWELVE

JOHN HAWK

"**T**WO POLICEMEN WANT TO TALK to you, John." My sister Anne stands at the foot of my bed, her arms crossed, eyebrows raised. She's wrapped her slender figure in a faded pink robe. Her short, curly auburn hair falls in front of her face.

I bolt upright, sweating, panting, my heart thrashing. Gloomy light seeps into my bedroom through two windows. I have no idea what time it is. Mid-morning? Afternoon?

I nearly always waken to the same nightmare: The lights of an oncoming truck glaring off my car's windshield. The sounds of a wailing horn, of Riley's screams, of metal grinding against metal. The whirl of a spinning, tumbling car. The smells of gasoline and diesel fuel. The sickly taste of my own blood. Then blackness.

Right after the accident, while I was in the hospital for a week with a concussion, two broken ribs, and the gash in my cheek glued shut, I could barely remember anything that had happened. I remembered driving on a dark road at night and bright, glaring headlights blinding me, but everything else seemed to have been deleted from my mind, even being at the bonfire with Riley. My doctor told me that memory loss was common among trauma victims and my memory of that night's events would likely return. Anne said I'd be lucky if they didn't. Dad said what the hell difference did it make. I'd screwed up again.

Fuck!

How right the doctors were.

Over the next three months, vivid, horrifying details in HD color popped back into my mind randomly and without warning, often leaving me weak, sick, sweating, and breathless. I'd actually hear Riley's scream, feel the pain in my ribs, and swipe at my face, expecting to feel blood. If I were home, I'd dash to my room. If I were driving, I'd pull off to the side of the road. The worst, though, was when the flashbacks happened in class. That had only happened twice, but both times, I bolted from my desk, sprinted to the restroom, and locked myself in a stall until I stopped sweating and started breathing right. The principal slapped me with detentions each time because I refused to explain what was happening. I didn't want him or anyone else to think I was crazy. But I think everyone did, anyway.

"You all right?" Anne swipes her hair away from her face.

"The nightmare." I shake my head, trying to clear my sleep-drugged brain. "What time is it?"

"Nine thirty." Anne's voice softens. "You left your light on all night again."

"Sorry."

"You've got to get over your fear."

"I know." I reach for the glass lamp on the night table and click off the light.

"You hear what I said? Two policemen are here."

I blink, still hazy. My eyes feel heavy-lidded and gritty. "What two policemen?"

"Don't know. But they want to talk to you." She stares at me, her dark-brown eyes flashing, arms crossed again, thin lips pursed. It's her motherly get-tough look. "They're dressed in suits. The big burly one looks mean. You're not in trouble again, are you?"

"No." I glimpse my rumpled prom clothes thrown on the chair.

"Dad's not here to protect you."

"I don't need his protection."

"What time did you get home?" she asked.

"Four o'clock."

"You didn't party at someone's house and trash the place, did you? Or a motel room?"

"Hell, no."

"I'm not that old. I remember what it's like to be eighteen. I remember the prom."

"I'm not into stupid stuff like that anymore."

"Right," she says, rolling her eyes. "I forgot."

"I'm serious."

"Get dressed. They're waiting." Hand on the doorknob, she asks, "You sure there's nothing you want to tell me?"

Only what a great night I spent with Megan, but that's private. "Nothing."

"Whatever those cops are here for better not be serious. If Dad finds out, he'll have your neck. Again."

I sit on the edge of the bed in my jockey shorts. When my feet hit the cold tiled floor, a chill shoots through me, sending me back to the wet coolness of early morning. After Megan and I decided to leave Credit Island, she got her car stuck in the mud. Out in the cold rain, I pushed and pushed—it seemed like forever—until I finally shoved her out.

I look out the window by my bed and realize the rain is still pouring down. My mind skips through the night's other events. No way could I be in trouble. Even the scuffle with Cole wasn't my fault. I'd been provoked. Everyone saw and heard that.

A pang of fear jolts my brain. *Megan.* Maybe driving home in the rain, after she dropped me off at my house, she slid through an intersection and slammed into another car. A tree. A telephone pole. Maybe she rolled her car into a ditch like mine rolled over.

Shivering, I yank on clean jeans and a T-shirt.

When I shuffle into the living room, my heart thumping, the two cops rise from the sofa. I'm a bit wary, but why should I be? For once, I've done nothing wrong, and I have nothing to hide. Besides, I know from past experiences that the best way to get along with these guys is to be polite and cooperative. Answer their questions simply and directly. Never volunteer more information than the question requires. Avoid sarcasm. Be cool. Don't smirk. Seriously, I have nothing to worry about.

I recognize Officer Striker, a red-haired, slender young guy who works part time at River Valley High in the morning as a liaison officer. Most kids like him, but he's tough on troublemakers, and sometimes his temper flares. I've seen him break up several fights. Once he slammed a kid against a locker, his forearm jammed across the kid's throat and the kid's eyes bulged. Police brutality, no doubt, but I don't think the kid had enough guts to report the incident. He didn't want to tangle with Officer Striker again.

"Hi, John," Striker says, friendly enough, and indicates the older man by his side. "This is Lieutenant Garske."

I nod hello and shake Striker's hand, three easy pumps. Heavyset, taller than me—he's maybe six three—Garske looks forty-five or older and grizzly, like a grizzly bear. He thrusts out a paw, and we shake. One hard pump. His grip is iron.

"Live here with your sister?" Garske asks.

"Yes, sir."

The kitchen and living room in Anne's house are connected, only a small island separating them, so she can see and hear everything going on between the cops and me.

"Why don't all of you sit down?" Her voice comes out high-pitched and nervous. "Make yourselves comfortable. I've got coffee made."

"Thanks," Striker says.

He and Garske sink back onto the worn sofa, and I slump onto the edge of the lumpy lounge chair by the door and face them.

"So how are you this morning?" Striker asks. "You look beat."

"Late night?" Garske says.

"I'm fine."

"Who would like coffee?" Anne calls.

The cops say they would, but I decline. I don't like coffee.

"What's this all about?" I ask.

Striker leans forward. "We need some information, John. You went to the prom with Megan Jones last night?"

"Yes, sir."

"What time did you take her home?"

I feel wary. Hair bristles on the back of my neck. "I didn't take her home."

The two cops exchange a glance. My eyes shift from one to the other, and my mind churns as I try to figure out what's going on. *Stay cool. Don't panic.*

Garske's steely gray eyes pierce me. "You didn't take her home. Is that what you said, boy?"

"Yes, sir."

"Why is that?" Striker says.

"I don't drive."

Garske nods. "Really? You don't drive?"

"I do not drive," I say slowly, as if I'm talking to a three-year-old. *Stay cool.*

"Lose your license?" Garske asks.

"Yes, sir."

"It wasn't his fault," Anne says, scurrying in with two mugs of coffee, the aroma strong. She sets them on coasters on the coffee table. Her hands shake a little. "The truck driver was at fault. He admitted that."

I shoot my sister a look. She doesn't know about not volunteering information. She sits at the kitchen table with her own mug of coffee.

"So tell me," Garske says before he tastes his brew, "how did you and your lady friend get to the dance? Somebody else take you? You walked?"

"Megan drove."

"Big boy like you, a girl drives you to the prom?"

Heat rushes to my face; my ears burn. "So what? What do you guys want?"

Striker studies his hands for a moment. Then he looks at me. "Megan's dad called us," he says softly, as though he's sorry about the information he's about to deliver. "She didn't come home this morning, John."

Shock rockets through me. Anne's coffee mug *clunks* on the kitchen table.

"That must be a mistake," I say. "She left here and headed home."

"What time?" Garske asks.

"About four." I stare at the cops. "If you guys talked to her dad, you already know she drove last night."

Garske's smile is almost invisible. He's been toying with me. "Her car's home, but she's not. How would you explain that?"

"I can't."

Striker sips his coffee then sets down his mug. "Dr. Jones got home from the after-prom party at six this morning. He was a chaperone. He looked in Megan's bedroom to check on her. Her bed hadn't been slept in."

"Weren't you at the after-prom party?" Garske asks.

"No, sir. We didn't go."

"Something better to do?" Garske smiles.

"What's that mean?"

"Her father tried calling here," Striker cuts in. "But all he got was a busy signal. Someone had taken the phone off the hook."

"You do that?" Garske says, looking at me.

"I did." Anne fishes a pack of cigarettes from her robe pocket and fumbles one out into her fingers. "When my ex gets drunk, he calls here. The only thing I can do is take the phone off the hook and turn off my cell." She lights the cigarette; it twitches between her pale lips. "That's why there's been a busy signal. He called. I hung up and left the phone off the hook. It's still off."

Striker nods again. "Megan's father called other friends, and everyone said the last person they saw Megan with was you, John. They didn't know where you two were going. Megan's father kept calling here"—Striker gestures at Anne—"but got a busy signal. He called us. We thought we'd talk to you before we did anything else. Unofficially, of course."

Sitting on the edge of the sofa, Garske laces his fingers and stares at me. "So that's where we are, boy. Megan Jones goes to the prom with you but doesn't come home." Garske bends his laced fingers back, cracking his knuckles. "You want to tell us where she is?"

Breathe. Breathe. "I don't know."

Anne's cigarette smoke drifts into the living room. I swish my hand in front of my nose.

She says, "Better tell us what's going on, John."

"I don't know. I'm telling the truth. Megan dropped me off here and drove home." My face feels on fire. My cool is fading. "Maybe she drove to her girlfriend's house."

"Her car's in the drive," Garske says. "Remember, we told you that."

My head dips; my shoulders slump. *What the hell's going on? Megan's not home, but her car's in the drive? Where is she?*

Striker clears his throat. "Did you know Megan ran away from home once?"

I look up and nod. "She told me last night."

"Maybe she's run away again," he says. "Anything bothering her?"

"Early in the evening she was uptight. Something happened at home that upset her, but she didn't say what."

"You're sure?" Striker says. "She didn't tell you anything?"

"Something about her dad, I think."

"That's all she said? Just something about her dad?"

"She was complaining about him, about his gambling too much. He must've done something else yesterday to seriously upset her."

"She didn't say what upset her?" Striker asks, still pressing. "No details?"

"She wouldn't talk about it."

"Maybe some guy followed her home." Anne taps cigarette ashes into the ashtray. "Maybe when she got out of her car, he kidnapped her and—" Anne stops abruptly. "Sorry." She shakes her head. "That sounds horrible. I didn't mean that."

A picture of Megan lying dead in a ditch off a lonely gravel road flashes through my mind. Goose bumps pop out on my arms.

Striker sips his coffee again. "How long have you and Megan been dating?"

"This was our first time."

"And you don't come home till four in the morning?" Garske says.

"Prom night. Everyone stays out."

Garske shakes his head. "I don't understand kids these days."

"Who did you guys talk to last night?" Striker asks. "What did they say? What did Megan say? Tell us everything."

I'm not sure I want to do that, so I say nothing.

"Where did you go after the dance?" Striker asks. "What did you do? What was she wearing? If she turns out to be a missing person, we'll need every scrap of information we can get. We'll post an Amber Alert."

"Why don't you do that right now?"

"To issue an alert," Striker says, "we need a description of the captor or of the captor's vehicle."

"What he means," Garske adds, "is we have to confirm that an abduction has taken place."

"Makes sense," I say and study the pattern in the worn brown carpet.

A tight ball of fear knots in my stomach. Megan has to be all right. She has to be. Two different towns, two different schools, two different girls—tragedy can't strike another girl I've dated. Megan is too young to die. Riley was too young too. I hate talking to cops, but I have to cooperate. I need to find out what happened to Megan as much as they do. More than they do.

THIRTEEN

JOHN HAWK

As I tell my story, every detail of my time with Megan on Credit Island flashes through my mind. I tell Garske and Striker about the note I found in my locker and the threat: *IF YOU GO TO THE PROM WITH M. J. YOU'RE DEAD MEAT.* I tell them about Megan and her stepmom not getting along very well. I explain my scuffle with Cole Wainwright at the dance and how his threat when Megan and I were leaving echoed the note I found in my locker: *You're dead meat! Both of you!*

But I halt my story the moment I tell them Megan parked on the island and killed the lights and engine. What we talked about, her saying I would be her semester project, her sitting on my lap, and what happened after—her quick favor—they don't need to know any of that. But I tell them about Megan getting her car stuck in the mud and my having to push her out, which took a long time.

Striker and Garske exchange glances.

"Let me get this straight," Garske says. "You guys parked at Credit Island and just talked. That's it? Nothing else?"

I sit on the edge of the lounge chair, staring at my hands, my fingers laced between my knees. "Nothing else."

Striker drains his coffee mug. "Credit Island woods is not a good place to be after dark. Gang members hang out there. Drug deals go down. Megan didn't tell you that?"

"Maybe she doesn't know."

Striker shakes his head. "Everybody who's lived around here awhile knows that."

"Tell me," Garske says, "what time did you get to the island?"

"I wasn't keeping track of time." *Don't get smart.*

"Estimate."

I tip my head back, thinking. "We started to leave the dance at ten thirty and had a little trouble with Megan's ex-boyfriend. I told you that. We went home to change, then we drove to the island. It's not very far… I don't know. We got there at eleven thirty, midnight maybe."

"Did you see anybody you know?" Garske asks. "Anybody stop by to talk to you?"

"I told you, a car followed us but drove by."

"Look," Garske says, "let's say you parked on the island at midnight. Then the girl drops you off here at four in the morning. Think about it." He counts on his fingers. "That's four hours in a car in the dark, a boy and a girl. You were just talking?"

I look at Anne at the kitchen table.

She crushes out a cigarette in the ashtray. "Tell them the truth." Her brown eyes jab me.

"When you were stuck, nobody came by to help?" Striker asks.

"No one."

"And all you guys did was talk?" Garske asks again, three grooves streaking across his forehead as he frowns.

"Yes. And we parked in front of this house and talked a little while longer."

Garske turns to Anne. "Did you get up during the night, look out, see them?"

Anne lights another cigarette and blows smoke at the ceiling. "I came home about two forty-five. I work nights. I had Donnie with me from the babysitter's. He's my little boy."

"You brought him home at two forty-five in the morning?" Garske says.

"Like I said, I work nights. The babysitter's a friend of mine. I have a key to her house. I go in, bundle Donnie up, and bring him home."

"Go on," Garske says.

"When we got here, Donnie woke up, then his dad called. I had to deal with that. I didn't get Donnie back to sleep till after three. That's when I went to bed. I slept straight through, till I heard you knocking-slash-pounding at the door this morning."

Garske turns back to me. "Did Megan say anything about running away? When we talked to her dad this morning, he suggested that might be a possibility."

"She was mad at him. Like I said, I don't know about what. It seemed serious, but I don't think she ran away."

"Why not?"

"We'd had a nice time. I promised to call her today. We talked about getting together and doing something—a picnic at Westlake if the rain stopped. Why would she make plans then run away?" I stand. "I have to use the bathroom."

In the hallway, I open a bedroom door and peek in at Donnie, a chunky boy with hair so blond it's nearly white. The kid knows his ABCs already and can count to a hundred. He's sleeping in his bed. If he knew a cop car sat in front of his house and cops sat in the living room, he'd go wild with excitement. I ease the door closed.

Damn! The cops are taking the wrong approach. Cole Wainwright is the guy they should be grilling, not me. Why don't they realize that? Can't they see beyond their badges? I shake my head.

When I return to the living room, I find the cops standing by the door. Anne scurries about, clearing off the coffee table. Relief washes over me. Thank God these guys are finished here.

"You going to check out Cole Wainwright?" I ask and hope at least one of them will say yes.

"We'll check him out," Garske says.

"You say he wrote you a note?" Striker says.

"I think it was him."

"Still got it?" Garske asks.

I rub the back of my head. "Threw it away."

Garske nods. "Get a coat. Some shoes. Socks."

"Why? I told you everything that happened last night."

"Right," Garske says. "And now you can show us where it happened. Get a coat, shoes, socks."

I look at Striker for help. He seems the friendlier of the two, more my age. Like I hope he could be my ally in this mess. "What's happening?"

"John, I believe you," Striker says. "We just want to see where you parked. There should be tire tracks, shoe prints. Maybe you threw something out the window: a tissue, a candy wrapper. Anything to prove you were there."

"Beer bottles," Garske says. "Condoms loaded with DNA."

I bite my bottom lip. I'd like to punch him in the mouth. "We didn't eat a candy bar, blow our nose, or drink beer. Or anything else."

"John, go with them," Anne says. "Prove to them what you said is true. Stop making a fuss."

Cheeks puffed, I blow out a long breath. Anne is right. Why make a fuss? Why be paranoid? I have nothing to fear. Or hide.

FOURTEEN

JOHN HAWK

GARSKE TURNS AND SQUINTS AT me through the wire grid that separates the front seat from the back of the police cruiser. I catch the scent of an orange air freshener. One of these guys smokes and is trying to hide it. Garske, probably.

"Let me ask you something again." A grin lights his growly face. "What were you and Megan Jones doing in her car this morning all that time?"

"Talking."

"I mean, I understand why you didn't want to say much in the house, with your sister there. We're alone now. Just us guys. You making out with Dr. Jones's little girl?"

I jerk my head away from Garske and stare out the cruiser's side window at the rain. "We were talking."

"Big boy like you… you were getting a little, weren't you?"

My fists clench. If I could rip the wire grid separating us, I'd wring Garske's neck.

Striker eases the cruiser to a stop at an intersection. "Look!"

Rainwater floods the four-way intersection. It flows over curbs and across lawns. Water halfway up their hubcaps, two cars ahead of us have stalled. The drivers wade around, trying to push their cars to the curb, out of the way of the rest of the traffic.

"It's been a long time since I've seen this much rain in the streets," Garske says.

Striker coaxes the cruiser around the stalled cars. As he drives, I can barely see through the rain-blurred windshield. The taillights of cars in front of the cruiser wink at us.

When Striker makes the left turn off River Drive to the Credit Island causeway, he stops abruptly. City barricades, painted bright yellow, block access to the causeway. Peering through the wire grid and the windshield, I watch in disbelief as the river rages over the causeway. Credit Island itself, with its trees, courts, and picnic area, is drowning in rainfall.

"What a mess," Garske says.

Striker sits upright, staring and gripping the steering wheel. What he sees apparently stuns him: water pounding over the causeway, carrying gnarled tree limbs, a broken picnic table, and a dog house, all swept away from upriver. *Damn!* The sight is enough to alarm anyone.

"Unbelievable," Striker says. "Unbelievable."

Garske says, "A guy like you from Chicago has never seen real flooding, have you? Never seen what the Mississippi can do when it's on a rampage."

"Never," the young cop says.

I realize most of Credit Island must be underwater, especially the shoreline. That means my footprints, the tire tracks from Megan's car, and anything else that might verify Megan and I parked on the island is probably washed away. Even the mud under Megan's car was probably splashed away as she drove me home over the rain-filled streets.

I have no way of proving my story. What will the cops think now? *Liar!*

"I know exactly where we parked," I say and explain where the site was—just beyond the picnic pavilion, where a narrow lane cuts to the right, down close to the water.

Garske listens. Then he looks at Striker. "Nothing we can do now. Turn this thing around."

When Striker parks in front of Anne's house, I remain seated in back. I can't get out until one of the cops opens the door for me. There are no inside handles in the back of a cop car.

Garske turns to me again. "We'll let you out in a second. Wait on the porch."

"What for?"

"Wait on the porch."

I nod. After Striker climbs out of the car and opens the back door, releasing me, I dash through the rain, leap the puddles on the walk, and stand on the front porch, chilled. I wish the cops would drive away, but they don't. *What the hell do they want now?*

Striker ducks back into the car and talks on the radio, the mic to his mouth. He's probably asking headquarters what to do since Credit Island is flooded, and he can't verify my story.

Bring the kid in. Book him.

For what? I didn't do anything!

The front door to the house opens behind me. I turn. Behind the screen door stands Donnie, his blue eyes nearly popping out of their sockets. He's the most curious kid in the world.

"You riding in a police car?" he asks, clapping.

I smile at him. "Close the door, tiger. You'll catch cold."

"Real policemen in that car?"

"Real policemen." I bend down in front of the screen. "You bet."

"Make them give me a ride. Pleeease?"

"They don't have time. Close the door."

"Make them."

Anne hurries to the door, and I stand up.

"Why are you standing out here?" she asks.

"They wanted me to wait a second."

Donnie's face sparkles. "They're getting out of the car!" He clenches his little fists. "Make them give me a ride. Pleeease?"

Hunching in the rain and tiptoeing around the puddles on the walk, the cops walk toward the porch. Anne grabs Donnie's arm, draws him into the house, and closes the door.

Striker mops the rain from his forehead with the heel of his hand. "What did you wear to the prom last night?"

"A tux. Why?"

"And after the prom?" Garske asks. "You came home and changed, right?"

"Right."

"What did you wear then?"

"Jeans. T-shirt. Hooded sweatshirt." My eyes narrow.

Lacing his fingers and bending them, Garske cracks his knuckles. "We'd like to take everything you wore last night with us."

"Why?"

"Routine," Striker says.

Garske says, "You don't mind, do you?"

I fight the urge to tell them both to get screwed. "Everything?"

"Everything. Your tux. All the stuff that goes with it. Your jeans and whatever else you wore." Garske indicates the front door. "Officer Striker will go with you. We want it all."

The jeans, shirt, socks, and underwear I changed into after the prom are stuffed under my bed. They were wet and muddy, and I didn't want Anne to spot them. I didn't want to explain what happened. I intended to wash them when Anne went to work today. She'd never know.

Kneeling, I pull a throw rug out from under the bed, and there huddles my pile of wet clothes, smelling of river mud and rain. Striker stands over me, hands on his hips.

I get up. "There's my jeans, shirt, and everything else. The tux is on the chair. Do you have to take it?"

"We need everything."

"I'll be charged ten dollars a day for the tux," I say, rolling my eyes. "A late fee, starting Monday."

"Can't help it. Call the rental place. Explain. Maybe they'll give you a break."

"Like I'm going to explain to a stranger the trouble I'm in."

"Can't help it," Striker says again.

"What do you want with my clothes anyway?"

"We'll process them for blood, alcohol, drugs. Any DNA we can find."

I stare at Striker. "You think I did something to Megan?"

"Look," he says, rubbing his jaw then patting my shoulder, "I believe your story. Maybe Garske doesn't, but I do. If your clothes are clean, it helps us eliminate the possibility that you were involved in any kind of mishap with her. Lighten up. You got nothing to worry about."

Running, Donnie stumbles into the room and nearly falls, but I catch him. "Easy, tiger. Not so fast. You're supposed to be with your mom."

"She's on the phone. Daddy called."

"Go talk to him." I gently push Donnie back into the hallway.

Striker places my muddy clothes into one plastic evidence bag, my tux into another. He hesitates then says, "Listen, I'll tell you something. Maybe it'll help."

"What?"

"Garske's wife was injured a year ago. She liked to jog at nighttime with her German shepherd. She used to run by the high school. One Friday night—it was after a basketball game or a dance, I can't remember which—a car hit her. Broke her back."

"That has nothing to do with me."

Striker holds up a hand. "Listen to me. She's in a wheelchair now. Dog was killed. Garske always figured it was some kid roaring out of the school parking lot then down a side street. The driver clipped her and the dog and kept going. Only one witness, who gave the make and model of the car but no plate number." Striker shrugs. "It's pretty fresh in his memory. That's why he's tough on you. Besides, he doesn't have any kids. He doesn't understand teens, but I remember being one. I know what you're going through."

I absorb all that. "So now he hates kids?"

"Hey, this is just between you and me, as friends. Okay? Don't mention it to him. He's sensitive about it. You don't want him on your case any more than he is. He's a good cop—try to understand."

"They ever find out who drove the car?"

"No."

"This cop who can't find out who ran over his wife and her dog is going to find Megan?"

"Chances are Megan's run away. We'll find her in a day or two."

"I hope." I look at the evidence bags then at Striker. "Why take my clothes?"

"We've got to cover all bases. Everything'll turn out okay." This time he pats me on the back instead of the shoulder. "I'll let you know as soon as we hear anything. Okay?"

I've done nothing wrong, so why not let the cops take what they need? They can have my whole wardrobe if it helps find Megan. "Right."

Donnie waits for me in the hallway, jumping up and down. He grabs my hand. "Make them, John. Make them give me a ride in the police car."

Smiling, I hoist the chunky boy into my arms and give him a squeeze. "I can't make the cops do anything, tiger."

Striker steps onto the porch, the screen door slamming behind him. I follow with Donnie in my arms and stand in the doorway.

Garske lingers on the porch. "Got everything?"

Striker nods. "Looks like the rain's stopped."

Garske steps toward the door, holding up a pair of muddy shoes. "These yours?" he asks me. "Full of mud. Found them here on the porch behind that potted plant with some other muddy shoes. Must be your sister's and the kid's."

"Pleeease, John, make them."

"Be quiet." I squint through the screen at the shoes. "Yeah. They're mine."

"Ask them!"

"We'll take them along," Garske says.

"Please, John! Please! Please! Please!"

I cup a hand over Donnie's mouth. "Shhh, tiger!"

Already headed for the squad car, Striker skips around the puddles.

Garske turns to follow. "We'll be in touch."

Pulling my hand away, Donnie wails, "They're leaving!"

"Be quiet," I say and shift Donnie from one arm to the other. "Don't forget to check out Cole Wainwright!" I yell at Garske's back.

Without turning around, he gives a single wave. Does that mean *Okay*? Or *Forget it*? Donnie rubs his tear-filled eyes. I let out a long low breath, and a sinking feeling grips me.

FIFTEEN

JOHN HAWK

"You should call Dad," Anne says as she pulls a skillet from a cupboard under the sink. She clunks it on the stove. "Are you going to make toast?"

The cops are gone—finally. But I still can't relax. "Sure."

"Scrambled eggs okay?"

"Fine."

"Talk to him while I make breakfast. Tell him what's going on."

I shake my head. I hate dragging Anne into this. My sister's life is filled with enough stress.

Dad's a hotshot county prosecutor, and while Anne was in high school, he convinced her she should be a lawyer too. He was paying her way to law school, but in her sophomore year of college, she got knocked up. I can't tell you how much that pissed off Dad. The guy who did the deed was a walk-on stud of a football player who didn't live up to his potential. Not on the football field, anyway. He and Anne dropped out of school, got married, and ended up in River Valley because it's his hometown. He works with his dad as a carpenter and barely keeps up with child support. He has Donnie every other weekend but doesn't show up sometimes. Because of work, he says.

Now I'm dumping another huge problem on my sister to worry about.

I grab a loaf of wheat bread from the breadbox in the cupboard. "Where's Donnie?"

"In his bedroom pouting and looking at his books. He's starting to read."

"Not riding in the police car broke his heart. He'll probably never speak to me again, but I couldn't ask them."

"I know." Anne turns to the refrigerator for eggs and milk. "Call Dad. Now."

"I'm not giving him another chance to go off on me."

"You can be *so* stubborn."

"Look, if I call, all I'll hear is, 'I knew you couldn't keep out of trouble for a semester. I knew you'd screw up. Why am I giving you an allowance every month, your sister money to feed you? You're a joke. You're wired to fail. Like your mother.'" I drop two slices of bread in the toaster and slam down the lever. "I don't need more shots like that. I've heard them before."

"Hey! Easy. That's the only toaster we've got."

"Remember what else he kept yelling last time?"

"He didn't mean that."

"That's why he said it, like, a million times, right? *I wish you'd never been born!*'"

"I'm sure he's sorry he said that."

"So am I. Because I really believe he is sorry I was born."

Anne picks a whisk out of a drawer. "If Megan doesn't turn up today, the story will be in Monday morning's newspaper. It might make the Des Moines paper."

"So what?"

"Do you want Dad to read about it in the newspaper? 'Principal's daughter missing. Last seen with John Hawk.'"

"I'm not calling him."

Anne adds a bit of milk to the eggs then beats them to make them light and fluffy. "Then I'm calling him. I'm the one who's responsible for you."

"He's going to yell at you too. He'll remind you you're just like Mom, getting involved with a loser and screwing up your life."

Anne dumps the eggs into the skillet. Her shoulders slump. I wish I hadn't said that.

She pushes her hair out of her eyes. "All right, don't call. But if something bad has happened, *I'm* calling him no matter what he might say to me. Whether you like it or not."

"If something turns out bad, I'll call. You won't have to."

SIXTEEN

CHARLOTTE COTTON

S UNDAY MORNING AT CHURCH, MY conversation with Megan's dad swirls in my mind. The horrible question knifes deep into my gut: *Where's Megan?* Mom, Dad, and I always go to ten o'clock Mass at St. Anthony's on Sunday.

Thank God the rain's finally stopped, though the sun's having a tough time battling the clouds. Had the rain kept up, the Hut might have been flooded. That happened ten years ago when I was a kid. What a mess. Two feet of river water on the floors, leaving behind a foot of squishy, stinky mud.

I never ask God for much. Well, once I prayed for a bow so I could go turkey and deer hunting with Dad, and my prayers were answered. But this morning in church while I'm sitting, kneeling, or standing, I'm praying like crazy for Megan. I figure that's all I can do right now. *Dear God, give Megan a break. I know she's got her faults, plenty of them. We all do. But let her be alive. Let her be okay. Let her come home.*

Megan and I became friends in ninth grade. I hate bullies. On my third day of high school, before class by my locker, a burly girl named Claudia Murphy—a shot-putter on the high school varsity track team when she was an eighth grader—ripped little Leroy Leonard's notebook out of his hand so she could copy his homework. His locker was right next to mine. We all knew each other because we'd gone to Frank L. Smart Junior High, and Claudia had a reputation of bullying anyone she wanted to.

I thought, *Man, if she gets away with this, she's going to harass Leroy all through high school.* I wasn't much bigger than Leroy, but I didn't care. I gave Claudia a push. She didn't budge—it was like shoving a tree stump.

I yelled, "Leave him alone! Do your own damn homework."

"You want to get knocked on your ass, girlfriend?" Claudia said and shoulder-rammed me into my locker with a bang.

"How about a trip to the principal's office, porky!" Beautiful, black-haired Megan Jones halted by us, hands planted on her hips.

I nearly fell over.

"Who you?" Claudia snarled.

"She's the principal's kid," Leroy blurted, his freckled face bright red.

Scowling at Megan, Claudia gave that announcement a moment's thought. I didn't know why she didn't know Megan was the principal's daughter. I thought everyone knew, even though Megan had gone to the other junior high in town.

Anyway, her head cocked, Claudia scowled at Megan, evidently trying to decide if she believed Leroy or not. She didn't. "When's the last time you was bitch-slapped, bitch?"

Claudia probably thought that shot would make Megan disappear. *Wrong!*

Megan dropped her backpack and whipped out her cell phone. "Got my dad's number—the principal—right here on speed dial. You sure this is the way you want to start high school? Dragged to the principal's office?"

Claudia's ugly, narrow-eyed glare ricocheted from Megan, to me, to Leroy. "Who gonna take me? None of you twerps."

Megan stepped into Claudia's space, forefinger ready to stab at her phone. "Won't have to take you. He'll come get you. Last chance."

Big bad Claudia exhaled a gush of air. "Fuck you!" She hurled Leroy's notebook to the floor and stalked off, never to bother him again that I know of.

It turned out that Megan and I had a study hall together that semester and the same lunch period. She belonged to a clique of popular girls who drank and smoked. But she made time for me, and she didn't smoke, thank God. Gradually we ended up talking on the phone, texting, and emailing. She always confided in me. Like I knew she'd lost her virginity when she was thirteen and had gone all the way with a couple of other guys before Cole latched on to her.

Once she coaxed me into painting my fingernails and my toenails purple. She always wanted me to wear makeup—especially line my eyelids, darken my eyelashes, and smear my mouth scarlet. But I balked. It's not who I am. Megan finally understood and let it go. That's how she is—understanding. Though she's never given up hoping I'll hook up with a guy. It's like I'm her *real* friend outside of her circle of popular friends.

And now no one knows where she is.

Like I said, I can't do much, but if I find out Cole or John hurt her, I'll be on the bastard like a fly on horse crap.

Excuse me, God. Sorry.

SEVENTEEN

JOHN HAWK

BLOWING FROM THE SOUTH, A breeze pushes me along as I ride my bike to Dr. Jones's house. The sun muscles through partly cloudy skies. I'd be making good time if not for the low spots that are still full of rainwater. The water flows over curbs, drains into people's front yards, and spills into their basements, no doubt.

Wary of another downpour, people wear raincoats and carry folded umbrellas as they scurry along the sidewalks. Passing cars splash me. Twice I stop to help push stalled cars. Motorists cuss, and horns blare. Streets smell like sewers.

A weatherman on TV, apologetic because he wasn't quick enough with the flash-flood warnings yesterday or last night, explained the flooding this morning. Heavy two-day rains north of River Valley, plus an unexpected six-inch local downpour during the past twenty-four hours, produced massive flash flooding in creeks, streams, and rivers that all flowed into the Mississippi River.

The Mississippi itself rose six feet in twenty-four hours and has gone four feet over flood stage. Flood waters from Black Hawk and Duck creeks—both cut through River Valley—swamped the houses built on the creeks' flood plains, forcing hundreds of residents to abandon their homes, cars, and other personal belongings. In many cases, boats were the only way of escape.

"Fortunately," the weather forecaster says at the conclusion of his report, "we have no reported casualties due to flooding."

Where's Megan?

My heart beats like a trip-hammer when I lean my bike against the oak tree in the front of Dr. Jones's house, and my mouth turns dry. I want desperately to convince Dr. Jones I have nothing to do with Megan's disappearance. I'm innocent.

I told Mr. and Mrs. McGinnis how sorry I was for what had happened to Riley, and I begged for forgiveness. I thought surely they would understand I was hurting, too. I thought they would realize that after the accident, my heart felt as though it had been ripped from my chest. I loved Riley like they did.

But as I explained my regret and sorrow, Mrs. McGinnis only cried harder.

Mr. McGinnis's face flamed, and he roared, "Do you think your pathetic '*sorry*' is going to bring her back? That's what we want! We want her back! Look at you! Not even hurt, except for a gash on your ugly face. God, I pray your life is cursed the way you cursed us! Wherever you go, whatever you do—cursed!"

That curse has been haunting me, sending shivers through me, ever since Mr. McGinnis blasted me with it. I have no idea how to escape it.

As I stand under Dr. Jones's oak tree, I touch my scar. Maybe this scar is my everyday reminder of my cursed life. There is no escape. *You're doomed, John.* Shaking my head, I scatter those thoughts.

Megan's red Mustang sits in the double-wide driveway. The police have probably processed it already.

I swallow when I ring the doorbell. Stephanie opens the door and stares at me with ice-blue eyes, her eyelashes way long and black. Fake. Like maybe she's a fake too. She wears billowy white slacks and a pink fuzzy sweater. Gold hoops dangle from her ears. "What do you want?"

"I'd like to talk to Dr. Jones."

"You're dripping wet."

I look down. Rainwater soaks my jeans from my knees to my shoes.

I feel as if I'm standing in full buckets. "I rode my bike. Got splashed. I'll stand outside if he'll come to the door."

"Step inside." Her voice sounds chipped, edgy. "I'll tell him you're here."

She marches down the hallway. I close my eyes for a moment. Being here, facing another set of parents, getting ready to explain myself again—I'd rather burn in hell. Yet here I am.

Stephanie marches back, her lips thin. "He'll talk to you in his study." She points at my feet. "Take off your shoes."

I kick off my shoes and stride barefoot behind Stephanie through the living room and down a hallway to an open door. The carpet feels thick and warm under my cold, wet feet. Stephanie moves aside so I can step into the room. The office smells of fine leather and wood. Pictures and gold plaques hang on the walls. Hardcover books crowd tall wooden bookcases. A hand of solitaire is laid out on a small table in a corner, the cards placed in precise rows.

Seated at his desk in a high-back, leather swivel chair, elbows perched on the chair's arms, fingers forming a steeple, Dr. Jones stares at a computer screen. "A remarkable game, chess." He looks at me with tired eyes, his face drained. "Not a game of chance. A game won through skill. Not like roulette or dice. I like that, a game of skill. Do you play chess?"

"No, sir."

"Life is a chess game. Everyone makes a move. Everyone else reacts to somebody else's move. Action and reaction." He leans back in his leather chair. "Why are you here? Can you tell me where Megan is?"

"No, sir." My palms sweat. "I told the police that, and I've come to tell you myself. Megan left my house at four this morning. She was fine. She was headed home. We'd had a great time. We parked a while but just talked."

"Were both of you drinking?"

"Nothing. Not a drop. I don't drink."

Dr. Jones looks at me sideways. "I'd like to believe that. Megan's had a problem with alcohol in the past."

"We didn't even talk about drinking. We talked about... stuff. But

I don't know what happened to her. We had planned to get together today. A picnic, maybe."

"Had anything upset her?"

I hesitate and decide all-out truth is my only option. "Something that happened in this house Saturday was bothering her."

Dr. Jones's gaze shifts to his wife, and I detect a flash of annoyance in his eyes. "Were you quarreling with her again?"

Stephanie's chin rises defensively. "Not at all, and don't ask me what was wrong with her. I have no idea what goes on in that girl's mind. She's too unpredictable."

Dr. Jones's gaze returns to me. "Did she say what upset her?"

"She wouldn't tell me exactly, but she said she'd like to run away forever. I know she's run away before. She told me that. And the police told me."

"That's true. We found her after she called her friend. I called the girl this morning."

"Charley Cotton?"

Dr. Jones nods. "When Megan ran away the first time, she called Charley, and Charley called the police. The police called me, and we got her back."

"You think that's what'll happen this time?"

"I'm hoping so." Dr. Jones clears his throat. "Let me say this about my daughter. Her personality often wavers between that of a charming schoolgirl and that of an angry juvenile delinquent. She's an enigma."

"She's a brat," Stephanie says.

Dr. Jones fires an icy stare at Stephanie. "Sometimes. Megan's gone through periods when her behavior has been quite irresponsible."

"Like when she drank a fifth of cherry vodka, and we rushed her to the hospital to have her stomach pumped," Stephanie says.

Dr. Jones gives his wife another icy look, then his eyes slide to the computer screen. "I appreciate your stopping by, John. Is that all?"

"I'll do anything to help find Megan."

"I believe you will."

"Um... one other thing, Dr. Jones."

"What is it?"

I shift from one foot to the other. "Um… did the police lock Cole Wainwright up last night?"

"I don't believe so."

"He threatened Megan and me—you heard him. He could've been waiting for Megan when she got home. He could have taken her some place, harmed her."

Dr. Jones leans back in his chair. "I talked to his father last night on Cole's cell phone—I made the boy call his parents. Mr. Wainwright assured me Cole would leave the dance without further disturbance. He insisted Cole would come straight home."

"Do you think he did?"

Dr. Jones's lips purse. "I have no way of knowing. Perhaps he didn't."

"He could've waited in front of this house until Megan got home."

"I've thought of that too, but I don't want to believe it. Just as I don't want to believe you harmed her."

I sigh. "I didn't."

"I want to believe she's run away," Dr. Jones says, tilting back and closing his eyes for a second. "She'll be found and brought home safely."

"I hope so."

"She's probably gotten herself into serious trouble," Stephanie says. "That's my guess."

Ignoring his wife, Dr. Jones rests his elbows on the arms of his chair. "Thank you again for stopping by."

I realize my dismissal is final now. I mumble good-bye and follow Stephanie to the front door, where she turns to face me. She's beautiful, her face smooth, clear, unblemished but flushed now. She glances over her shoulder then looks at me, her eyes daggers.

"There are several things Megan's daddy didn't tell you about his precious baby girl." Her voice is raspy.

"What?"

"She's a slut. She never parks with a guy and just talks. You lied."

"I told the truth."

"I'll be honest with you," Stephanie says, her lips thinning. "Megan's not a brat—she's a bitch. She probably lied to you about me. God knows I've tried to be a good stepmother to her, but she's determined to cast me as a Disney villainess. What did she say?"

"Nothing."

"Are you sure?" Stephanie's eyes are slits under those spider-leg lashes. "Whatever she said, don't believe her."

I cock my head. "Why are you worried? What do you think she said?"

"No telling what that girl will do or say."

"I know one thing..."

"What?"

"She doesn't like you very well either." My eyes lock with Stephanie's. "Something about her dad upset her yesterday. Something that happened in this house. Maybe *you* were involved."

The muscles in Stephanie's neck tighten. She yanks open the door. "Get out!"

I've hit close to something, but I don't know what. I slip my warm feet into my wet shoes and tromp down the porch steps and across the soggy grass to the oak tree, where I leaned my bike. The soft southerly winds have shifted to winds from the north, bringing with them more clouds.

I feel cold and empty. *Where's Megan?* Why did Stephanie Jones seem so pissed at me? *Does she think I know something I shouldn't?*

EIGHTEEN

JOHN HAWK

I FEAR RETURNING TO SCHOOL. How many kids know Megan is missing? Hundreds saw me at the prom dancing like crazy with her. They saw my scuffle with Cole. How many rumors have spread behind my back?

Anne and Donnie sleep late every morning. My sister works at the Vanishing Point as a cocktail hostess, mostly nights. She has to dress like a skank: lots of makeup, short skirts, low-cut T-shirts or blouses so every guy can sneak a peek whenever she leans over. But the tips are good, she says. I babysit for her whenever I can, saving her money and helping earn my keep. I owe her that and a lot more.

I climb out of bed at six a.m. and fix my breakfast. I splash milk over cornflakes and whip up a toasted English muffin smothered with crunchy peanut butter and grape jelly. While I eat, I usually watch cartoons on the fourteen-inch color TV on the kitchen table. Not this morning. Instead, I turn on the local news. I watch for a story about Megan's disappearance.

There is none.

The TV features stories about the flood. Angry residents living along creek banks face TV cameras and demand to know why they weren't given any warning. Cameras catch homeowners rowing down their streets, their cars left behind in driveways and half submerged in swirling water. The newspaper shows an aerial view of Credit Island's flooded shorelines. The caption reads: **FIRST TIME IN NINE**

YEARS. I recognize the roof of the picnic pavilion Megan and I passed on our way to park. I was sure the directions I gave Garske pinpointed the spot where Megan and I had stopped.

Hallways, cafeteria, study hall, and classrooms—kids' stares smart like bee stings. I suspect everyone knows about Megan's disappearance and that I'm the last one to have seen her. But if I turn to look, eyes dart away from mine.

I remember that being-stared-at feeling from when I went to school after Riley's death. But back in Des Moines, because everybody knew me, I caught a lot of in-your-face verbal abuse too: "You are a major screw-up, you know that?" Or "Why didn't you leave Riley alone? She was an awesomely nice girl!" Here at River Valley High, I hear only whispers: "That's him... He probably got her drunk... No telling what else he did to her."

Like I had after Riley's death, I feel as if I want to curl up inside myself and disappear. But this time, I try to carry my head high. Nobody is going to push me around. I'm responsible for Riley's death, but not for Megan Jones's disappearance. *Don't mess with me.*

During C lunch, I spot Cole Wainwright in the cafeteria. I amble up to his table. My heart rate picks up several beats. Maybe I can wring some answers out of him. If something bad has happened to Megan, this guy is surely to blame.

One of Cole's buddies eyes me, taps Cole's shoulder, and Cole looks up. He brushes his brown hair back and tucks it behind his ears.

"What do you want?" His thin face is dark, sullen.

I square my shoulders. "We need to talk."

"Got nothing to say to you, asswipe."

"About Megan."

Cole shoves his plate of ketchup-drenched french fries aside and stands. "You heard from her?"

His friends stare at me, their eyes flashing hate.

"Let's talk outside. Alone." I walk out through the open fire-exit doors.

The weekend's dark clouds and rain have given way to blue skies, soft winds, and a warm sun. A lot of kids from C lunch sit in the grass under oak trees, eating sack lunches, laughing, and talking. Three tall blue spruces grow close to the school building, and their strong pine scent fills the air. I halt by one of the trees, and Cole shuffles up next to me.

He stuffs his hands deep into his jeans front pockets. "What do you want?"

"I haven't heard from Megan. I thought you might know something. You were her boyfriend."

His hands fire out of his pockets, and he jabs a finger at me. "I'm *still* her boyfriend. If you think some big-city asswipe like you can horn in… if you think we're all lowlifes living on the river—"

"Listen, I'm not trying to steal Megan. I went out with her because she asked me, if you really want to know."

He jabs at me again. "You think you're the only new guy who's come to school here that Megan's had an eye for? Don't flatter yourself."

"I'm not. I'm simply telling the truth—and get the finger out of my face, dickhead."

"She always comes back to me," he says, the finger dropping. "But this was the prom, man." He swipes a hand across his face. "Our last one."

I hate this guy and can't believe Megan liked him, but at that moment, I feel for him. I mean, if I thought someone had been trying to steal Riley from me, I'd be in his face just like Cole's in mine. "Look, let's not fight. Maybe we can't be friends, but let's put our heads together. Let's figure out where she might be."

He glares at me. "You parked with her on Credit Island, didn't you?"

"Man, let's focus on what's important."

"I swear, if I find out—if she tells me—"

"I didn't hurt her in any way," I say. "If I had, I wouldn't be talking to you right now. Her car's home, but she isn't. You think she parked it, walked into the rain, and melted? Does that make sense?"

"I don't know what the hell happened to her."

"Let's figure it out."

He bites his lower lip, looking miserable. "She's run away before.

She does freaky shit like that. Doesn't care who she worries. No telling where she went."

"Prom night, she was pissed at her dad."

He whips a hand through the air. "She's always pissed at him."

"But she wouldn't tell me what happened. And I know she doesn't like her stepmom."

"She totally hates the bitch."

I rub my jaw and the back of my neck. "I think there's a connection between Megan's dislike for her stepmom and Megan's disappearance. Something happened at the house that made her mad as hell at her dad and stepmom."

"That's possible."

"What could it be?"

Cole shrugs. "How the hell do I know?"

"*Think!*"

"Look, I'm tired of all this. Megan'll be back today or tomorrow, and it'll be like nothing happened. She'll come back to me. So why don't you leave me the hell alone? Forget about Megan while you're at it."

"You wrote me a note the other day and left it in my locker. Said I was 'dead meat' if I took Megan to the prom."

Cole glances at his shiny black biker boots. "Yeah? So what?"

"I kept the note. If something's happened to Megan, I'll show it to the police. They'll figure out it's your handwriting, even if it is left-handed."

"No, they won't."

"It's a threat they'll take seriously, and then they'll be on your butt."

Cole's smile twists into a wicked grin. "I saw you tear the note up and throw it away, asswipe. I was watching."

Damn!

"Megan's okay," he says. "Unless *you* did something stupid. You were the last one seen with her."

I shake my head in frustration.

Cole's chest puffs up. "When Megan shows up, you stay away from her. You might think you're tough and you can shove everybody around, but I've got four or five guys who'll pound your sorry ass into the ground."

"You better recruit more than four or five."

"None of us like strangers coming to our school and messing with our women. River kids stick together." Brushing by me, he heads back to the cafeteria. "*Dead meat!* Don't forget it."

NINETEEN

JOHN HAWK
CHARLOTTE COTTON

I SIT IN SEVENTH PERIOD AMERICAN lit and study Charley Cotton as she trudges into the classroom, looking whipped. She looks as if she hasn't slept in forever. Like me.

She wears cutoff jeans, a red T-shirt, and white sneakers. She's tiny but shapely, with a pointed nose and chin. She plunks into her seat to my right, the row by the windows, four seats from the front. Sunlight streaming through the windows bounces off her short, kinky, brownish hair.

Maybe Megan called Charley. Maybe Megan told her where she is. I couldn't wring any information out of Cole, but maybe I can coax some out of Charley Cotton.

After class, I follow Charley into the hallway. I manage to keep sight of her in the horde of students galloping for the doors. I intend to talk to her in the parking lot before she hops on a school bus or into her car.

I trail her to her locker and wait ten feet away, by the library doors. She shoves some of her books onto the top shelf. She crams a couple into her backpack. After she finishes, I tail her through the hallways. We pass my locker, so I grab a second to drop off my books then scoot after her into the parking lot.

As cars and trucks rev up, tires squealing and the air filling with exhaust, she skitters along, talking to no one. But she looks back twice.

I catch a glimpse of John Hawk trailing thirty feet behind me. *What the hell's he doing? Stalking me?* I weave between cars, approaching my truck, and decide I can't take it any longer. I mean, I caught him staring at me all during seventh period. What's with him? I'll bet the police have been questioning him and asking tough questions. Like they did me.

This morning, the cops came and dragged me out of study hall—everyone stared—and took me to a conference room in the counseling suite, where we could sit at a table and be alone. One was Officer Striker, the school liaison officer. He has pretty red hair and awesome blue eyes. He's a nice guy, but don't cross him. He can be mean. The other, a Lieutenant Garske, was fat with a face like a bulldog's. They basically wanted to know about Megan and who she hung with.

"What's her relationship with John Hawk?" Garske asked. He did most of the questioning. "How long has she known him?"

"Not long. Two or three weeks maybe. The prom was their first date."

"What do you know about him?"

I felt nervous sitting there talking about Megan's personal life, my hands fidgeting in front of me on the table. "Not much. I read a little bit about him in a newspaper article on the Internet. He's been in a lot of trouble."

"We're aware of that. Has he been abusive to Megan? Was she afraid of him?"

"I don't think so."

"This Wainwright kid, what's he like?"

"Mean sometimes. Gets jealous easy. Sneaky."

"Abusive?"

"Verbally. I think he pushed Megan around a lot. I've seen bruises on her arms like he grabbed and shook her. She keeps her mouth shut about stuff like that though. But I think if he got pissed enough..."

Striker said, "Go on."

"If he got pissed enough, he could hurt her. Maybe bad."

Garske asked, "Any reason why Megan might've been upset on

prom night? Why she might've done anything… unusual? Like run away?"

I kept my face expressionless. I figured it was none of their business about Stephanie Jones. Megan was in enough trouble without my blabbing stuff about her stepmom. Besides, how could the cops' knowing about Stephanie and her lover help find Megan?

Striker leaned toward me, seeming friendly. I supposed if I were to be buddies with a cop, it would be him. He seemed ready to help.

He said, "Tell us if you know anything, Charley. John Hawk says Megan was upset prom night. Something to do with her dad. Something that happened at home."

"So what else is new? She's always upset with her dad. And her stepmother. She doesn't much like her home life."

Striker and Garske looked at each other then asked me other stuff, like where Megan hid out when she ran away. I told them she'd ended up in a St. Vincent's shelter in Chicago. The cops wanted to know if she was promiscuous. I said I didn't think so, which was a big lie. But I had to protect her. They didn't need to know that.

"Does she drink?" Striker asked.

"Not after her dad hauled her to the ER about six months ago and they pumped her stomach. She had tangled with a fifth of vodka at a party. At home, she fell in the bathroom and made a lot of noise. Woke her dad up. He took her to the hospital."

"She quit drinking?" Garske asked.

"Cold turkey. She realized how stupid it was to lose control of herself like that. She didn't want to mess up her whole life."

"Good thinking," Striker said.

"You have to admire her," I said, "getting sober by herself."

"But where is she?" Garske asked.

The million-dollar question!

Then they said I could go but to call if I heard from Megan. I promised I would.

"Don't keep any secrets," Striker warned. "The minute you hear anything, let us know. We can help."

I nodded and shoved my chair back, hoping they were finished with me.

"One other thing," Striker said. "God forbid, but if something bad has happened to Megan—like if there's a rapist out there, maybe a killer—you and every other girl in this town need to watch out. You understand what I'm telling you? There might be a real bad guy hanging out in River Valley."

My hands clenched. I gulped and nodded again. I hadn't thought about that. "I do. I understand completely."

Now Hawk's stalking me and seriously creeping me out.

I stop in front of my pickup—Old Blue—and swing around to stare at him. "What's with you?"

Startled, he stops but nearly bumps into me. I back up. He backs up.

The bright sun is blinding him, so he cups his hand above his eyes. "Hi. I'm… I'm John Hawk."

"I know who you are. We're in seventh period together, remember? Why are you following me?"

He clears his throat and turns his head to the side, trying to avoid the sun's glare. I stare at him.

"I need to talk to you," he says. "Megan told me you guys are best friends."

I don't say anything.

He says, "So I figure the two of you probably talk a lot. I'm in big trouble. She might be too. I thought you could help."

"Probably not." I fish in my pockets and pull out my keys then walk around to the driver's side of Old Blue and unlock the door.

He trails me. "Hey! Wait a minute."

"I'm in a hurry."

"Look, no one knows where Megan is. I thought you might have talked to her since the prom. Do you know where she is? Is she okay?"

I ignore him. I'm about to climb into my truck when he grabs my left wrist and pulls me away from Old Blue. His putting his hand on me totally ticks me off! I snap my wrist, hoping to yank it free, but his grip is like an iron clamp.

"Let go of me!" I yell.

"You've got to talk to me," he says, his eyes flashing desperation.

"Let fucking go of me!" My face feels as hot as the sun. "You have no right—!" I claw at his fingers. "Let go!"

"I will, but talk to me!"

"I don't know where Megan is!" I dig at his hand, but my fingernails are too short to do any damage. "I told her dad that, the cops, and now I'm telling you! So let go, you asshole!" When I bare my teeth, ready to bite, he releases me, and I stumble backward against my truck. I'm furious, my blood pumping hard. "Don't ever touch me again! You might have put your hands on Megan, but not on me. I'm not a jock-toy."

"I'm sorry. I didn't mean to hurt you." He lets out a long breath. "Let's start over." He holds out his hand to shake. "Name's John Hawk. I took Megan to the prom—you already know that. Now no one knows where she is. I'm worried about her." He extends his hand farther. "Can you help me find her?"

Ignoring his hand, I glare at him and rub my wrist. God, he's good-looking with that reddish hair and those deep brown eyes. *Oh my!* The scar—I'm curious about the scar. *But good-looking guys can sometimes be the biggest pervs.*

"You don't care about Megan," I say. "You're like all the rest of the strays she takes into her life. She's loving and caring and kind and generous, and all you guys take advantage of her."

"I didn't."

"I don't know what she sees in losers like you. I told her not to get involved with you."

"I tried to avoid her," he says.

"You're no better than that brain-dead scum-sucker Cole Wainwright. And now *you* ask *me* where she is? I don't know where she is. What did you *do* to her? You're a wrestler. Did you break her bones?"

A scowl creasing his face, John looks disgusted. "I did *nothing* to her. Were you at the prom? Did you talk to her there?"

"I didn't go."

"I've talked to her father, stepmother, and Cole trying to find out about her."

"None of those people really know Megan," I said.

"I believe that. That's why I'm talking to you. I know Megan ran away once, and she called you. Tell me about that."

"She wanted to punish her dad for marrying that stupid bimbo Stephanie. What I'm telling you is I haven't heard from Megan, and I'm worried about her. I don't know where she is."

"I'm worried too."

"For your own hide maybe."

"For Megan's. Believe me."

I study John Hawk again, reappraising him. Maybe he isn't so bad. He appears honest, genuine. Maybe he is concerned. But he's a wrestler. A sweaty, stinky wrestler who slams people around and bends their arms and legs backward. Who could even like a wrestler?

"Megan says you're different. Are you?" I ask.

"I didn't take advantage of her, if that's being different."

"Like I believe you." I open the door to my truck.

"Think she's punishing her dad again? She was pissed at him prom night."

"Could be." I shrug out of my backpack and sling it into the passenger's seat. I bounce up into the truck and sit behind the steering wheel, leaving my door open. "Look, I've got to go. If she calls me, I'll let you know, okay?"

"Good, that's good."

"When she ran away to Chicago, it took three days before she called. This has been only two days."

"Thanks!"

I slam my door closed. I grind Old Blue's starter for nearly half a minute before the engine fires. The truck backfires and belches a cloud of blue exhaust before I finally get it rolling toward the exit. I glimpse John Hawk shuffling across the parking lot to the east side of the building, where he's probably chained his bike to the rack. Though he grabbed my wrist, he doesn't seem like a guy who would deliberately hurt anyone. But you can never tell about guys. Like I said, he's a wrestler.

What am I going to do with Megan's secret about Stephanie?

If something really bad has happened to Megan, maybe I should tell someone Stephanie Jones has a lover. Maybe there's a connection between Megan's finding out and her disappearance. Everyone knows Megan hated Stephanie. But who'd believe me? My accusation would be only hearsay, a rumor from a girl no one can find.

I stop Old Blue at the parking lot's exit, ready to turn right, and the brakes squeak. *Please, Megan, call me. Or I'll have to tell.*

TWENTY

JOHN HAWK

FROM TWO BLOCKS AWAY, WHEN I'm pedaling home Wednesday after school, I spot a gleaming police cruiser parked in front of my sister's house. I've seen them parked in front of my house before, the cops just itching to talk to me. Wolves circling their prey. The sight always jolts me.

Sweat drips from me. My skin prickles. *Four days since the prom. No Megan. Let it be good news. When I walk through the door, let everyone be smiling. Let Garske be grinning. "Hey! Guess what, boy! Megan's dad called us. She's home. She's fine. We thought you'd like to know. Everything's cool. Sorry we harassed you. Obviously you're a good kid. The best. We had you all wrong."*

I drop my bike in the middle of the front lawn. I sprint and hit the porch with one bound. I yank the screen door open and stand in the living room, the door banging closed.

I feel all eyes on me. Arrows. Daggers.

My sister sits at the kitchen table, a cigarette burning in an ashtray, with Donnie on her knee. She shouldn't smoke around Donnie like that. Garske and another cop, a skinny bald guy I don't recognize, sit on the couch.

"This is Officer Regan," Garske says.

Regan stands and offers his hand. "How do you do, John?"

Hardly able to breathe, I shake the cop's hand. "Megan's home?" *Let it be true.*

Garske gives me a cold stare. "Not quite."

My gaze swings to Anne. She sucks smoke into her lungs. Then turning her head, she blows smoke out through her nose, away from Donnie. She nails me with her worried, pissed-off look. "They haven't told me anything."

I spot a manila envelope on the coffee table. "What's that?"

Regan picks it up.

Garske says, "You've got quite a list of priors, boy."

I square my shoulders. "So what?"

"You want us to refresh your memory?"

"No."

"Officer Regan would like to anyway." Garske points at the envelope in Regan's hand. "Read to the boy."

Regan seems nervous, embarrassed. He glances at me then pulls a sheet of paper out of the envelope. He clears his throat. "John Hawk, age thirteen, convicted of violation of moped-motorcycle laws. Also convicted of driving without a license. Age fourteen, expelled twice from school for fighting. Age fifteen, ticketed for possessing an alcoholic beverage as a minor. Age sixteen, ticketed for possessing an alcoholic beverage as a minor and for possessing a fake ID."

Crushing her cigarette in the ashtray, Anne stands, Donnie cradled in her arms. "I think I'll read to him in the bedroom. Excuse me."

"There's more," Garske says. "It gets worse. Don't you want to hear?"

Anne hurries down the hallway; the bedroom door closes. I'm grateful she took Donnie out of earshot.

"You don't have to read anything else," I tell Regan.

"I want you to listen to the rest of this." Garske nods at his partner. "Go ahead."

Regan clears his throat again and coughs into his fist. "Age sixteen, ordered by the court to attend a nine-week CADS program: Center for Alcohol and Drug Services. Dropped out and had to start over. Age seventeen, convicted of speeding, twice. Age seventeen, charged with criminal mischief, setting off firecrackers on the Fourth of July in violation of state and local ordinances. Fined three hundred fifty dollars. Age seventeen, involved in a fatal auto-truck accident. License is suspended by state for five years. Habitual offender."

Heat spirals into my face as if it's on fire. "Did they tell you I wasn't at fault in that accident? I wasn't charged. They took my license anyway. I didn't have proof of insurance in the car, but I had insurance. They nailed me just to nail me."

"Sure," Garske says. "And they told us you were trapped in the car for four hours. You were on a country road. By the time they got you out, hauled you to the hospital, and somebody thought to run a blood alcohol test on you, your test said you were clean."

"That's because I wasn't drinking."

"You were found with a beer cup in the backseat of your car. Whose was that?"

I could tell him the truth—it was Riley's. But he won't believe me. Why the hell bother? "I don't remember."

"Des Moines PD says you've got a rich old man. A lawyer who's spent a fortune to keep you out of jail, pay your fines—and provide you with a fast car and a nice big house to live in. Maybe that's how the test turned out negative. Daddy paid someone to fix it."

"If my dad has that kind of pull, why didn't he get my license back too?"

"Only so much a guy can do," Garske says. "There's one more item." He nods at Regan. "Read it to the boy."

The slender cop clears his throat once more and coughs into his fist again. "Charged with assault with intent to commit injury. Ordered by the courts to write a letter of apology to the victim."

Garske studies me, his bushy eyebrows bunched together. "They said you got in a fight and practically squeezed some guy's head off in a chokehold."

I glance at the ceiling then at the floor. "Someone was sending me black roses to punish me for Riley's death. I couldn't handle it any longer. I figured out who was doing it."

"Her older brother?"

"That's right."

"They said you almost killed him. You were a state wrestling champion?" Garske asks.

"What about it?"

Garske laces his fingers. "You got quite a record, boy. Angry, hostile, aggressive—that's how the folks at the Des Moines PD describe you."

"My record doesn't prove I harmed Megan. You can't use it in court against me."

"The boy's smart," Garske says, nodding several times. "Very smart. Let me ask you, you beat up girls too?"

"Give me a break."

The two cops exchange a glance.

Garske cracks his knuckles. "A commercial fisherman found the body of a young female with black hair this afternoon in the Mississippi River. Found the body tangled in his fishing net."

The bottom drops out of my stomach. I feel dizzy. "What?"

"You're not getting any breaks, boy. Megan's dead."

TWENTY-ONE

JOHN HAWK

MY MIND EXPLODES INTO A million pieces. Tears sting my eyes. The words ricochet in my head before I can say them. "Megan's dead?" I lick my lips and fight a sickening, rising sense of horror. "Megan's dead?"

"Dead," Garske repeats. "She's…"

I think he says something else, but I hear only my own breath coming fast and hard. I glare at Garske. *I hate this cop.* "You're lying! Why are you lying?"

"I've seen the body," Garske says. "As we speak, Megan's father is making a positive identification."

Is this really happening? "Must be a mistake!"

"After four days in the river, the body is bloated and chewed up a bit—turtles, catfish—but still identifiable."

That picture sends shivers through my body. Clamping my eyes shut, I blast the image out of my mind and hold my breath for what seems like forever. Then I force myself to exhale slowly. "I didn't do anything to her. I've got nothing else to say."

Rising to his feet, Garske stares down at me, nodding. "We're not reading you your rights yet, boy. The coroner has to examine the body. We haven't got word about your clothes from the crime lab."

The tears rushing into my eyes feel like lava ready to burst down my cheeks.

Garske asks, "You sure there's nothing else you want to tell us about prom night? What you and Megan really did? What happened to her? Now's the time."

I drop my chin to my chest, squeeze my eyes shut again, and stab at my tears. "I told you everything."

"Megan's body was nude."

My head jerks up, my eyes wide open. "Nude?" The word is a croak.

"How do you suppose she ended up in the river nude?"

"I don't know!" The tears flow, and I knuckle them off my cheeks as fast as I can. I hate crying in front of this stupid cop.

"You were the last one seen with her," Garske says.

"I wasn't the last one. Somebody else—"

"Who? Tell me that? And why?" His voice grows louder. "Motive, means, opportunity—that's what it takes to pin a murder rap on someone. You had the opportunity."

I fire back with, "What about motive and means?"

"You almost strangled your girlfriend's brother," he says, bringing his hands together as though his fingers are squeezing someone's neck. "Your hands and strength are your means."

"Why did I do it?"

"She wouldn't put out."

I laugh and knuckle my tears again. "You don't know what you're talking about."

His eyebrow cocked, he says, "Are you telling me she *did* put out?"

"That's none of your damn business."

"Don't worry. Her body and your clothes will answer all our questions." Garske motions to Regan. "Let's go." At the door, Garske turns. "Don't even think about running away. Hear?"

I don't answer.

"You paying attention, boy?" he says, pointing at me.

"Not much."

"What did they want?" Anne creeps into the living room with Donnie trailing behind her. "They're gone, aren't they? I heard the screen door close, a car drive away."

"Where are the policemen?" Donnie asks.

I sit on the edge of the lounge chair. "They left." I sag back.

"You look horrible," Anne says. "What did they say?"

I shake my head.

"Is there any word about Megan?"

"Are the policemen coming back?" Donnie asks. "Huh? Make them give me a ride in the car."

"It's that bad?" Anne frowns. "Have you been crying?"

"It's worse than bad."

"She's... been found?"

I slam my eyes shut for a second then look at her. "Yes."

Anne's fingers jump to her mouth. Her lips quiver. Her face turns stone white. "She's...?"

I nod. Tears burn my eyes again. Angry tears. I glance at Donnie to see if the boy understands, but I can't tell. I quickly look away. I don't want him to see me cry.

"Oh my God," Anne says, her fingers still in front of her mouth. "Oh my God..."

"Found in the river," I say. "A fisherman's net."

"Dear God..."

"Can we go fishing?" Donnie says. "You promised, John. Pleeease?"

"Not now." I stand slowly. I'm like a zombie. Numb. I still can't believe it. Riley's death left me in shambles, nearly destroying me. Though I wasn't in love with Megan, Megan's death seems worse than Riley's because I had nothing to do with it, but I'm being blamed. I mean, Megan's death isn't my fault, is it?

The painful truth slinks into my brain. *Yes, it is!* I'm to blame for everything. I've made mistakes I can never take back.

If I hadn't accepted Megan's invitation to the prom, none of this would have happened. She would have dated Cole. She'd still be alive. I'd be an anonymous kid at River Valley High. Not a suspect for what? Murder?

Riley would be alive too, if I'd had my act together.

Cursed because I'm a curse to others. Guilt leaps onto my shoulders.

I shuffle toward the front door.

Anne frowns. "Where are you going?" Alarm rings in her voice.

The weight of guilt is so heavy I'm barely able to shrug. "I don't know."

"Can we go fishing, John?"

"Stay here," Anne says. "Please? You've got to call Dad."

I stumble out the door. Ignoring my bike lying on the lawn, I plod down the street. The sun is bright and warm on my back. I have no destination in mind. I know only that I can't sit in the house. I have to keep moving. If I stay and stare at the walls, I might turn to stone and never move again. I have to keep thinking. I can't let my mind morph into stone. I have to keep figuring it out. *Means. Motive. Opportunity.*

It's about five o'clock. I walk by neighborhood houses. Tall oaks and maples shade green lawns. Flowers bloom in front yards: tulips, roses, pansies. People are arriving home from work, climbing out of their cars, slamming doors. Dogs tied to front porches bark at me. I smell hamburgers grilling on backyard barbecues.

Did Megan commit suicide? Did she jump from a bridge into the black river? *No way.* Who strips before jumping into water to drown? How did she get to a bridge to jump? Her car was at home. Did she walk from her house in the rain? *Not a chance.*

Who wanted Megan dead? Who had the opportunity? *Cole Wainwright!* His parents may have told him to come home from the dance, but he didn't. He followed Megan and me to Credit Island. I recall again the car lights following us as we drove onto the island. He wanted to check on her. *On us, Megan and me.* He wanted to see for himself what his so-called girlfriend was doing.

He left the island and waited for Megan at home. She got into his car, and they fought. Maybe he raped her and killed her accidentally. He stripped her then threw her into the river. He buried or burned her clothes so they wouldn't reveal who she'd been with. No hair or fibers or blood stains to give the cops a clue.

I tremble at the thought.

Or maybe a stranger followed her home. Maybe a stranger did all those things.

And then Cole Wainwright is innocent. But I'm still guilty.

Two questions plague me: If the cops accuse me of murdering Megan Jones, how can they prove something I didn't do? What evidence can link me to her murder?

I walk all the way to Rockingham Road, a narrow, twisting street on the edge of town, not far from the Mississippi River. Semis often use Rockingham as a thoroughfare, and a giant sixteen-wheel flatbed piled high with crushed cars lumbers by, filling the air with the stench of diesel fumes. It's the same smell that filled the air as I lay trapped upside down the night Riley died, a smell that lingered in my nostrils months after her death.

I feel my whole body swelling with anger, a fierce fire spreading through me. No one will blame me for *this* death. *Not this time! I am* not *the guilty party!*

I glance at my watch. Five fifty. Anne has already taken Donnie to the babysitter's and gone to work. I whirl and start home.

TWENTY-TWO

CHARLOTTE COTTON

I CAN'T STOP CRYING. HOT TEARS burst out of my eyes like liquid fire, soaking my pillow. I'm lying in my bed in semi-darkness. A breeze blowing through my open window and a shaft of moonlight penetrating the darkness offer me no comfort.

I heard it on TV, the ten o'clock news. I'd just finished my homework and switched on the TV.

I shudder and shake and cry.

The TV anchor said, "Breaking news: a River Valley commercial fisherman, Raymond Klein, reported to police Wednesday morning at about eleven a.m. that he'd discovered the nude body of a young woman with black hair snared in one of his nets. 'Water was down enough I thought I better check 'em,' Klein told police. 'There she was all tangled up. From the looks of her, she must've been there a day or two. Maybe longer.' Police have not released the identity of the young woman."

It's got to be Megan.

I am so fucking pissed! Anger boils in my belly. I roll around on my bed, kicking the air, and land on my back, flinging my forearm over my eyes.

Megan's dead! I can't believe it. I don't want to believe it. It can*not* be true.

But it has to be. Who else's nude body? *Nude!* Someone stripped and maybe raped Megan and killed her and threw her body into the Mississippi River like garbage.

I am so fucking pissed I will never get over this! *Fuck!*

Who would do that to Megan? John Hawk? Cole Wainwright? Probably not John. My feelings for John are up in the air, but Megan liked him. He wouldn't have had to rape her to satisfy himself.

That stupid sonofabitch Cole! He did it. He raped and killed my best friend forever.

Or maybe a stranger did it. How? Why? I am never, ever going to get over this, or forgive the bastard who did it.

A light rap sounds at my bedroom door. The knob clicks. I bolt up and flick on the table light next to my bed, casting a dim glow across the room. The door squeaks open, and Mom pokes her head in.

"Charley...?" she whispers then steps inside my room.

I blink two or three times, more tears gushing out of my eyes. I swipe them away. Looking at my mom is like looking in a mirror. We have the same build and same fizzy hair, except my forty-year-old mom has curves where I have lines and her hair's a bit gray at the temples. She's wearing red flannel PJs.

"Did you have the TV on?" she asks, still whispering.

"I heard." I sob, crouched on the edge of my bed, and throw my hands over my face.

"I'm so sorry, sweetheart."

Mom knows Megan and I have been best friends all through high school. Megan goes to a lot of rowdy sleepovers with her popular friends, but she always tells me—told me—the ones she liked best were the ones in my tiny room, the two of us alone where she didn't have to pretend to be anybody else. We talked about what it's like to be a girl—wishing your body was different, wondering if a guy liked you for you or because he wanted in your pants, trying to remember that you could be happy and complete even if the boy didn't come along. Who are you, really? What are you going to be?

"I'm so sorry," Mom says again, shuffling across the room. She sinks down next to me on the edge of my bed. "Do you know anything about this?"

She flings her arms around me and squeezes. My head lands on her shoulder, my face buried in her neck. Her scent is citrus from her soap. Mom and I haven't hugged like this since Grandpa died a year ago.

"I know she was involved with two boys." I suck in deep breaths of air. "But I'm not sure either of them did anything to her. I don't know. I'll kill him myself if I find out—"

"Shhh!" Mom hisses. "Megan doesn't have any real enemies, does she?"

"Cole's out-of-his-mind mad at her. She went to the prom with a new guy at school, and that guy's... got a skeevy reputation."

"Oh Lord. I can't understand why someone would do this."

"I feel so guilty. I wish I would've said something or done something to change what happened."

"Sweetheart, it's not your fault," Mom says, running her hand across my head, flattening my hair.

"The minute Megan dumped Cole, I should've talked her out of going to the prom with John. Then none of this would've happened. She'd still be alive. I should've told her we'll have a sleepover. She liked sleeping over here." I push out of Mom's embrace and sit straight. "I should've told her prom wasn't worth it. I should've tried really hard to talk her out of it, but I didn't. Why didn't I see something like this coming—Cole or John or some other stupid freak doing something bad to Megan?"

I'm hiccupping. I slam my hand over my mouth, and Mom gently pats my back.

"Charley, sweetheart, you can't blame yourself. No one could've seen this happening. You're not to blame. Don't go there. That's a treacherous road."

"I know, but I could've saved her if—"

Still hiccupping, I look up, and Mom pats my back again lightly. Dad stands in the doorway dressed in blue sweatpants and a white T-shirt, arms crossed over his wide chest. He's a big, handsome, jovial, always-smiling Irishman whose black hair turned silver practically overnight. He's not smiling now though. He's scowling, eyebrows bunched together.

"What the hell's going on with kids these days?" he says.

The scent of his aftershave wafts into my room. He always shaves before bedtime. I think Mom likes that.

She says, "Megan apparently dumped Cole and went to the prom with someone else. But it's so hard to believe either of them would—I mean, a young boy…"

Dad heaves a sigh and shakes a finger at me. "Look, Charley, I'm sure as hell sorry about Megan. I think she's the best girl—I really liked her—and I know you'll want to get to the bottom of this, but I'm telling you, stay away from that Wainwright kid. He's trouble. And that other kid—whoever he is—stay away from him too. If either one did this and he thinks you know something—well, you can just never tell what might happen." Another big sigh escapes Dad. "You understand what I'm saying?"

I nod and wipe my nose with the balled-up tissue.

"Dad's right." Mom kisses my forehead. "Stay away from them. Don't do anything foolish."

Both say again that they're sorry and if they can help, let them know right away. They tell me to get some sleep, they'll see me in the morning. They love me.

But I can't sleep. I toss and turn while scenes of the fun times Megan and I enjoyed flash through my mind like a highlight reel. With Dad driving the boat, I taught Megan how to water-ski on the river that first summer we were friends. She popped up out of the water on her first try, skimmed along for about forty yards, then nosedived. But she jumped right back up on the skis and tried again. Last year, she was skiing on one leg.

I talked her into catfishing with me only once though. She wouldn't bait her hook with a night crawler. When I held the squirming worm under her nose, she scrunched up her face, clenched her fists to her cheeks, and squealed, "Ewww!" She caught two nice flatheads, but she nearly jumped out of the boat after she hauled each fish in and it flopped around at her feet. Of course she wouldn't take the fish off the hook and covered her face when I did it for her. A true girly girl. But one of a kind.

I love you, Megan.

One moonlit night, we sat outside the back of the Hut in lawn chairs, and she told me I had a really great life with a loving Mom and Dad and the river for a friend. She hoped nothing ever happened to fuck it up. Of course, I knew what she was talking about. She didn't have to tell me. Her mom's death, her dad's gambling, and his marriage to Stephanie had fucked up her life.

I lock my eyes shut now, squeezing out more tears. I'm afraid Megan's death has already fucked up my life.

Everything's my fault.

TWENTY-THREE

JOHN HAWK

A T THREE A.M., ANNE'S TOYOTA grinds to a rattling stop in front of the house. I lie flat on my back in bed, the light on my night table filling my bedroom with a soft glow and stubby shadows. I'm so tired I can hardly think, but I can't sleep. That terrible weight of guilt and frustration is dragging me down. *Riley: dead. Megan: dead.* Why have people I liked and loved died? Or left? Why has my life turned out so rotten? What do you do when your life is cursed, tragedy everywhere, and you're helpless? Guilt weighs so heavily on you that you can hardly breathe.

If I don't uncover the truth about Megan, I'll never have a life, and I'll never learn to forgive myself. Though I'm innocent, I'll always be blamed for Megan's death. People will say I was the last person to be with her. I have to be the killer. Look at my record. Didn't I kill Riley too? How can I live with the weight of my own guilt and everyone else's blame and suspicion? What about justice for Megan? Whoever did this terrible thing needs to pay. *I'm not running again. Not this time.*

The front door creaks open then closes. Anne's footsteps shuffle into the hallway. She opens the door to Donnie's room, across from mine. Donnie cries, probably still half asleep and confused in Anne's arms, as she lays him in his bed and covers him. I don't have to be there to know she drops a kiss on his forehead.

A few seconds later, my doorknob clicks. The door inches open, and Anne pokes her head into the room. Wearing only my jockey shorts, I sit up, pull the sheet up to my waist, and rub my eyes.

"Oh!" Anne says. "You startled me. I thought you'd be asleep. I was going to turn your light out." She steps into the room. She's wearing a white T-shirt with THE VANISHING POINT printed in bold purple letters across her chest. She's also wearing a short, pleated purple skirt.

"Can't sleep," I say.

"Your eyes are red and puffy like you haven't slept for weeks. Maybe if you turned out the light."

"That won't help."

"Where did you go this afternoon?"

"Walking. Thinking. Sorry I ditched and wasn't home to babysit."

Leaning against the doorjamb, she says, "What are you going to do?"

"I'm not sure. Go to school. Ask questions. Find out what I can. I'm not calling Dad. Not yet."

"I told you if something bad happened, I'd call him myself."

"Don't. Please. Give me a chance to work this out."

"I don't know, John. That's all people talked about tonight at the lounge. The high school principal's daughter is dead. Found nude in the river."

I smooth my sheet over my legs. "What do they think happened?"

"Most people think she went to a party after the prom, someone assaulted her and accidentally killed her, then panicked and threw her body into the river, hoping it would float away in the flood waters."

I bite my bottom lip. *Cole Wainwright.*

Shifting against the doorjamb, Anne says, "Could she have done that? Gone to a party after she left you?"

"Someone must've picked her up at her house, but I don't think she went to a party."

"But you don't know that."

"We both said we were tired, needed sleep, and that we were going to do something later in the day. Maybe a picnic."

Anne hesitates a second, then says, "You might need a lawyer. Dad's your best chance. He's always been there for you."

I frown. "The cops haven't charged me with anything, and I don't want to listen to Dad's rant again. Not unless I really have to."

She steps closer to my bed. "But you're still in trouble. I don't think you should go to school this morning."

"I've got to. Somebody at school knows something."

"Kids at the dance saw you with Megan." Anne kicks off her high-heeled shoes and bends to pick them up. "Everyone in school—I mean *everyone*—will know she went with you. Now she's dead. They're going to be angry. Maybe violent. You should stay home."

"For how long?" I clutch my sheet and pull it up to my chest. "A week? A month? The rest of my life?" I shake my head. "I can't do that."

"You have to. It's the only wise choice."

"I can't let everyone think I'm afraid or that I have something to hide. I'll take my chances."

"I'm so worried about what's going to happen to you."

"I'll be all right. I'm sorry you and Donnie have been dragged into this."

Anne purses her lips and shifts her shoes from one hand to the other. "I'll wait a day. Give you time to get your thoughts together. Then if you don't call Dad, I will."

"I'll do it."

"Promise?"

"I promise," I say, dragging my hand across my face. "Good night."

"Good night." With that, Anne ducks out of my room, closes the door softly, and leaves me alone.

I roll around in bed, land on my stomach, punch my pillow, and flop onto my back again. I screw my eyes shut, but I know I'm facing more sleepless hours of wondering if my life will ever be good again. When I was Donnie's age, I had a mom and dad, lived in a great house, and everybody liked me.

TWENTY-FOUR

JOHN HAWK

THUMBS HITCHED IN HIS JEANS, Cole Wainwright is the first one to ambush me at school.

"You read the paper this morning?" he asks, sneering. "Watch any television?"

I stop my bike in front of the bike rack at the east side of the school building by the entrance. "Yeah. I read the paper. Watched television. We need to talk again."

It's seven forty-five a.m. The morning is sunny, warm, the grass wet with dew and glistening in the sunlight. School starts at eight. Obviously Cole has been waiting for me. I swing my leg over the bicycle seat and push the front wheel into the rack. Grim and silent, five other kids—three guys, two girls—fall in behind Cole, their fierce eyes glaring at me.

I swallow and stroke my chin.

The morning paper and TV stations officially identified the body discovered in the fisherman's net as Megan's. Authorities wouldn't comment on the cause of death until after further investigation. My name wasn't mentioned in any of the stories, but I'm sure that when the cops have all the evidence they need to hang me, my name will create a media explosion. Probably tomorrow. *But what evidence?*

Glaring at Cole, I hit him with, "Prom night, did you follow Megan and me to Credit Island? Were you spying on us?"

"You *did* take her there, didn't you?" His fists clench.

"After you spotted us, you left the island and waited for her at her house."

"You asswipe!"

The crowd swells. A voice in my head says, *Get your back to the building so no one can jump you from behind!*

I jerk back too late. More students run across the lawn and gather to witness the excitement. Some have already broken apart to surround me, cutting me off from the building. Whipping my head back and forth, I try to glimpse what's happening on all sides.

Cole steps into the circle of students. "We wondered if you'd be stupid enough to show up this morning."

"I've got nothing to hide."

"Tell us, how did you kill Megan?"

My hands ball into fists. "*You* killed her and dumped her into the river. Admit it!"

Cole swears and throws a quick right-hand punch, catching me by surprise. I raise my left hand, partially blocking the blow. Still, it bounces off my mouth, snapping my head sideways and stinging. I dance away.

A girl behind me yells, "He's afraid to fight!"

"He's a coward!"

"He's not afraid to kill girls!"

His fists in front of his face like a boxer's, breathing heavily, Cole circles me. "Killer!"

I can't win a fight against him and this mob. A fight will get me kicked out of school, leaving me no chance to talk to Charley and Striker again. But I can't run. Hadn't I told myself I wasn't running anymore? And I can't take more taunting from Cole Wainwright and this mob.

Crouching and staying as low as possible, I launch at Cole like a missile. My chest collides with his legs and thighs; I lock my arms around his legs. Pulling his hips in close, I lift him off the ground with the power of my own legs then slam him to the ground on his back. A perfect double-leg takedown, one of the most basic wrestling moves. I release him.

Cole sits up, surprise and anger registering in his wide eyes. "You're dead—"

Before Cole can scramble to his feet, I pounce, attacking him from the back, and hook my arms under his armpits, locking him up in a full nelson. It's illegal in high school wrestling but not in a schoolyard brawl. With the strength of my legs and upper body, I stand and hoist Cole to his feet. I keep him locked in the full nelson, my fingers laced, my palms pressuring the back of his head. His arms, from his elbows to his fingertips, flap like limp chicken wings.

The crowd holds back, I guess giving Cole a chance to escape and prove himself. He kicks at my shin with his right foot then stomps viciously on my instep. I take the blows, grit my teeth, and grind Cole's head down, burying his chin in his chest, a move that wedges his Adam's apple against his windpipe, cutting off his air.

"*Aggg...*"

"Somebody stop them! He's going to kill Cole!"

Cole sucks air into his lungs. "*Aggg... my neck... I can't...*"

His words finally reach my brain and wrench me back to the reality of what I'm doing, the stupidity of it.

I release Cole, hurling him to the ground. "Tell your friends to back off!"

He bounces on the ground. He rolls onto his back, grabs a single ragged gasp of air, and begins hacking and clawing at his throat. I face the crowd. I know what they're thinking. Not only have I killed Megan, their principal's daughter, but now I've also nearly broken her boyfriend's neck. Someone body-blocks me in the back of my knees, buckling my legs and toppling me over backward onto the dew-wet grass.

"Get him!" someone else shouts.

In an instant four guys swarm, kicking me in the back, the legs, the ribs, the stomach, and the head. *Whop! Whop! Whop!* Each blow jolts me with pain. I wrap my arms around my head and cover my ears with my biceps. I roll away and scramble to one knee. Someone kicks me between the shoulder blades, pitching me forward, face first. I smell grass and taste dirt before another kick to my head ignites a bright light in my brain.

TWENTY-FIVE

JOHN HAWK
CHARLOTTE COTTON

WHEN I COME TO, I'm sitting on the concrete step to the east entrance of the school, my head against the building's brick wall. All is black and quiet in my brain, but something wet and cool—a towel maybe—swabs my face.

"John!" A soft hand strokes my cheek. "Can you hear me?" A girl's voice filters down from far away. "Do you want to go to the hospital?"

Stupid question. I'm not hurt. I shake my head no, then wince. *Damn!* A terrible noise fills my head—like the buzzing of a thousand angry bees. A shaft of pain shoots through my shoulders.

"We can take you to the school nurse," the girl says. "I got this towel from her. You can come in and lie down if you need to."

I fight my way out of the blackness and force my eyes open. Striker's face blurs at first but moves into focus. I want to smile and say I'm okay, but my face hurts, and I can't find the words. I'm dizzy and sick to my stomach.

If I could stand up.

"Easy," Striker says and places a hand on my shoulder, holding me in place.

"Sit down." The girl's voice again.

I turn my head her way. Kinky hair. Pointed nose and chin. Freckles. Frowning. Charley Cotton.

She wipes my face with that wonderful wet towel. "At least you should see the nurse and lie down."

"I'm all right." I plant my palms on the cool concrete to push myself up—my butt won't budge.

She strokes my face with the towel. "Let me get this blood off your mouth. And the grass and dirt off your forehead."

"What started this?" Striker asks.

I shrug and wince. "I don't know." I feel along my nose, my cheeks, and the sides and back of my head. Though my face feels tender, everything seems to be intact. I'll be okay. "Where did everyone go?"

"Charley came running to get me," Striker says. "Said you were getting beat up. When I got here, kids darted in every direction."

"Period one was starting," Charley says. "Everyone ran to class."

"What happened?" Striker asks.

"I don't know. Cole Wainwright and I were talking…"

"Cole started it," Charley says. "When he couldn't finish it, his scum-sucking friends jumped in."

Still shaky, I brace my back against the rough brick wall and push myself up. Once on my feet, I lean on the wall to steady myself. A wave of nausea rolls over me, but it passes. "I'm all right."

"You don't look like it," Charley says.

I suck my bottom lip, tasting blood, then probe the nick with the tip of my tongue.

Charley swabs my forehead. "Your coming to school today was dumb."

"You need to stay out of trouble," Striker says.

"Story of my life. Did you check out Cole, where he went after the prom? Did he go home?"

"He went riding around with his buddies in his car. They didn't see Megan after the prom."

"What time did he get home?"

"Before four."

"Who said?" I ask.

"His parents."

"They'd lie for him." I rub my forehead. *Ouch!* "His buddies would too."

Striker says, "I think the best thing you can do for yourself and for the rest of us is go home. Keep a low profile."

"Like I've got something to hide? Like I'm guilty?"

"Stay home till we get a break in this case." He drags a hand through his thick red hair. "There'll be more details on TV tonight. Probably a picture of Megan."

"Her graduation picture," Charley says.

"That'll stir up more emotions," Striker says. "More resentment."

"I don't give a damn."

The cop grabs my shoulder and squeezes; he's getting pissed, showing his temper. "John, think! Kids are crying in this school today. Mourning. There's a lot of grief here. You understand what I'm saying? I'll help you all I can, but you've got to cooperate."

I shrug out of his grip. "I get it, but I've got to defend myself."

"This is a small town. All these kids grew up together. Everyone liked Megan. They want somebody to pay for her death, and you're their target."

"He's right," Charley says, folding the towel and dabbing at my cheek.

God, I pray your life is cursed. Wherever you go, whatever you do— cursed! Mr. McGinnis's words ring in my ears.

Striker says, "There's no way I can guarantee your safety here. Go home. Stay there for a day or two till things simmer down. I'll take care of things."

Charley says, "That makes sense, John."

My head dips. I don't want to go home, but I don't have much of a choice. My fists clamp together, and frustration eats at me again. "All right."

Striker says, "I'll explain to Dr. Jones what happened this morning and why you're not in school." He pats my shoulder. "You sure you're all right?"

"I'm fine. Just sore." I rub the back of my neck and rotate my shoulders.

"You ride a bike this morning?" Striker asks.

"Yes."

"I could call a cruiser to give you a ride home. I don't know what to do about your bike."

"I can ride it."

"Throw it in the back of my truck," Charley says. "I'll take you home."

"Why are you doing this for me?" John asks as I grind Old Blue into gear and the truck creeps across the parking lot. He rolls down his window, inhaling the still-fresh morning air, probably trying to clear his battered brain.

"Because I feel like it," I say.

"I know you don't like me. And you're missing school."

"I skip once in a while."

"You're one of these small-town kids. You're Megan's best friend… *were* her best friend. Sorry… You must hate me more than anyone else, except maybe Megan's dad. Or Cole Wainwright."

I don't answer. *Why* am *I doing this?*

Mom and Dad's warning to stay away from Cole and John rushed into my head the instant I said I'd take John home. But I ignored it. John is the last known person to see Megan alive. He may be my best chance to find out what happened to her. If I can do that, maybe some of this horrible guilt that's eating at me will go away. And truthfully, I don't feel he's dangerous. Besides, I can take care of myself.

I peer straight through the windshield as Old Blue crawls along. I feel John's eyes nailing me. *Crap!* I know what he sees: someone who barely weighs over a hundred pounds, freckles covering her nose and cheekbones, wearing a yellow T-shirt that drapes over a body that could pass as a boobless, assless twelve-year-old girl. Cutoff jeans. Sneakers. Not much of a picture. No chance of making the Louvre.

I say, "Most kids think you raped Megan then killed her."

"That's probably what the police think too."

Old Blue's brakes squeak as she stops at the edge of the parking lot. I shift gears, turn right, and the truck lurches into the flow of traffic on Locust Street.

"You liked Megan?" I ask.

"A lot. She says exactly what's on her mind. She's full of surprises.

She—" He stops and clears his throat, realizing he's been talking again about Megan in the present tense. As though she's still alive.

"I don't think you raped and killed her," I say.

"Thanks." He looks at me again. The scar on his left cheek is jagged like a crooked check mark. "Why? Suddenly you think I'm a nice guy?"

"If you wanted sex with her, you wouldn't have had to rape her. She liked you. She would've… cooperated…"

I simply nod.

"You wouldn't believe how incredibly kind she could be. Understanding and loyal." I'm tempted to tell him the Leroy Leonard bullying story, but I don't want to cry. I've barely stopped from last night.

John props his arm on the passenger's door, his elbow sticking out the open window. "I feel so bad about Megan"—his voice cracks—"so rotten. I still can't believe it."

I glance at him. For a second, I think *he* might cry.

Then he says, "Could Cole get so mad at her because she went to the prom with me that he'd kill her? Could he get that pissed, that drunk maybe?"

"It's possible." I catch John looking at me for a third time—staring and appraising me. *Holy crap! Why does he keep doing that?*

"You saved me this morning," he says. "Thanks. Um… where are we going? I didn't tell you where I live."

"You want to see where they pulled Megan's body out of the river? It's not far from Credit Island."

His mouth snaps open. "They found her body by Credit Island?"

I look straight ahead, both hands high on the steering wheel. "That's right. You want to see where?"

He hesitates a second then says softly, "Sure."

I press my foot harder on the accelerator, coaxing another five miles an hour out of Old Blue. As I look straight ahead, fiery tears teeter at the corners of my eyes. The thought of Megan's body snared in a fisherman's net chills me. But I'm not going to cry. No way!

"The spot in the river," I squeeze the words past a lump in my throat, "is close to where I live."

TWENTY-SIX

CHARLOTTE COTTON

FTER I DAB AT MY eyes, I explain to John that my mom and dad own the Catfish Hut, a bar and grill on Harbor Road close to the Mississippi River. The Hut's on high enough ground and far enough from the river that it's been a flood victim only once in the last ten years. The river has been my front yard and playground since I was a kid.

"My dad is 'Catfish' Charlie Cotton, the best fisherman on the river," I tell John with pride in my voice. "When I was a kid, he called me Minnow. We fished together all the time. Now it's hard to find time. I mean, the Hut is a popular place and keeps my whole family busy. There's just my mom and dad and me. I'm going to be a master chef someday. I—" I stop abruptly, catching my breath, my face warm. I don't know why I babbled like that. I got started and didn't know when to quit, like Megan.

Turning left off River Drive onto Harbor Road, I direct Old Blue across bumpy railroad tracks then down a potholed road. I park under a sprawling sycamore tree. We jump out, and John follows me onto a weathered wooden dock. A soft breeze blows in our faces. Three hundred yards to the left, a huge island full of green trees squats in the river, the treetops waving in the breeze.

"The river looks like a lake here, it's so smooth," John says.

"This is Credit Island Harbor. The main channel runs on the other side of the island along the Illinois shore." I point. "That's Credit Island you're looking at."

John stands motionless and stares across the water as if he doesn't believe me.

"That's where you parked with Megan, on that shoreline in those trees facing us."

"How do you know that?"

"Megan always parks on the island. It's her favorite spot. *Was* her favorite spot."

"Cole Wainwright knows that too, right?"

"He's been there, yeah."

"Someone followed us onto the island that night and drove by as we pulled off to park. That had to be Cole. I can't believe he didn't follow us. Then he was waiting for Megan when she got home."

I brush back the hair blowing in front of my face. "The fisherman who found Megan was working his net in the harbor right out there." I point again, shielding my eyes from the sunlight with my other hand. "About a hundred yards out from that giant locust tree."

"And the net caught Megan?"

"You know what that means?"

"What?" he asks.

"Think about it. Right in front of you is the harbor. The island's causeway is way, way off to your left, around that horseshoe bend. From your left, there's no entrance into the harbor. The mouth of this harbor is to your right, then the river itself, flowing south."

He stares at the island once more. "What are you driving at?"

"It means the fisherman's net couldn't have snagged Megan's body floating down from upriver."

"I still don't get it."

I hope I'm not looking at him as though I think he's stupid. "When rain flooded everything Sunday morning, Megan's body probably floated from the island into the harbor then into the fisherman's net."

"Megan and I left," he says, his eyebrows bunching together.

"She ended up back there."

"That's crazy!"

"Look, if someone threw her body in upriver, with all this fast water, she'd be in Muscatine by now. Thirty miles from here."

John takes a wobbly step forward, as if to get a better look across the water. "That means someone killed her and brought her back to the island."

"That's what I think. And left her where you guys parked. Probably not very far from the water's edge, never realizing the river was rising so fast and her body would be washed away."

"Why would someone do that?" John answers his own question. "To frame me." He blows out a long breath. "Cole... he killed her, stripped her, and stuffed her body into the trunk of his car. Dumped it where we parked." John shakes his head in disbelief. "My God, when the police came to my house Sunday morning looking for Megan..."

"What?"

"I took them to the island, but the causeway was flooded. If it hadn't rained so badly, if we could've driven across the causeway, I would've taken them right to Megan's body."

Charley says, "Maybe that's what the killer planned."

"But Cole had no way of knowing the river would flood and wash Megan's body into the harbor." John looks sick, dizzy, as if he's been beaten up again. Teetering, he turns and starts for the bank.

I grab his shoulders, steadying him before he staggers headlong off the dock into the water. We go sit on the riverbank in the shade of the sycamore, ten feet from the water. Air circulating under the tree cools us. I'm unbelievably sad and pissed about Megan's death. I will be for the rest of my life. I'm sure John feels the same way. He sits with his legs splayed across the clumpy grass. He's staring at the river, his face expressionless, his jaw tight. The guilt rushing over him must be overwhelming, like a tsunami. A coal barge far across the choppy water churns into view, and we watch it move southward.

I finally say, "You all right?" I'm sitting close to John, hugging my legs and looking at him.

John exhales as if he's deflating and bows his head. "My life's been carved into a jigsaw puzzle and all the pieces dumped into my lap. Will I ever be able to put them back together? You suppose the cops know Megan's body floated off the island into that fisherman's net?"

"They're probably bright enough to at least realize that."

"They'll never be able to prove Cole did it. His parents will say he was home and tucked in bed when Megan was killed. Unless the cops can find blood in his car. The trunk, maybe. Fibers. Hair."

"Maybe he *was* home in bed."

John frowns. "You believe him?"

"Look, I'll tell you the truth about Cole. I've known him since grade school. I felt sorry for him once, though I've never liked him. In second or third grade, he got meningitis. I don't know much about it—just that it's an inflammation of the brain and spinal cord or something."

"Sounds serious."

"Potentially deadly. He lost a year of school. He'll be nineteen when he graduates. He's grown up pampered and privileged. He was the first kid in high school to drive a brand new car—a dark-blue Pontiac Solstice. Then a Harley."

He blinks as though that news surprises him. "I mean, Cole and I are sort of alike. I grew up with money and without a worry in the world too. Really, I was better off than Cole. I didn't have a life-threatening disease attack me. I was gifted with muscle, a knack for wrestling, a love of the sport, and a great future. Now I've blown everything."

I say, "I think the car and especially the bike first attracted Megan." I pick up a little stone and toss it into the water. *Plink!* "And she liked to party. Anyway, what I'm telling you is Cole's never had to do anything for himself. My gut reaction was that he killed Megan. I mean, I can picture him drunk and jealous, waiting for Megan to come home, and getting into a fight with her when she climbed out of her car. Hitting her. Maybe accidentally killing her."

John says, "Like she hit her head on the driveway."

"Right." I plink another stone into the water. "But he'd panic and run. He'd leave her lying there. I swear there's nothing but air between his ears. He wouldn't be smart enough to take her back to Credit Island and try to frame you."

"Then who? Who would want Megan dead?"

I shrug.

We're silent again. Off to the right, far across the river, near the Illinois shore, another coal barge chugs along.

John asks, "Did Megan ever tell you her father is addicted to gambling?"

"She tells me everything." My eyes close. Tiny tears squeeze out, and I blot them with the heel of my hand. "I can't get the verbs right, either—I can't think of Megan as dead."

John stands and kicks at the grass. "Megan's dead. I'm the last person known to see her alive. I'm the only real suspect. I had the opportunity. The cops probably think my motive was to cover up a rape." He gushes out a big breath of air. "Man, it sucks to be me."

"You wouldn't have had to rape Megan." I remain seated, arms planted on my knees, staring at the ground.

"You know that and I know that, but the cops don't. They probably think I killed her and panicked. Like you said Cole would. I left her on the island and drove her car away. I parked it at her house and walked home." John's head drops. "I shouldn't have dated her... for her sake. I knew better. I told myself not to." He finds a stone the size of a golf ball half buried in the grass, digs it out, and hurls it fifty yards into the water. "Before we went to the prom, Megan was upset, especially with her dad. His gambling. I thought she was going to break down. You think he's in debt really bad? Gambling debts, big time?"

"He might be. He always goes to Dubuque to bet on the greyhounds. He gambles on the riverboats too. There are two on this side of the river and another one across the river at Rock Island. You want to know how really whacked he is?"

"What else has he done?"

I flail a hand. "The woman he married is a blackjack dealer on the *Rhythm City.*"

John nods. "Megan told me."

"For a guy who's addicted, how stupid is that?"

A mallard drake and a hen come quacking and paddling along the riverbank, poking their bills into the water and shoreline weeds as they glide by.

John watches the ducks a moment. "Maybe whoever Dr. Jones owes money to killed Megan because the doctor couldn't pay. A big-time hit man from Chicago, maybe Las Vegas. You know, if Dr. Jones doesn't pay now, he's next kind of thing. Megan's death is a warning."

"Why frame you? A hit man would just kill Megan and throw her in the river. No elaborate frame-up. At least that's the way they do it in the movies." I let out a breath. "I don't know if I should tell you this."

"What?"

"There's something I haven't mentioned."

"What?"

I look at him. He's leaning against the sycamore, right foot propped back against it. He's watching me intently with slightly narrowed eyes, as if he senses what I'm about to say might be important.

"Prom night, Megan wasn't so much pissed at her dad as she was at Stephanie," I say.

"How do you know?"

"Megan called me that afternoon. Before the prom."

"And?"

I hesitate. *Should I? I've got to tell someone. Eventually.* "Megan had this big secret."

"What? What was it?"

"The day of the prom..."

"What?"

"Megan found out her stepmother was having an affair."

I'm still looking at John. He jumps to attention, his eyebrows arching.

"Are you kidding? That's crazy!" he says.

"Not as crazy as you think."

"An affair?"

"I'm sure it's why she was so upset prom night. But she wouldn't tell you," I say.

"Have you told the cops?"

"No. The last time I talked to them, I didn't think it was important. But I think I'm changing my mind."

John scratches his head. He's thinking hard, trying to process this.

I stare at the ground. I'm glad I've finally told Megan's secret. I feel relieved, but what good will my telling do? Who will believe me besides John? Striker and Garske won't because Megan, the only witness, is dead. My story is hearsay. The Mississippi could run dry before Stephanie would admit to cheating on her husband. I stifle a sigh.

Megan's dead, probably murdered, John Hawk's life is at stake, and Megan's killer might go free. What a mess. And there are no answers in sight.

TWENTY-SEVEN

CHARLOTTE COTTON

"AN AFFAIR? WITH WHO?" JOHN asks.

He plops down next to me again, so close that our arms touch. His is hairy. A quiver ripples through me; a hot flush grips me. *Oh my! Am I crazy? This is Megan's boyfriend. But she's…* I don't even want to *think* the word.

A blue bruise swells slightly under John's left eye. The bruise and the scar on his cheek make him look like he's taken a lot of punishment. Maybe his heart is bruised and scarred too.

An impulse to touch his scar sweeps over me. I rub my thumb across my fingertips. *Don't be stupid.* I swallow and shift out of his space. "Megan didn't exactly say who. Somebody she knows at school. A teacher probably."

"She tell anybody else?"

"She didn't know what she was going to do. She hates Stephanie… hated… sorry… but she didn't want to see her dad hurt. I think she needed to vent to me, no matter what else she decided."

"Have you told anyone else? The cops?"

"Her stepmother's affair isn't something I'd blab about. I *almost* didn't tell you."

John picks up a twig and snaps it in two. "Prom night, we ate at the Rusty Pelican. She was telling me about her dad's gambling problem. In the middle, she said, 'And then today—' like she was going to tell me what happened, but instead she nearly started to cry. She said she talked too much. She stopped, smiled, and said she wanted to go dancing. How did Megan find out?"

I explain about Megan's wanting black nylons and different shoes, forgetting her credit card, driving back home.

"Was the guy's car in the driveway?" John asks. "A car she recognized?"

"I asked her about a car. She didn't see one."

"Did she walk in on them and catch them making out?"

"She heard them in the bedroom," I say.

"Did she see the guy?"

"I think she recognized his voice. She didn't really tell me if she saw them, but I think she might have."

John scoots around in front of me and sits back on his haunches. His face is intent, lines creasing his forehead. I can practically see his brain churning behind his eyes.

He says, "Megan listened to them. She got all pissed off. Then she flung the door wide open. That's what the Megan I know would do. She saw them. Then she screamed at them."

That sounds exactly like her. "All right. So...?"

"So if that's true, Stephanie and her lover would have a reason to kill Megan. They'd want her mouth kept permanently shut."

"Stephanie couldn't have killed her. Wasn't she at the after-prom party with Dr. Jones?"

"Her lover could've. He'd want Megan's mouth kept shut too. He framed me to remove any suspicion from himself."

I think about that.

Just when I decide it makes sense, John throws his hands in the air and says, "Is this all true? Or am I going crazy, thinking all this weird stuff?"

I squint at the sun high in the sky. "Must be eleven o'clock. It's getting hot."

John pops up and looks at me. "Thanks for telling me these things. Thanks for listening."

"No problem." I push myself up.

"Um... could I ask you a big favor?" he says.

"What?"

"Think we can get onto Credit Island? Has the water gone down enough?"

"We can probably get onto the island in Old Blue." I point at my truck parked on the road. "Or we can take a boat across the harbor. My folks have one. I use it all the time. I live just down the road, above the Catfish Hut."

"Let's try Old Blue," John says. "Water's not my friend."

"Can't swim?"

"Never learned," he admits.

"What do you expect to find on the island?"

"I want to see in daylight where Megan and I parked. I want to see if there's any evidence we were really there, though I imagine the flood washed everything away."

"Maybe not," I say. "We'll check things out."

TWENTY-EIGHT

JOHN HAWK

As Charley spins the truck's tires on the gravel road, Old Blue lurches forward. The heap is beat up on the inside and the outside. The dark-blue plastic upholstery is tattered and cracked; the glove compartment door is missing. I swear I'm inhaling dust filtering up through the floorboard. Far different from Megan's sleek, red Mustang.

"Some vehicle," I say. "Doesn't start very well though."

Charley had to grind the starter before the engine finally coughed and fired to life.

"Needs work on the carburetor," she says. "And brakes. The radio doesn't work either. Old Blue's been in the family fifteen years. Over two hundred thousand miles on it. Not bad for an old pickup."

"Not bad at all."

"Dad bought it at a farm auction, but it gets me around. Bluie has never let me down in a pinch." She glances at me. "I know what you're thinking."

"What?"

Wisps of her reddish brown hair curl across her forehead. She's pretty in a different sort of way that it takes a minute or two to notice. She has nice eyes. They're sparkly green, like emeralds.

"Most girls wouldn't be caught dead driving this piece of junk. They'd want something like Megan's Mustang. But I grew up on the river. River people are different."

"How did you and Megan get to be such good friends?" I ask.

She tells me a story about a kid named Leroy Leonard and a girl who tried to bully him out of his homework.

A smile pushes onto my face. "Sticking up for a little guy—sounds like Megan. You too."

"I hate bullies. It's another reason I don't like Cole and can't understand why Megan dated him. He wasn't good for her."

"Sometimes people don't realize what's good for them. Or they know, but they look the other way. I know that for a fact."

"Anyway, it was the first and only time I've ever seen Megan use her relationship with the principal as leverage." Charley adds with a shrug, "We just hit it off, I guess. Different in many ways, but buddies all the same. I always told her the truth. Exactly what I thought."

"She probably liked that."

"I think so."

I hang on as Old Blue lurches around potholes and bounces over the railroad tracks, my bike rattling and clunking in the bed. Charley swings the truck sharply to the right then into the traffic on River Drive.

"Can I ask you something?" she says.

"What?"

"This is personal…"

"Go ahead. Ask."

She clears her throat. "Did you do it with her? I mean, I know you didn't rape her, but I just wondered…" Charley stares through the windshield, her eyes on the cars ahead.

"No. I didn't."

She shoots me a look. "Are you gay?"

I smile again. "I'm not gay. We… just didn't, that's all."

She turns onto the causeway and stops where the cops and I stopped the other day when it was pouring rain. Yellow traffic barricades still block the causeway, but it's no longer submerged. I peer down its length to the island. Floodwaters have littered it with sand, pebbles, tree branches, and a car hood. Tire tracks through the sandy debris indicate that other vehicles have driven onto the island. Whoever went ahead of us pulled the debris aside, clearing a path.

"What do you think?" I ask.

She bites her bottom lip then says, "Let's go."

I jump out of the truck and shove the barricades aside. After Charley drives onto the causeway, I drag them into place and clamber back into the vehicle.

"Keep to the right," I say. "We parked just past the picnic pavilion."

"Uh-huh. Okay," Charley says. "See the water mark on the shoreline trees? It tells you the low-lying areas were under about three or four feet of water."

As we pass the picnic pavilion, I stare through the windshield. My heart jumps. Two blue-and-white police vehicles are parked ahead of us on the side of the road. One of them is a regular cruiser, the other a minivan. Goose bumps pop out on my arms.

"Oh, no!" Charley says. "Trouble ahead."

"What are the police doing here?"

"They're not digging for worms."

She pulls up alongside the two vehicles. Black lettering on the driver's door of the minivan says POLICE EVIDENCE TECHNICIAN. Both vehicles sit empty in the shade of tall trees along the roadside. The cops apparently got out of the cars and followed the short lane through the woods toward the river, where Megan and I parked.

"Do you still want to take a look?" Charley asks.

"That's what I came for."

Pulling ahead of the cop cars, she parks her truck.

"Stay here," I say.

She tilts her head. "Think again."

"I just want to see what the cops are doing."

"I do too."

So we both get out. I peer into the empty police cars, see nothing interesting, and move on. I wonder if they're locked. As a fourteen-year-old, if I'd found one of them unlocked with keys in it, I'd have driven it away. Pretty stupid.

The muddy lane cuts through the brush and tall trees toward the water. I stop and try to imagine Megan and me driving down it. Floodwaters have leveled the tall grass and erased the tire tracks. The deepest ruts, where Megan spun her tires backing out, are still there, but there are no tracks or footprints except for the cops'.

"We have company," Charley says, moving up to stand beside me.

Three cops approach in a single file across the flattened grass. Garske heads the trio. A grin spreads across his growly face when he recognizes me.

"Well, now, ain't this something?" He's breathing hard, his red cheeks puffed—the lane is slightly uphill—and sweat glistens on his forehead. "No school today, boy?"

I don't recognize the other two officers. The second one is a blond woman. She carries a Ziploc evidence bag with something dark in it. Dirty rags, maybe. The last cop carries a camera slung on his shoulder. Garske's wearing a rumpled short-sleeved white shirt and baggy slacks, but the other cops are in uniform.

"Took a day off," I say.

"What you mean is that you were in a fight this morning and got sent home. I was at school earlier, looking for you. Couldn't find you at your house either."

"What did you want?"

"Just to talk. Fill you in a bit. And take you out here with us. Make sure we were at the right place." Garske mops his head with a wrinkled white handkerchief that he pulls from his back pocket. "Now I find you 'returning to the scene of the crime.'"

"Was a crime committed here?"

"This is where you told me you parked, isn't it?" Garske asks.

"Yes."

"Then a crime was committed here, all right. Soon you'll be begging to tell me about it. Plea bargaining." Garske smiles at Charley then looks at me. "See you got yourself another pretty little lady friend."

Charley stiffens. I shake my head. I can't believe this guy.

The cop eyes her T-shirt and cutoff jeans. Then he turns to me once more. "What brings you here, boy?"

I shrug. "Came to look around. Same as you."

Garske motions to the officer behind him. "Loretta, let me see that bag." She hands it to him. "Know what's in here?" Garske shifts the bag from one hand to the other a couple of times then shakes it in front of me. "Panties and bra. Found them tangled in the brush."

"They look like muddy rags," I say.

"I expect we can prove who they belonged to. All we need is a bit of DNA, one tiny hair. You want to know something else?"

"What?"

"Megan's body floated off this island—just enough rain—into the river from the end of this lane. Somebody killed her right here. She didn't jump into the water off a bridge up river. Didn't drown. No water in her lungs."

Anger snakes through every muscle in my body. "If I killed her and left her here, do you think I'd have told you where we parked? That I would've tried to take you here? Think about it."

Handing the bag back to Loretta, Garske jerks his head toward the road, and the other two cops trudge ahead to the police cars.

"You're lucky we couldn't find footprints," Garske says.

"I didn't kill her, I'm telling you," I nearly yell. "Besides, I'm not the only guy who wears size fourteen sneakers."

Charley touches my shoulder. "Calm down, John."

"Not many others got feet that big." Garske's steel-gray eyes penetrate me. "What did you do with the rest of her clothes, boy? Bury them around here? Or in a cornfield? Is that why your clothes were so muddy?"

"Why would I leave her bra and panties behind?"

"Carelessness," Garske says. "It was dark, raining, miserable. You were in a hurry and frightened. This is a new low, even for you." The cop's eyes dig into me deeper. "Want to know something else?"

"What?"

"Maybe you wouldn't want your new lady friend to hear this."

"Say it."

Smiling, Garske says, "According to the crime-lab people, your jockey shorts contain traces of semen."

I flinch. Maybe I should have seen that bit of news coming, but I didn't think about what they might find in my underwear. I can't let him know I'm alarmed. "So what's unusual about that?"

"When the state's forensic pathologist finishes," Garske pushes on, "we expect to find a match in the corpse." Garske's eyes narrow. "Sure you got nothing to say?" Lacing his fingers, he cracks his knuckles.

My throat tightens. "Nothing!"

"Found a condom on the floor by the front seat of Megan's car," Garske says. "Probably nothing unusual about that either, huh?"

Fire races across my face. I'd forgotten about the condom. It must have slipped off the dashboard and landed on the floor. I glance at Charley. Her face reveals nothing, but what a liar she must think I am. Just like the cops.

Garske says, "You're eighteen, right?"

Fuck you! dances on the tip of my tongue, but I bite it back. "So what?"

"You'll be tried as an adult, boy. No lightweight juvie sentence for you."

"I won't be tried for anything."

"Next time I see you, I'll be reading you your rights."

TWENTY-NINE

JOHN HAWK

A S THE COPS TROMP BY me, my jaw clenches. I shake my head and march up the lane toward the road. Charley follows me. I kick at the ground along the way. The stupid, kid-hating, narrow-minded, blind jerk of a cop doesn't know what he's talking about.

At Charley's truck, I turn to watch the three policemen. They linger by the minivan, conferring and nodding. Garske climbs into the cruiser, the other two into the minivan, and they drive away.

I'm beginning to sweat. The sun hovers straight overhead now. The river breeze can't find its way to the dappled shade where Charley and I stand. I look at Charley. The freckles spattered across her pointed nose shine like flecks of copper. Her eyes roam my face.

What she thinks about me matters to me.

"Look, Megan and I didn't do it," I say. "I'm not lying. I don't care what Garske says about my underwear. Or about a condom in Megan's car."

"I didn't say anything."

"I see you looking at me. I know what you're thinking."

"No, you don't," she says.

"I'm not lying to you. We kissed. We talked. I was telling her about myself… I admit, she offered me a condom. I set it on the dash."

"John, you don't have to explain."

"When we got ready to leave Credit Island, she surprised me…" I simply can't make myself say *hand job*. I feel too sheepish. I swallow a huge lump in my throat and shrug. "I hope you believe me."

"You don't have to draw me a picture, and don't get bent out of shape. I know how Megan is... *was*..." Charley whirls and starts down the lane. "C'mon. Walk down to the water with me. There'll be a breeze. You can cool off."

Tromping over the grass the cops flattened, we follow the lane about fifteen yards. The river appears right in front of us, covering the shoreline weeds.

I study the area. "Cops probably found the bra and panties somewhere here in the weeds and brush."

"There are probably bras and panties everywhere on this island." Charley points to the left, out across the water. "See that tiny dock across the harbor? That's where we were talking earlier."

"I see it." The breeze feels good. I wipe the sweat off my forehead with my palm. "It's nice here in the shade, the breeze blowing."

Kicking off her shoes and wading into the muddy water, Charley asks, "What's that fat cop's problem?"

"Garske? I think he hates kids." I tell her the story Striker had told me about how a hit-and-run teen driver left Garske's wife a paraplegic. "They never caught the guy. Garske wants a kid to pay for once, I think."

"They haven't got anything on you, even if the bra and panties are Megan's."

"They won't find my semen in Megan either."

"Garske's scaring you. Cops do that. And they lie," she says.

"I know."

"I'll bet Megan's body's been in the river too long to reveal anything."

"You're probably right."

Charley wades into the river up to her knees, sunlight glinting off her hair. I hadn't noticed the hues of gold and copper in it before. Nice.

"The water's cool. Feels good. Take your shoes and socks off," she says.

I shake my head and smile at her, my anger slowly draining away. "You are a minnow, aren't you?"

Cupping her hand, she skims it across the top of the water, whips it forward, and splashes me. Surprised, I jump back and duck too late.

"Knock it off!" I say and laugh. I study her a moment.

She has a sweet little body: excellent pointy breasts under that T-shirt, great smile, green eyes—mischievous. *Uh oh!* She's Megan's best friend—*was* Megan's best friend. She's my only friend in the world but for Anne and Donnie. *Cool it!* I don't want to be attracted to her like that.

"Um… what's your boyfriend going to say about you hanging out with me all morning?"

"Fresh out of boyfriends today."

She looks at the muddy water, and I look back up the lane.

"Let's go," I say. "I need to get my bike out of your truck."

As she steps from the water onto the muddy bank, mud squishing between her toes, I grab her hand. She starts, glancing at me as though she's surprised I helped her. Then she picks up her shoes and carries them.

"What are you going to do?" she asks.

"Ride my bike. Think."

At the road, I reach into the truck's bed and drag my bike over the side. "Thanks again for saving me this morning. And for the information about Mrs. Jones. You've been really helpful."

"You're going to call her, aren't you?"

I swing my leg over the bike seat. "I didn't say that."

"You're going to call her and go see her, aren't you? I want to go too."

I shake my head a definite no.

Charley drops her shoes on the road and grabs my bike's handlebars. "Put your bike back in the truck."

"You're not going with me."

Heat flashes in her face. "I have as much right as you do to find out what happened to Megan. *More* of a right, in fact. We've been best friends forever."

"I know that. I understand. But I don't want you involved in *my* problem."

"I *am* involved." Charley jerks on the handlebars.

"I've got to do this alone."

"I'll tell you something, John Hawk. I'm not a skinny, helpless female. I can fish and hunt—shoot a pistol, rifle, and shotgun. I can bag a deer—gut it, drag it out of the woods, hang it, and skin it."

"And I'll tell you something: the last two girls I hung with are dead. Ever think of that?"

"Not your fault!"

"So I don't want you involved anymore. Let go of the bike."

"What, you going to break my fingers? My arms?" She releases her grip with an angry shove, her face red and freckles dark.

"Look, I like you. I know you were Megan's best friend and you have a right to know what happened to her, but I can't let something bad happen to you too. Try to understand that."

"I'm a big girl. I can take care of myself."

"I just can't. You don't know how awful this is for me," I say.

"Yes, I do! It's awful for me too. My cell phone's in the truck. I've got the Jones's landline on speed dial. Call Stephanie right now. She's probably home. She deals blackjack at night. We'll both go talk to her."

"No way." I ease back on the bike's seat. "But thanks again for your help." I shove off and pedal, pumping hard. "I'll call you!" I yell over my shoulder, but I realize I don't have her number.

"You're not ditching me," she shouts. "I'm following!"

"You'll never catch me!"

I look back and glimpse Charley picking up her shoes, jumping into her truck, and slamming the door. I hear her grind the truck's starter. Bending forward to stand on the pedals, I whip the bike back and forth between my legs as I gain speed. By the time Charley gets that truck started, I'll be off the island, out of sight, and on my way home. Where I intend to make my call.

THIRTY

CHARLOTTE COTTON

"D AMN YOU, OLD BLUE!" So much for never letting me down in a pinch.

Crap! I sit there like an idiot in Old Blue, grinding her starter and cussing, while John speeds away. Old Blue's flooded. I pound the steering wheel. Nothing I can do but sit and wait until the gas drains out of the stupid carburetor.

Damn you, John Hawk! I absolutely *hate* when guys act superior, like when John wanted me to stay in the truck while he got out and talked to the cops. What a butthead! Now he's going to confront Stephanie Jones. I'll bet he'll blurt out that he knows she has a lover. Maybe he'll accuse her of Megan's murder. Just how he's going to do it all, I don't know, but he has no right to leave me behind. I don't even know his number or where he lives.

I'm so pissed I could bite off a bat's head.

But two girls he dated are dead. That's got to be tough to deal with. A warm feeling invades my stomach when I remember our arms touching on the riverbank earlier. I recall that hot flush that rippled through me and how I wanted to touch his scar. I remember him taking my hand as I stepped out of the river. Though I certainly didn't need his help, I felt something electric in his touch. It probably felt like nothing to him.

Maybe I shouldn't have splashed him.

Why does he keep staring at me? What does he see? I pound the steering wheel again. *Get a grip.* It's stupid to have feelings for John Hawk—he's so handsome, yet flawed. He for sure has girls falling for him everywhere he goes, like Megan fell for him. But there's no way he killed her.

I'm about to twist Old Blue's key again when I spot a squad car prowling toward me. It pulls up alongside me, and that fat, mean cop Garske lumbers out and slams the door.

He stands there, scowls at Old Blue as if she's a piece of junk, then strolls over to my window. "Troubles?"

"Nothing I can't handle."

"Saw your friend pedaling off the island like a bat out of hell."

"You were waiting for us?" I ask. "Hiding and getting ready to follow us?"

"Might've been. Didn't see you though. Thought I'd come back and make sure you weren't in trouble."

"Like what kind of trouble?"

"A kid like John Hawk is capable of anything," he says.

"Well, I'm fine, thank you. My truck wouldn't start. I have to let it sit for a while."

"I smell gas. Old clunker like this—probably your carburetor."

He thinks he knows everything. "Thanks."

He puts a hand on the cab and looks in. What he expects to see, I don't know. I'm not driving a Cadillac. That's obvious.

He asks, "What's your relationship with John Hawk? I thought he was Megan's boyfriend. How would she feel knowing you two are so close these days?"

He has no right making an assumption like that. "We're not close— we're trying to figure out what really happened to her. Nobody else is."

Garske scowls, three long creases streaking across his forehead. "What's Hawk told you lately?"

Lifting my chin, I say, "I'll tell you one thing—John had nothing to do with her death. I know that for a fact."

"For a fact? Is that so? I'll tell you something."

"What?"

"If you're hiding anything, like concealing evidence, you can be charged as an accessory *after* the fact."

"So?" I ask.

"Makes you just as guilty as the accused. Did you know that? That's something you don't want to ignore."

"Why don't you harass Cole Wainwright? Or better still, Megan's stepmother."

At the mention of Stephanie Jones, his big piggy ears perk. "What about her?"

"She and Megan weren't in each other's fan club." I wonder how much I should tell him.

"Stepmothers and stepdaughters often don't get along. Nothing unusual about that."

Why not tell him? The information might get him off John's back and send the cops in the right direction. *Sorry, Megan, but I've got to do this.* I bite my bottom lip. "The day of the prom, Megan found out her stepmother was having an affair."

That really snags his attention. He pulls out a notebook and pencil from the breast pocket of his shirt. He scribbles as I tell him everything Megan told me, the same stuff I told John.

When I finish, he flips his notebook closed. "Why didn't you tell me this before when we talked?"

"I didn't think it was important. I thought Megan had run away and that she'd be home soon. Now I... know differently."

"This doesn't prove Stephanie Jones or her lover harmed Megan though."

"But it gives them a reason."

He nods. "Maybe. Look, I'd be careful around John Hawk if I was you. The boy's had some serious problems. Been in some major trouble."

"I know that."

"Wouldn't want any harm coming to another pretty girl."

I stiffen. I *hate* being patronized. "John didn't harm anyone, and Megan deserves to have someone find her real killer." I give the key a twist.

Old Blue fires up, and Garske jumps back.

"Good luck, officer," I say and peel out. If I only knew where to find John.

THIRTY-ONE

JOHN HAWK

ANNE SHAKES HER FINGER IN my face. "I told you you shouldn't go back to school till this mess is over."

"I had to."

"I told you that this morning." She rises from the kitchen table to clear the dishes from our late lunch of grilled cheese sandwiches and noodle soup.

I lean back in my chair. "I didn't have any other choice. I can't sit around doing nothing."

She clanks our bowls into the sink. She's already put Donnie down for his afternoon nap. "Then this morning that cop Garske shows up and wants to know where you are. Tells me you'd been in a fight at school and sent home, but you're not here, and I don't know where the hell you are. I'm responsible for you."

"I'm okay, I'm all right," I say, hoping I sound convincing. "Don't worry about me."

She stands in front of the sink, arms crossed, eyes narrowed—her ultimate get-tough stance. "Look at you! Your face is bruised. You've already got that terrible scar on your cheek. I don't think it'll ever be safe for you to go back to that school."

"I can't stay away. I want to graduate. I want to be somebody, not what everybody thinks I am—a loser and a killer."

Anne turns to the sink and rinses off the dirty dishes.

Though she knows about my getting beat up at school and how

Charley Cotton saved me, I didn't tell her anything about Stephanie Jones's affair or my meeting Garske on Credit Island. I decide to keep my mouth shut about the really, really bad stuff: the bra and panties found where Megan and I parked, the condom in Megan's car, my semen-stained underwear, Megan's body floating off the island into the river, and no water in her lungs. Telling Anne all that would totally freak her out and make her call Dad for sure.

I wonder if Charley knows where I live or my cell phone number. Megan knew. She might have given it to Charley.

Leaving Charley stranded was mean. I feel bad about it, but she's safe. Maybe even safer because I'm not there. She doesn't need to hang with me. I doubt any of the other kids at school know where I live. Anne's last name is Dexter, so if anyone tries to find my address or number in the telephone book under "Hawk," they'll draw a blank.

Anne turns off the faucet and wipes her hands on a dishtowel. "After you eat supper tonight, put everything in the dishwasher and start it. Empty it too."

"All right."

She reaches for her pack of cigarettes on the counter. "Dad has a right to know what's going on before he reads about it in the newspaper."

"How many times are we going to have this argument? Do you really think he cares?"

Anne lights a cigarette, smoke billowing in front of her face. "He's a prosecutor, but he'll still help you, like he's done before."

"He's probably tired of helping me."

Anne drags an ashtray across the counter toward her. "He's damn tired of all of us, don't you think? Mom. Me. You."

Tipping my head back and gazing at the ceiling fan above the table, I heave a big sigh. Then I shift in my chair. She's right—Dad's had it. I've known that for a long time.

I don't think Dad ever experienced failure until he married and became a family man. He was an Eagle Scout at fifteen, a high school all-state linebacker. At Iowa, he was an academic all-American his senior year. At age twenty-eight, he became a lawyer, then married at thirty. But Mom ditched us. A guy knocked up Anne, and I was in a car accident that killed a girl. Dad's probably thinking, *My wife! My kids! What the hell did I do wrong?*

Unable to deny what Anne said, I change the subject. "You should quit smoking." I stand and shove my chair up to the table. "It's not good for you. Not good for Donnie either."

"I smoke when I'm nervous, and you're making me damn nervous."

"Relax. I've got some ideas about what really happened."

"Like what? Put the crackers away, will you?" she says, gesturing to the table.

"They're... just feelings I have. Hunches."

"Don't go nosing around. Let the police handle this. Promise me?"

I don't answer. I seal the crackers' cellophane tube with a twister and slide the tube into the box. "I won't be home this afternoon to babysit. Sorry."

"Where are you going?"

"I'm not sure yet."

"John, somebody maybe very dangerous is responsible for Megan's death," Anne says. "Somebody maybe very evil."

"I know that."

"Stay out of it. I mean it. If you don't call Dad today, I'll call him tomorrow and send you back to him. That's what I'll do—I'll send you back! You hear me?"

"I hear you."

"I don't want to. I love your being here. Donnie absolutely adores you. Why do you think he follows you everywhere? It's almost like you're his dad, but I can't handle this any longer." She shoves a hand through her tousled hair. "I'll send you back if you don't talk to Dad."

"I said I heard you."

Leaving for the babysitter's at three thirty, Anne pauses at the door. "I don't like leaving you alone, thinking I can't trust you."

"Bye, John," Donnie says and waves.

"I'll see you tomorrow, tiger. Be good at Marge's," I say.

"I will."

"Call Dad," Anne says.

"We'll see."

"I'm not kidding, John. I'll ship you back to Des Moines."

"I know."

As soon as Anne closes the door behind her, I whip out my cell phone, punch in the numbers for Dr. Jones's house, and sit at the kitchen table. I decide that if by some chance Dr. Jones answers—he should be at school—I'll hang up. I want this encounter to be between just Stephanie and me.

She answers on the third ring. "Hello?"

I breathe a sigh of satisfaction before I clear my throat. I elect to be neither cute nor mysterious. A straightforward approach is the way to handle this. "Hello, Mrs. Jones. This is John Hawk."

Instant silence. I wait her out.

"What do you want?" Her voice is brittle.

"Um… I want to say again I'm sorry about what happened to Megan."

"I imagine you want to talk to Dr. Jones—he's not here. He's at school. Shouldn't you be in class?"

"Not today. I want to talk to you actually."

Silence strikes again.

"We have nothing to talk about."

"It's horrible what happened to Megan," I say. "I know what you must think, but I didn't have anything to do with her death."

"The police will determine that. What do you really want?"

I clear my throat and rub my neck. Accusing her won't be as easy as I thought. "The night Megan and I went to the prom, we talked a lot. We told each other"—my mind races for the right words—"secret things about our lives. You know, things we wouldn't ordinarily tell other people."

"I don't understand," Stephanie says impatiently.

"Megan told me a secret about you."

Silence again. Tension crackles.

Stephanie says, "I have no secrets. Even if I did, they'd be none of your business."

Saying this is the hardest part of all. "You're having an affair, Mrs. Jones."

"What?" She sounds startled.

Good. I've surprised her. Score a point for me. "Megan told me."

"She lied! I told you she was a filthy liar."

"She was in the house last Saturday afternoon when you were with him." *Don't hesitate.* "She told me who he is." Now for an even bigger lie. "I didn't tell Dr. Jones the other day because I thought Megan was still alive. I was protecting you because I didn't want to embarrass you or Dr. Jones."

"You're out of your mind!" Stephanie's voice is low and menacing.

"Everything's making sense now. I have to tell the police—I want Megan's murderer caught."

"You want a murderer? Look in the mirror!"

The connection breaks—she's hung up. I look dumbly at the phone. What now? I toss the phone on the table with a clatter. *Call her back, dummy!* But why would she answer when she hung up a moment ago?

I slump back in my chair. I've been stupid. Did I really expect Stephanie Jones would admit anything? *You blew it, John.*

What now? Get a hold of Striker? He seems to be a friend. Call Dr. Jones? Tell him about the affair? Call Charley? Call my dad? *I don't think so.* I can imagine how the announcement that I'm suspected of murder will blow his mind.

The phone's ringing startles me. I grab it and slam it to my ear. The caller has to be Charley.

"Hello?" I say.

"I want to talk to you. Not over the phone. Alone. But not at the house." Stephanie Jones sounds tense, frayed.

"All right." I'm breathless, my heart hammering.

"You have no right sticking your nose into matters that are absolutely none of your business. If you persist, you'll be in worse trouble than you are now."

"I'm not in trouble, Mrs. Jones. The police can't prove I killed Megan because I didn't." I suck in a breath. "But we know who did, don't we?"

Her breath catches sharply. I've rocked her world. I'm sure of it. *Good!*

"You really are crazy," she says. "Absolutely *crazy!* I can't talk about this over the phone."

"All right."

"Meet me at Westlake. You know the place?"

It's a little county park and lake with lots of camping slots. I've ridden by it on my bike. Megan and I had planned to have our picnic there. "Yes, I know the place."

"There are picnic tables at the edge of the woods and on the bank where we can talk. Can you get there on that bike of yours?"

"I'll be there in a half hour," I say.

"Have you talked to anyone else about this?"

"No one. It's still our secret. For now."

I wait for her to deny we share a secret, but she doesn't.

She says, "I'll wait for you in the parking lot by the fishing dock. A maroon Chrysler. Be there!" She hangs up before I can say she can count on it.

As I pump my bike along Y48, a hilly ribbon of blacktop leading to the Westlake Park entrance, I guess the time to be about four thirty. I'm making good time, I think. I haven't met a single car along the way, only two girls a mile back who were riding ponies side-by-side on the road's wide shoulder.

Fence posts and telephone poles slip past me. Red-winged blackbirds scold me from the grassy ditch on my right. The day has turned out to be the warmest day of spring. Heat radiating from the blacktop blasts me; sweat drenches me. But I feel good, though tense. I'm on to something big. I can feel it in my bones.

Stephanie didn't want to talk over the phone. She seemed scared, but she's willing to meet me alone in a secluded place. *Why?*

I lower my head and let the wind rush over me. I sweep downhill, ready to attack the next hill with a burst of speed, my legs pumping like mad.

I wonder if meeting Stephanie alone is a major mistake. What if she carries a gun in her purse, whips it out at a picnic table near the edge of the woods, and blows me away? What if a sniper hides behind a tree and picks me off—shoots me through the back of the head and dumps my body into the lake?

I barely hear the car zooming up behind me, but I've had enough experience riding that I can judge the speed of an approaching car behind me and its distance. This one sounds close. *Maybe sixty-five miles per hour. Thirty yards directly behind me. Closing in hard. Get off the road!*

I swerve onto the gravel shoulder and glance behind me. The roaring car is a black blur. Not until the driver swerves onto the gravel do I realize what's happening. The idiot punches the accelerator. The car's tires rip the loose gravel, and the vehicle is a rocket launched at me. The notion that I should leap from my bike into the grassy ditch strikes me at the same time the car does. The impact catapults me from my bike, the handlebars stripped from my grip, and hurls me cartwheeling through air.

Am I ever going to land? Arms and legs flailing, I crash to the ground with a mighty bounce. A bright yellow light flashes in my brain. Pain streaks across my forehead like a knife plunged into my skull. Then I wonder why I don't smell diesel fuel like the last time I was in an accident. Or hear Riley screaming.

THIRTY-TWO

JOHN HAWK

I LURCH UPRIGHT IN BED, MY heart thundering. I take deep breaths, struggling to fight off the effects of the nightmare. My mouth feels dry as bone.

I know I'm in a hospital bed.

This is a new nightmare. The worst nightmare ever.

I'm riding a bicycle built for three—three seats, three sets of handlebars—Riley seated in front of me and Megan behind me. A semi bears down on us in the darkness, headlights blinding me, while a car zooms up behind us, its hood and windshield glaring in the sunlight. I try desperately to turn my handlebars to swerve the bike off the road and save the girls and myself, but I can't budge the handlebars. I swear and cry out in desperation and fear, my throat hot, just as the vehicles crash into the bike from the front and rear and crush the screaming girls and me, splattering us like chunks of watermelon on the roadside.

Now I find myself sitting up in bed, panting and sweating. No one else is in my hospital room. I blink because the sunlight streaming into the room burns my eyes, making them throb. I fall back, my head sinking into the pillow. I try to breathe deeply, evenly, and calm my pounding heart. My eyes slowly close.

I recall flashes of what happened—how long ago? A roaring car crushing my bike and me. An ambulance's screaming siren. Paramedics lifting me out of a grassy ditch and bundling me onto a gurney. The smell of the exhaust as paramedics shove me into the vehicle. Pain streaking through my head.

My eyes pop open. I clutch my bedsheet. My pillow feels wet with perspiration. My body is banged and bruised. Voices outside my open door float into the room.

"How is he?" Anne's voice is nervous, high-pitched. "Is he going to be all right?"

"You'll have to ask the doctor." A nurse's voice, probably. It's soft, friendly.

"Can't you tell me anything?"

"Honey, I think it's a miracle he's alive."

"Oh, Lord," Anne says.

"He has a concussion, some bumps and bruises, but that's all. The police estimated he flew thirty feet before he landed in a ditch full of grass. The ground was soft because of all the recent rain. If he had landed on the gravel or blacktop, he'd be dead for sure."

"Oh, thank God."

"You can go in if you'd like."

I close my eyes again and hear Anne shuffling into the room. I try to think. I need to figure out who ran over me. My mind churns. *Beat up at school. Hit by a car on the road. Talk about a bad day.* My head hurts so badly—a sharp pain across the top—I can hardly think, and thinking makes the pain shoot into my eyes and ears.

A gentle touch lands on my hand. I start.

"John," Anne whispers. "You awake?"

My eyes flutter open, and I blink at the brilliant sunlight streaming through the window.

"I didn't mean to wake you."

I squint at my sister. She leans closer and kisses my cheek. She smells of cigarettes and flowery perfume.

"It's all right." My voice sounds shaky. I look past her, out the window at blue skies, bright sunshine, and the brick walls and windows of the hospital. The sun still burning my eyes, I turn away.

"I'll close the blinds," Anne says. "How do you feel?"

I move about in bed, testing my arms, legs, and neck. "My head hurts, but that's the worst. Um… what day is it?"

"Thursday. Ten o'clock. The police called me at work at about five yesterday. Said you'd gotten hit on your bike. Two girls riding horses found you along the roadside in a ditch. They called nine-one-one. I was here last night, but you were out of it."

Running my forefinger lightly over the lump on my head, I say, "When can I get out?"

"You have a concussion. You were nearly killed."

"Your sister's right," a man says.

I roll my eyes toward the doorway.

A thin, bald doctor in a white coat, clipboard in hand, strolls into the room, smiling. A stethoscope dangles from his neck. "Hello. I'm Doctor Bennett."

"Hi."

"How is he?" Anne says.

"A nasty bump on his head." The doctor flips a page on his clipboard. "No broken bones though. Lacerations and contusions are all minor."

"I can get out of here soon?" I ask.

The doctor takes my wrist to check my pulse, staring at his watch. "Hmmm…" he fishes a penlight out of the breast pocket of his white coat. "Open your eyes wide. Look at me and don't blink."

Doctor Bennett shines the piercing light into each of my eyes. I flinch a little. The light seems terribly bright and makes my eyes water, but I don't blink.

"Hmmm…" The doctor writes something on his clipboard. "Is your vision blurred?"

"No."

"Tell the truth," Anne says.

Bossy older sisters! "It's not blurred," I say.

"Your head hurt?" Dr. Bennett asks.

"A little."

"Probably a lot," Anne says, "considering the size of that knot on your forehead."

"You want some medication for pain?" the doctor asks.

"No. Can I leave today?"

"We'd like to keep you at least one more day for observation." He writes on his clipboard again. "That's a nasty lump on your head, but you'll be fine." He pats my shoulder. "You're a mighty lucky young man." He steps back. "I'll be in again this afternoon."

I close my eyes and let my head sink back into the pillow. I listen to the doctor shuffle out of the room. I realize that while I'm lying here in bed, I'm like a wounded duck on a pond. Someone tried to run me over, kill me, and whoever it was might sneak into the hospital and finish me off. Or do murderers only do that in TV movies?

"What happened yesterday?"

I open my eyes to see Anne sit on the edge of the chair at the foot of my bed. "What did the police tell you?"

"You were a hit-and-run victim. A car. No one saw it," she says.

"That's it. I was a hit-and-run victim."

Anne leans in closer. "What were you doing on that road?"

"Just riding."

"Were you going to see someone? Who lives out that way?"

I stare at the perforations in the ceiling tiles. Now more than ever, I can't tell Anne about Stephanie Jones and her lover. Stephanie set me up. Either she or her lover tried to kill me and make my death look like a traffic accident. I really am messing with dangerous, evil people. I guess that's knocked into my skull now.

Lying to Anne is rotten, like ditching Charley, but involving my sister will only jeopardize her and Donnie. I can't do that. I need to talk to Striker. Bad. Right away. All this thinking has wiped me out and makes my head hurt worse.

"Do you hear me? Were you going to see someone?" she asks again.

"Umm… I was going to feed the ducks at the lake."

"I hate it when you lie to me." Leaning back, Anne crosses her arms and scowls at me hard. The big-sister, get-tough act once again. "I called Dad."

I turn sharply and wince. "You shouldn't have."

She flaps a hand. "For God's sake, you were in the emergency room, unconscious after being hit by a car. I had no choice."

Sighing, I grab for the cord to raise the back of my bed and push the button. "What did you tell him?"

"You had an accident on your bike. Someone hit you with a car. You were in the hospital."

"Nothing about... Megan?"

Anne looks at her hands as if she's ashamed. "Nothing."

I offer a smile of gratitude. "Thanks. I appreciate that."

"Don't thank me!" she says sharply. "I expect you to call Dad as soon as you're out of here and explain everything."

"I haven't got all the answers yet."

Anne balls her hands into fists. "John, any minute the police will be in this room saying you're a murder suspect."

"They haven't got anything on me. If they did, they would've been here already, and I would have woken up cuffed to the bed. What did Dad say?"

"He wanted to know how you were. If you were hurt bad. He... asked me to keep in touch. He was in a hurry. He's very busy, you know that."

"A client? Or a woman? Both?"

"John, please..."

A flash of anger zaps me. "Why the hell do you make excuses for him?"

She says, "He's been good to both of us. He sent me to college, and he stands up for you all the time. We've both fucked up."

She's right again. Anne and I have made major mistakes. I blow out a tiny breath. Even that makes my head hurt worse, as if a vise is squeezing it. My gaze drifts to the ceiling, my eyelids heavy. Thinking and talking are totally wearing me out.

A skinny, gray-haired woman—a candy striper—bustles into the room, carrying a long, thin, glossy green box tied with a red ribbon. "For you," she says to me, beaming. "Somebody left it at the desk. Do you want me to open it?"

I yawn, rub my eyes, and yawn again. "No. Leave it on the table."

Does Charley know I'm in the hospital? Has she sent me something? A gift? Why would she? She's probably still fuming because I ditched her on the island.

After the candy striper marches out the door, Anne says, "Who would send you a gift? Who knows you're here?"

I gingerly touch the bump on my forehead once more. *Man, is it getting bigger?* "They probably delivered it to the wrong room. They'll come back for it later. I can't stay awake."

"All right," Anne says, shoving her chair back and standing. "I'll see you tomorrow. I'll bring clean clothes."

"Tell Donnie hello and I'm fine."

"I will."

I close my eyes. I don't even see Anne leave. Before I can lower the back of my bed, I drift off to sleep, wondering, *Who tried to kill me?*

The same person who tried to frame me. *Somebody who's desperate and therefore dangerous. Someone evil.* Stephanie Jones's lover. *Who's Stephanie Jones's lover?*

THIRTY-THREE

JOHN HAWK

I WAKE WITH A START AND think for damn sure that I'm in the middle of another nightmare. Lieutenant Garske slouches in a chair pulled close to my bed, staring at me with his steely-gray eyes. His eyebrows bristle, one gray hair over his right eye longer than the others. He breathes like a shaggy bear with bad breath, as if he's been eating roots.

I feel groggy, but I'm awake enough to realize Garske isn't making a social call. "What do you want?" I reach for the cord to raise the back of my bed a bit higher, and the dull pain returns to the top of my head.

"Checking you out, boy. How you doing?"

"You don't have to worry about me. What time is it?"

"Eleven thirty. When they letting you out?"

"Tomorrow."

"Heard you had an accident."

Should I tell Garske I suspect Stephanie Jones's lover—or maybe Stephanie Jones herself—tried to kill me? Will the cop listen? Will he even consider the possibility?

"I'm not sure it was an accident," I say.

Garske's shaggy eyebrows rise. "You're not sure? You think someone ran you over on purpose?"

"I heard a car coming up behind me. I pulled off to the shoulder so it could pass without going into the left-hand lane. I was coming to the top of a hill. I turned around to look, and the driver pulled the car onto the shoulder too. He stomped on the accelerator and aimed the car at me. I *know* he tried to kill me."

"My, ain't you got some imagination? Who'd do this?"

I take a deep breath and exhale. Now is the time to lay out my theory: "I think someone tried to frame me for Megan's murder, but the frame's not going to work because Megan's body floated off Credit Island into the harbor. Now that someone wants me dead, the sooner, the better."

"Framed you?" Garske rubs his grizzly chin. "I don't think so. This isn't an episode of *Law & Order*."

"Someone *did* run me over on purpose. Stephanie Jones, maybe. Or her lover." I explain what Charley told me about Stephanie Jones's darling.

Garske nods. "The girl told me the same story when I talked to her yesterday."

"You talked to her yesterday? When?"

"I saw you leaving the island on your bike, but I didn't see her. I circled back to make sure she was okay. I didn't want another girl in your life turning up dead."

"You thought I did something to her?"

"Just making sure you didn't," he says.

"Thanks."

"She couldn't get her truck started. What she had to tell me is hearsay." Garske scoots his chair closer to me. "I also talked to Stephanie Jones and Dr. Jones. Stephanie says Megan tried to ruin their marriage from day one, first by not talking to her or her dad, then by running away. Dr. Jones agreed that his daughter was troubled, an attention-seeker."

"You think Stephanie's going to tell the truth?"

"So what if she has a lover?"

"Look, I called her and accused her of having a lover. I said he killed Megan."

Garske sits back in his chair, grimacing. "Stupid thing to do, boy."

"Stephanie wanted to meet me at Westlake to talk. She was scared. She asked if I'd told anyone. Why would she ask that?"

"Afraid of the unsubstantiated rumors you might start by saying shit like that?"

I shake my head then carefully rub around the knot on my forehead. "She knew I'd be riding there on my bike. She knew which direction I'd be coming from."

Garske waves me off. "I think you were riding in the middle of the road—"

"I wasn't!"

"You wouldn't pull over. That's the way kids on bikes are these days—you think you own the road. The driver came up on you too fast. Misjudged your speed. His speed…"

"That's not what happened!" My voice rises, the effort hurting my head once again. "Why didn't the driver stop? He knew he'd hit me."

"He was afraid," Garske says. "Happens all the time. He might show up at the station in a day or two. Guilty conscience."

"Didn't you find his tire tracks in the gravel on the shoulder of the road?"

"Tracks could be anybody's."

I study Garske with disgust. I wish I'd saved my story for Striker. The young cop would have listened. "Look, I passed two kids on horseback. The driver must have passed them too. Did you talk to the kids? Did they get a look at the car or its driver?"

Garske nods. "I talked to them."

"Did they notice a license plate number?"

"I was going to ask you those questions."

I close my eyes and rub my forehead carefully again as I try to think. I can see the car speeding at me, hear its roar and its tires spitting gravel. The make, the driver—my mind draws blanks. "It was a black car."

"Millions of black cars on the road." Garske leans forward, elbows on his knees. "Got some other news for you, boy."

"What?"

"The panties and bra we found at the scene…"

"What about them?"

"They're the same size and style and from the same manufacturer as the ones we found in Megan's dresser drawers at home."

"That doesn't prove anything."

"Remarkable coincidence though, don't you think?" Garske stands heavily and shoves the chair back. "One more thing. Remember when you beat up your dead girlfriend's brother?"

"What about it?"

"Well, the officers at Des Moines PD tell me you almost strangled him. Took three people to pry you loose. Wrestling skills come in handy, don't they?"

"So what?" I ask.

"Witnesses at that fight you had with Megan Jones's boyfriend at school say you almost broke his neck."

"But I let him go."

"Had him in a full nelson, I hear." Garske laces his fingers and cracks his knuckles, never taking his eyes off me. "The coroner says somebody hit her on the head with something like a wine or beer bottle, maybe a big stone. Then they strangled her."

I swallow as a horrible picture blasts into my brain. Alive after a blow to the head, Megan's squirming in the black night on the muddy ground, a hulk of a guy sitting on her. His hands clutch her neck, squeezing, strangling her, as she gasps for life and claws his face.

My breath catches. I blink two, three, four times, deleting the picture.

"My guess," Garske says, "is someone with strong hands—hands of a weightlifter, maybe a wrestler—strangled her and left her." Garske gives me another hard look. "What've you got to say about that?"

I look straight at him and stare. "Stephanie Jones's lover killed her."

"Doubtful. I'll be in touch, boy. When you get out of here, stay close to home."

Garske turns and leaves me in numbed silence. Every encounter with that cop pisses me off, and my past is now haunting me worse than any nightmare.

My chin falls to my chest. I know plenty of people in this world start out bad but turn their lives around. I read once that a terrible beginning in life or a tragic failure is simply an opportunity for a person to grow in a different direction and to learn more about himself. But what if your life is cursed? What chance do you have? *What the hell chance do* I *have?*

A nurse's aide brings my lunch at noon: cold baked fish, peas, sliced peaches, a roll, butter, and a carton of milk. None of my favorites, except for the milk, but I don't complain. I clean my plate, longing for a cheeseburger and fries.

Later, a nurse takes my pulse and temperature and says it's all right if I get out of bed and take a shower, which I do. I let the hot water blast me, massaging my sore spots. My head feels a bit better, though the lump on my forehead is still almost the size of a walnut, and I'm still hungry.

At one o'clock, everyone finally leaves me alone. I call River Valley High to leave a message for Charley. I use my bedside phone because it's convenient and I don't know where my cell phone is. When I was in the hospital after the truck driver plowed into Riley and me, they kept a telephone directory in a dresser drawer. I check there first and get lucky. The secretary who answers my call informs me it's normally school policy not to deliver telephone messages to students.

I knew that might be the case, so I have a plan. "My name's John Hawk…" I pause, letting that sink in.

The secretary's breath catches. She and everyone else in town surely know my name and of my involvement with Megan. I'm sure she knows that I'm a murder suspect, the last person to see Megan alive. Talking to me probably shakes her a little.

"I'm in the hospital. I'd like to leave a message for Charley Cotton."

The secretary surely knows Charley and Megan were best friends, but I get no answer, only the faint sound of the secretary's breathing.

"It's really important," I say. "Urgent, in fact. Charley could be in danger. I want to leave my hospital telephone number. That's all." One more pause. "Please? I want Charley to call me."

Hesitation again. "All right. Perhaps just this once."

My room and telephone number are posted in big black letters on a placard on the far wall. I read my telephone number off and say, "Thank you. Thank you very much, ma'am. You've done me a big favor."

I'd forgotten about the long, thin, green box tied with a red ribbon on the table until I picked up the phone to dial. Placing the receiver in its cradle, I sit on the edge of my bed. Who would have sent me a present? Maybe the hit-and-run driver sent me a box with a bomb in it. When I open the box, the bomb will explode, ripping off my head. *Do I really care?*

I pull off the ribbon and carefully unwrap the box. I lift the lid and push back the green tissue paper inside. I gasp and feel the roots of my hair prickle. An icy chill of confusion and horror sweeps over me. My hands shake. I should have identified the acrid fumes the moment I lifted the lid.

Someone has sent me a single long-stemmed rose, spray-painted black.

A black rose! My heart freefalls to my stomach. I stagger into the bathroom and throw up in the toilet.

THIRTY-FOUR

CHARLOTTE COTTON
JOHN HAWK

WHEN I TIPTOE INTO HIS hospital room on the fourth floor, John's eyes snap open like an owl's and form perfect sparkly brown circles.

"What are you doing here, Charley?" he says, alarm ringing in his voice.

"Visiting. I got out early today."

"You were supposed to call."

I'm wearing a denim miniskirt, white blouse, white flats, and my unruly hair is corralled with a blue ribbon. After school, I rushed home and changed. John shoots me a second look. Does he think I'm not completely unfortunate looking? Or is he simply stunned to see I own clothes other than T-shirts, cutoff jeans, and sneakers?

Am I being stupid? Yes!

He pulls a sheet over himself. I'll bet he's embarrassed in his wrap-around, tie-behind hospital gown with nothing on underneath, his butt hanging out. His really cute butt.

"Why didn't you call?" he says.

I stomp. "You left me a message that you're in the hospital. I'm not sure what the hell's happening, but it can't be good. I had to see for myself."

"I wanted to talk to you over the phone."

"Right." I clobber him with a narrow-eyed glare. "This way you can't ignore me like you did on Credit Island, ditching me."

He looks away. "Sorry about that."

"I was so pissed at you."

"Sorry."

I pull up a chair and sit. "When I read that tiny article in the paper this morning that said you had been in an accident, I got a feeling your accident was no accident at all."

"You shouldn't have come here," he says.

How many more times is he going to tell me that? Getting information out of him is worse than gutting a snapping turtle.

"What really happened? Are you all right?" I ask him again. "Seriously."

The shadows under his eyes are so dark they look like bruises. A bump swells on his forehead. Dark stubble grows around the livid scar zigzagging down his cheek. He looks like a gorgeous renegade ready to star in a pirate movie.

"I'm fine."

"Did you talk to Stephanie?" I ask.

John hesitates then tells me about calling Stephanie Jones, his bike ride to Westlake Park, and a car slamming him into a ditch.

While he talks, I keep saying, "Oh my God! Oh my God!"

He says Stephanie Jones is dangerous, and he wanted to tell me to stay away from her. That's why he called me. Then he describes Garske's visit. Finally, his face pale, John says, "Look in the box on the table."

I pick up the box and brush the tissue back. "A rose." My nose twitches. "It smells—" My face freezes in a frown. I touch the rose. "It's spray-painted black. Someone sent you this?"

"The killer is playing with my mind. That rose is a message. It says, 'John Hawk, you're still alive, but not for long. You'll never escape.'" John licks his lips. "The killer knows all about me, is close by, and can strike anytime. At his convenience. That's why you shouldn't be here. It's too dangerous."

"I don't understand about the rose."

"Somehow Stephanie Jones and her lover—or someone else who wants me dead—knows about my past." He explains about the black roses he received after Riley's death, how they finally forced him to leave Des Moines and come to live in River Valley with his sister.

"Who could possibly know all this?" I ask.

"Riley's brother knows, but how could he know what kind of trouble I'm in or that I'm in the hospital?" John shrugs. "I haven't told anybody but Megan, and now you, about the black roses. She's dead—and you need to get the hell out of here," he adds, shaking a finger at me.

His saying Megan is dead silences both of us. An image of Megan snared in a fisherman's net zaps my brain. *God! Will that horrible picture ever dissolve?* Tears sting my eyes, and I look away from John. I imagine the same kind of picture walloped him. I hear him shifting in his bed, clearing his throat.

He says, "I didn't mean to say it so abruptly like that—Megan's dead. Sorry."

I face him again, shrugging. "Who brought the box to your room?"

"A candy striper. Someone left the box on her desk."

"What time?"

"Ten this morning. Maybe ten thirty."

I get a bright idea. "I'm going down to the lobby to find the candy-striper office and find out who dropped off the box. I'll be right back."

❖

As Charley darts out of the room, I sit in my hospital bed, my shoulders bent. My would-be killer is a nameless face. I realize again that the killer could be waiting somewhere in this hospital, could be watching Charley hustle down to the candy-striper office. I shouldn't have called her. When she arrived, I should have kicked her out of my room, commanded her to go home. *Right!* As if she'd listen to me. *Stubborn little bitch.*

I'm no longer safe in the hospital. I never was safe here. I peer at the clock on the wall: 3:10 p.m. Doctor Bennett said he would be back in the afternoon. I'm sure the doctor won't discharge me, no matter how much I beg. But if I leave the hospital, where can I go? Not home. That would put Anne and Donnie in jeopardy.

I have to find Striker.

I have to ditch Charley so she'll be nowhere around me if the killer strikes again. That's the only way to keep her safe.

The grass-stained clothes I wore when I landed in the ditch hang in the closet. I close my room door and dress quickly, but I can't find my cell phone. It should be in the right front pocket of my jeans. I search for it in the tiny drawer in the night table by my bed, but it's not there. It probably flew out of my pocket and now lies in the ditch where I landed after the hit-and-run driver sent me cartwheeling. Maybe the kids riding ponies also found my phone and kept it.

A rush of nerves covers me in a light sweat. I can't waste any more time. Dr. Bennett might be here any minute.

My leaving Charley behind like I did at Credit Island will totally piss her off. I don't want to do it, but her safety comes first. Like Anne's and Donnie's. Once I get out of here, I'll hide, like, in the public library or some other place with lots of people hanging around where it would be hard for someone to shoot me. Maybe a cafeteria in a big grocery store would be good or the food court in the mall.

Then I have to find Striker, or at least call him. I'll need a public phone. Maybe I'll have to sneak home—Anne will be working, Donnie at the babysitter's. But that doesn't sound like a good plan. I don't know what the hell I'll do. Just disappear, I guess. *But how?*

THIRTY-FIVE

JOHN HAWK
CHARLOTTE COTTON

I open my hospital door a crack. Peering through the slit between the door and doorjamb, I search up and down the hallway. I need to make sure no one is around who might recognize me and try to stop me. Once I'm sure the way is clear, I'll scoot down the service stairs to the main floor and dash out into the parking lot. I don't expect to meet a doctor or a nurse on the service stairs. They ride elevators.

My eyes dart left to right. I repeat the maneuver twice. The hallways look clear. I spot only a few visitors wandering around, searching for the right room number so they can visit a loved one. Good. As I'm escaping, I'll appear to be a visitor leaving.

I feel someone's hand gripping and twisting the handle on the other side of my door. They push the door. Hard. *Doctor Bennett?* My heart leaps.

I slam the door closed, but not before I glimpse Charley Cotton's curly hair. *How am I going to get rid of her?*

"It's me! Charley!" I whisper loudly through the door and twist the knob. "What are you *doing?*"

John opens the door an inch but leans against it, holding it steady with his shoulder so I can't push it wide open.

"How'd you get back so soon?" he says.

"I didn't go to China! Let me in."

"Who's with you?"

"Nobody! Let me in! What are you doing?"

He opens the door six more inches, still blocking it with his shoulder. "What did you find out?"

"I'm going to scream if you don't let me in." *God, why is he so paranoid?*

He steps back so abruptly that the door pops wide open because I'm leaning into it.

I stumble past him into the room, nearly falling on my face. "What are you trying to do?"

I swing around to face him, ready to cuss him out, but I stop. *Oh my God!* He's dressed, grass stains on the knees of his jeans and the left shoulder of his white T-shirt. He thinks he's going to waltz out of here as if he's fully recovered.

"What's going on?" I ask.

"Did you find out anything?"

"I got a name and telephone number. The candy stripers work four-hour shifts. They're volunteers. The woman who brought you the box is off this afternoon. I begged the lady in charge for the woman's name and telephone number. I told her the truth, that the box contained a single rose spray-painted black. It was a totally mean act. We have to know who did that. Why are you dressed?"

He closes the door softly. "It's not safe in the hospital. I'm getting out."

"You can't. You have to be discharged first."

"No, I don't."

"You were going to leave without me?" *Sorry, butthead! Not this time!*

He looks away, avoiding my gaze.

I say, "Once you're out, what are you going to do?"

"Find Striker."

"Uh-uh. He had a sub at school today. He took a personal day."

"How do you know?" he asks.

"I talked to the sub. Striker went to Chicago to see his mom. She hasn't been well for a long time. He goes to see her often." I shake my head. "I can't believe you were going to leave without me."

"Chicago's only a three-hour drive. Maybe he'll be back tonight."

"That's what the sub said."

John goes to the door, opens it, looks into the hallway, and closes it. "Look, Dr. Bennett said he'd see me this afternoon. He might be back any second. I can't waste any time. I've got to get out of here. I'm going to use the stairs."

"You sure you can make it? We're four floors up."

"No problem."

"All right," I say. "We'll separate. I'll take the elevator. You take the stairs. I'll meet you in the parking lot."

He grasps my shoulders. "I don't want you hanging with me. How many times do I have to say it?"

His brown eyes piercing me, his strong hands clutching me—*crap!* My stupid heart lurches. But I don't look away or try to shrug out of his grasp. "I don't think you have a choice."

"I'm not involving you. I think someone's stalking me."

"You going to run to your sister's house and hang out there, knowing someone's after you?"

His hands drop from my shoulders. "I can't. That would be too dangerous for her and my nephew."

"I know a perfect place where you can hide till we find Striker."

"No way."

"You won't find a better hideout." At that moment, Mom and Dad's warning about staying away from John leaps into my mind, but I shove it aside. All John and I need to do is confide in Striker, send him on the right track, and we'll have this mystery solved. Megan's murderer will pay the price for his horrible deed.

John hesitates, as though he's still wondering how to get rid of me. Or as though he's wondering if he can trust me. "Where?"

"It's totally safe," I say.

"You sure you want to do this?"

"I don't do things I don't want to."

He gives me a wry, jagged-scar smile. "Will Old Blue start?"

I love his smile, and my heart thumps approval. "Of course." I smile back. "My dad and I tinkered with the carburetor. I'll leave first. Wait fifteen or twenty seconds, then you go. Okay?"

"All right. I'll meet you in the parking lot."

Sitting next to me as we rumble along in Old Blue, John says, "You're driving in circles."

Since leaving the hospital parking lot, I've been winding Old Blue through a neighborhood of brick homes with ancient oak trees growing in the middle of big green lawns. "I'm making sure no one is following us. Have you had anything to eat lately?"

He tells me about his cold-fish lunch and about throwing up in the bathroom. I make a face; his stomach rumbles.

"We'll get something good to eat at my folks' place," I tell him. "If I can't get to Striker tonight, I'll talk to him tomorrow at school. You can stay in hiding overnight."

"I'm not staying at your house."

"It's not my house."

"Where?" he asks.

"You'll see after you eat." I turn onto River Drive. The traffic is light, and no one seems to be following us. "I was wondering why the person who wants you dead didn't simply bring a gun and shoot you from the car window. I figure he—or she—wanted your death to look like an accident."

"I never thought of that."

"So why not shoot you? Why run you over? Why would a killer murder Megan and try so hard to frame you, then try so hard to run you over when he could've shot you?"

John blows out a long breath. "I don't know. None of this makes sense. Except maybe a bike accident would attract less attention than a shooting."

"In the whole world, who else knows about the black roses?"

"Everyone in my old school in Des Moines. My dad, my sister, the Des Moines cops."

"And someone in River Valley who found out about them, but who?"

"Lieutenant Garske. He's talked to the cops in Des Moines.

He'd like to see me crack under pressure." John tells me again about Garske's visit this morning.

Another astounding thought surfaces in my brain. "Garske could've sent the rose. Then he showed up at the hospital hoping you'd be crazy with fear, ready to crack."

"But I hadn't opened the box yet," John says. "I didn't know a rose was inside."

"Did he look at the box? Did he encourage you to open it?"

"He didn't mention it."

"He couldn't say anything without giving himself away."

"That could be it," John says. "Garske sent the rose, hoping to scare me into a confession."

We bounce over the railroad tracks onto Harbor Road. Leaning his head back, John sighs. I feel for him. How can an innocent person be in such a mess? Why did my best friend have to die? Why isn't life fair? Tears mist my eyes. Will I ever be able to think of Megan without crying?

After a moment, John sits up. "When we get to your parents' place, I've got to call my sister and let her know I'm all right. But I've lost my phone."

"You can use mine."

"The hospital and the cops will probably call her. She'll freak when she finds out I ditched."

"And I'll call Mrs. Anderson, the candy striper. Maybe she can tell us something about who delivered the black rose."

THIRTY-SIX

JOHN HAWK
CHARLEY COTTON

"I**S THAT YOUR FAMILY'S RESTAURANT?**" I ask.

Charley nods and turns her truck into the parking lot. "We live upstairs."

Crouched in the shade of tall trees, the Catfish Hut is a two-story, wood-framed building—painted barn-red—with white trim and narrow, horizontal windows on each side of a white front door. One window advertises WARM BEER in blue neon light, the other, LOUSY FOOD in gold neon. A gravel parking lot filled with battered cars and pickups surrounds the place. Looking at Charley, I smile and point toward the front of the building.

"What?" she asks.

"Those neon signs?"

"Warm beer, lousy food? My dad's sense of humor." She shrugs. "He's Irish. I'm more like my mom. She's German. She keeps my dad in line. Except when it comes to signs."

Charley drives through the parking lot and ends up in the back. She parks by a beat-up white pickup that looks just as weary as hers. I'll bet it's her dad's. She digs a cell phone out of her truck's doorless glove compartment. "Here. Call your sister. I'll go inside, fix something to eat, and bring it out. Wait here in Old Blue."

"Call that candy striper," I say, "and call Striker's apartment. See if he's home yet."

"I will." She hops out of the truck and scurries around the corner of the building.

Hunger gnaws my belly. I can't wait to eat something decent. Using Charley's cell, I stab in Anne's cell phone number—she'll be at work.

When she answers and realizes it's me, she screams, "Oh my God! Where *are* you? The hospital called and said they couldn't find you anywhere. John!"

"I'm all right."

"Where *are* you?"

"Have the police contacted you?" I ask.

"Not yet."

"Listen, if they get a hold of you, tell them you don't know anything. You haven't heard from me."

"What the hell are you doing?" she asks.

"Don't call Dad again. I'm all right."

"I swear—"

"I'm okay. Everything's going to be fine. I'll call tomorrow, I promise."

"John—!"

I break off the call. My head dips. I feel terrible, cutting Anne off like that. She'll be totally freaked now, but what else can I do? I can't tell her anything. The less she knows, the better off she'll be. At least she knows I'm safe for the moment, and I know she and Donnie are safe.

I peer out the truck's clouded back window across a grassy yard to a wood that starts maybe thirty yards behind me. I know beyond the woods flows the Mississippi River, but I'm not sure how far away the river is. I guess Charley's going to hide me somewhere in the woods, maybe in a tent. The thought of being alone at night in the woods makes me shudder. I'll have to ask for a flashlight, one with good batteries, and a lantern of some kind. Or I'll be scared shitless. I'll never sleep. *So hot, so manly.*

I turn back around, lay my head back, and close my eyes. My head throbs a bit, and I try to think of nothing, try to rest. I don't know how long I sleep. Ten minutes? Forty-five?

The truck's door on the driver's side pops open, and there stands

Charley, a picnic basket hanging from one hand, a small cooler on the ground by her feet. She's changed into cutoff jeans, a yellow T-shirt, and sneakers—her usual. But, man, did she turn out to be anything *but* usual in every other way. She's smart and fearless, someone I really need on my side right now.

She slides the basket next to me on the bench seat. "I deep-fried some chicken quick. I hope it's done, or you'll be back in the hospital. There's fries too."

The aroma fills the truck, and my mouth waters. All I'd hoped for was a cheeseburger, but fried chicken is awesome. She picks up the cooler and swings it into the bed of the truck.

After she climbs in next to me, I say, "What did your parents say about you bringing all this food out?"

"I told them a friend and I were going to eat down by the river. They're glad I have someone with me right now." Charley turns the key in the ignition, and Old Blue grumbles to life. "Did you get a hold of your sister?"

"I told her not to worry, that I was okay. How about the candy-stripe lady? Was she home?"

Charley backs the truck up slowly. "She said a tall woman with red hair, wearing mirror sunglasses, left the box on the desk in the office and asked that it be delivered to your room. She didn't give her name."

I frown. "Stephanie Jones has blond hair."

"Maybe she wore a wig."

"If it's Stephanie, that shoots down our theory about Garske sending me the black rose. Unless Garske is Stephanie's lover."

Charley shakes her head. "She'd want someone rich. And he's too fat and ugly."

"Right." I eye the aluminum-foil-covered food in the basket. The four cans of pop also look inviting.

"Help yourself," Charley says. "I called Striker's apartment. No one was home. I left a message that we want to talk to him. I also left my number."

"I hope he responds." I rip back the foil and grab a golden-brown piece of chicken breast. It's crunchy and delicious, a little spicy; I devour huge bites in seconds.

By this time, Charley has turned the truck around. "Ahead of us is a lane that cuts through the woods and leads to the river, which is maybe a quarter of a mile away. My folks have a dock and boat there and a little picnic area. You can finish eating at the picnic table, then I'll take you for a boat ride to an island in the river's backwaters and a cabin where you can hide and be perfectly safe."

I look at her. "A… boat ride?"

"The Mississippi's still fast and high, but we'll be okay. No one knows this part of the river better than I do. Except my dad."

A lump forms in my throat. I'm not sure I can swallow my last bite of chicken. *Shit!* I'm not looking forward to a boat ride on the Mississippi River.

Two battered oars lie in the bottom of the johnboat, along with several coils of rope and a rusty anchor. First thing, when we sit down, Charley apologizes for the boat's smell. She tells me her dad uses it to run catfish traps in the river; he baits them with a commercial cheese bait. She usually cleans the boat but hasn't had time lately. But a rotten-cheese-and-dead-fish smell is the least of my worries. I cast a wary glace over the river's choppy waters.

"You look a little pale," Charley says. She wears a Cubs baseball cap with the bill in back, plastic adjustable strap across her forehead. She snatched it from under her seat in Old Blue before we hopped out. "Did you say you can't swim?"

"Right. Isn't this a little boat for such a big river? Water looks little rough too."

"Seventeen-footer. It's safe." She smiles. "Just hang on so you don't bounce out."

Sitting in the bow of the boat in a swivel seat, facing Charley, I clutch the gunwales as she eases the boat out of the muddy waters of Credit Island Harbor toward the river's main channel. I wear a life jacket. Charley leaves hers draped over the back of her seat. The sun is bright, but clouds seem to be drifting in. The river breeze feels good across my body. The boat's motor purrs as I glance nervously left and right at the tree-lined shores.

"How far do we have to go?" I ask.

"Just a couple miles to Cotton's Island. You'll love it."

When she clears the harbor, she cranks the motor's throttle wide open. I feel the boat surge as the bow lifts. The boat planes, and I hang on tighter. The craft hits the choppy waves in the channel as if they're speed bumps, the wind rippling Charley's T-shirt across her pointed breasts. My butt bounces off the seat every other second, and my head jerks each time I land. I feel as if my insides are shaking apart.

Ten minutes after hitting the river's main channel, still driving at full throttle, Charley veers the boat sharply to my right. The boat tips, and I flinch as the river licks the fingers of my right hand. When Charley straightens the boat, she slows it to a crawl.

⤛⬥⤜

"Are we there yet?" John asks, like a kid.

"Almost."

Finally releasing the gunwales, he looks around and seems to relax a little. He didn't much like the ride. I didn't think I was going *that* fast. I motor us through a maze of backwater islands and sloughs. Everywhere along the banks, tall locust trees sporting huge white blossoms like lilacs grow at the water's edges. I love their perfume. It's not the ordinary fishy, muddy river smell.

"Cotton's Island is off the bow," I say and spin my cap around, bill in front, to shade my eyes from the sun.

We glide into what looks like a small lake, its glassy waters doused in late afternoon sunlight. A blue heron stalks minnows in the weeds along the shoreline. In the center of the lake sits a tree-filled island, fifty yards wide.

"You can't see it from here," I say, "but twenty yards back into the woods on that island is a duck hunters' cabin. My granddad built it over eighty years ago. That's why we call it Cotton's Island. You can stay in the cabin till I get back."

"Where are you going?"

"Back to wait in front of Striker's apartment building till he shows up. Then I'll bring him here."

"Suppose he doesn't show tonight?"

"If I'm not back before dark, I'll come back for you in the morning. I'll find Striker for sure by then. Stay in the cabin tonight. You don't have to worry. There are plenty of places to sleep and lots of blankets. No electricity, but there are Coleman lanterns for light."

"That's good," John says, and his eyes seem to flash a sense of relief.

I wonder what that's all about. "There's a pump for well water. More food and pop in the cooler. A two-holer."

"Two-holer?"

"An outhouse."

John's lips curve into a crooked smile. "Corncobs?"

"Regular paper," I say. "Unless the mice used it all for nests."

"Great."

I aim the boat between two trees on the bank. The bow slides up into the weeds and mud. "Grab the bowline and tie us to a tree."

Clutching the bowline, John leaps from the boat toward shore. But his leap pushes the boat backward, giving him no forward momentum. He flaps through the air a few feet and lands with a *plop!* in the thick mud and short grass, sinking in over his ankles.

"Damn!" he cries as his shoes fill with water and mud.

I can't help but laugh. "Not a very graceful leap."

John pulls one foot out of the mud. As he stretches for firmer ground, muck sucks at his shoes like tar. He pulls the other foot out, and two more sucking steps put him on solid ground. "My good shoes!" he grumbles. But when he sees I'm still laughing, he laughs too. "Talk about stupid and clumsy." He laughs again.

"Like a beached whale," I say, happy that despite everything, he still has a sense of humor.

He pulls the bow of the boat ashore and ties the line around a tree. I grab the picnic basket and cooler, and he takes them from me and follows me up a narrow path through the trees to the cabin, his feet sloshing in his shoes. Somewhere in the woods, a crow caws in alarm.

My dad and granddad painted the cabin dark green when I was three or four. I watched but mostly played in the mud. Peeling badly now, the cabin sits six feet off the ground on a cement-block foundation. Wooden stairs with a pipe railing on either side lead up to the door. Before he goes up, John removes his shoes and drops them on the ground. Inside, I open windows, allowing the musty air to escape. I show John the most comfortable bed and prime the sink pump for him.

"I should get going," I say as we go back outside and sit on the steps. "It's nearly six. You know how to light a lantern?"

"Yes."

"Matches are in the kitchen cupboard. I'll be back before dark or early in the morning. I'm not going to school tomorrow."

"Do your parents know what's going on?"

"They're too busy at the Hut. They don't have time to worry about me. I work for them every Friday, Saturday, and Sunday." I look at him. "What about your folks?"

"They're divorced."

"Seems like nearly all kids have divorced parents these days."

"My mom left us. I used to live with my dad, but I don't have a relationship with either of them now."

I look away from John. What I have to say next is tough. I bite my bottom lip and try to think of the right words.

"What?" John says.

I squeeze my hands together. "Megan's funeral is the day after tomorrow—Saturday. My mom showed me the paper when I was in the kitchen. There's a story about Megan's death with her graduation picture above it."

"What did the story say?"

"Nothing that we don't already know. Not as much as we know, in fact. The police say they're investigating 'promising leads.' They didn't identify you as Megan's date to the prom, probably because they don't have any solid evidence against you yet. They're still digging."

"I'm a person of interest though, the only one. I was the last known person to see Megan alive, and everyone knows that whether it's in the paper or not. Besides, Garske's been on my case since day one."

"He plays his bad-cop role well. The funeral is at ten o'clock."

"I've got to go," he says.

"And create a riot? Are you crazy? The church will be packed with school kids." I stand. "I'd better get moving."

At the bottom of the steps, John picks up his shoes, frowns at them, and sets them on a tree stump.

"You can wade out and wash them off in the water," I tell him. "Or use the pump in the cabin."

"They're the best pair of shoes I own." He follows me down to the boat. He grabs my hands and squeezes, his hands nearly swallowing mine because they're so big. "Thanks for helping me. I really mean that."

Again, his touch is electric. My heart thumps and bounces off my ribs. Way too much heat rushes through my body.

"Megan's killer has to pay," he says.

"He will." I puff out a tiny breath. I can't stand here forever holding hands with John, looking into his dark-brown eyes, with my hormones flying around. I wish I knew what to say. My eyes are drawn to his mouth. In a moment of pure insanity, *Kiss me!* pops into my head. My face burns; my breath catches in my lungs. *Uh-uh! No way!*

Abruptly, I pull my hands from John's, turn, and climb into the boat. He unties the bowline and tosses it to me. Slopping in mud over his ankles, he pushes the boat into deeper water. I hate leaving him alone. As big and tough as he appears, he looks vulnerable standing there on the bank, barefoot, arms hanging loosely at his sides. I wish I could stay with him. *All night would be nice.*

"See you!" I call as I swing the boat around, its motor humming. I hope he'll be okay, but why wouldn't he? No one can get to him here.

THIRTY-SEVEN

JOHN HAWK

C HARLEY'S RIGHT. I CAN'T GO to Megan's funeral. I didn't go to Riley's funeral either, for the same reason: no one would tolerate me there.

I wave good-bye at Charley's back. As the boat rounds a bend to the left, its wake rolls lazily in the sunlight. In a second, the boat is out of sight.

What if something happens to Charley? No one will know I'm on Cotton's Island. I'll be a modern-day Robinson Crusoe. Me as Robinson Crusoe? *Afraid of the dark. Can't swim.* What a laugh. I try to smile but can't. Will I be found? Weeks might pass before a fisherman wanders into this remote area of the river. I might die of starvation.

Shut up! You're paranoid. I know it! I know it!

I pick up my muddy shoes and stare at them. An odd feeling shoots through me—a mixture of enlightenment but also puzzlement. I cock my head. I turn the shoes over and study the mud-clogged bottoms. I pick at the mud with my finger. *Something's not right.*

I shuffle down the path to the water, wade in, and wash the mud off my shoes. In a far corner in my mind, a piece of this puzzle drops into place. I own two pairs of sneakers: the new ones I've been wearing since after the prom and the old pair I leave in my locker at school so I can wear them to gym class. Yet along with my prom clothes, jeans, and underwear, the cops took my old pair to the police lab to be processed. The shoes were sitting on the front porch of Anne's house.

How did my old shoes find their way to the front porch? I left them at school. In my locker.

Carrying my shoes, I trudge up the hill to the cabin and plunk down on the steps. I flash back to last Sunday morning when Garske stood on the porch and held my old shoes up to the screen door. I was cradling Donnie. He wanted a ride in a police car.

"These yours?" Garske had asked. "Full of mud."

The cops had confused me. Donnie had distracted me by insisting he wanted to ride in a police car. I remember acknowledging the shoes were mine, but in my confusion, I didn't tell the cops those shoes should be in my school locker, not on Anne's porch. How did they get there? I mean, my mind was a mess—Megan missing, the cops at my house questioning me, Anne pissed at me, Donnie begging me.

I frown and shift on the steps. Did someone take my old shoes from my school locker and leave them on Anne's porch? Someone with access to the school and the locker combinations. Or access to the master key that opens all school combination locks. But why steal my shoes?

The answer belts me in the face. I blow out a sharp breath. *To leave my footprints next to Megan's body on Credit Island. That's why!* Footprints that match my shoes perfectly—size fourteen—because my shoes made them. But somebody else was wearing them. Not me.

A shiver ripples up my spine. *Who?*

Doctor Jones? He has access to the school and lock combinations and the master key. Why would Doctor Jones kill his daughter? Garske? Could he be Stephanie's lover and accomplice? Charley and I already decided Garske isn't Stephanie's type.

I frown again. A chill grips the pit of my stomach, and my heart beats faster. *Striker!* Where was *he* the night Megan died? I've never asked that question. Neither has Charley. *Why would we?*

He surely knows about Riley's brother sending me black roses back in Des Moines. Striker's young and handsome. He could be Stephanie Jones's lover. While he was in Chicago—if he went to Chicago— Stephanie could have rammed me with a car. She could have worn a red wig and delivered a black rose to the candy-striper station at the hospital, just like Charley and I suspected. Striker is strong enough to strangle Megan. He could have attempted to assassinate me.

Another chill creeps through my stomach. Fear grips me. *Striker.* I shake my head. I have to get rid of these stupid thoughts.

I climb the steps to the cabin, slip on my shoes, tie them, and stagger inside. Immediately inside the doorway is a kitchen area with cupboards, a sink, and a water pump next to the sink. The next room is huge. A big oak table sits in the center, eight mismatched wooden kitchen chairs surrounding it, and two hide-a-beds are against the walls. Fishing poles lean against the walls in corners. The bare wood floor squeaks and groans as I shuffle to the table, pull out a chair, and collapse. I rub my fingertips along the surface of the table. Cigarette burns scar its worn finish.

Striker! I can't get him out of my mind. I shake my head again. I can't be right.

Striker's a cop. A young cop, not much older than me. We should be like brothers. He's the only adult besides my sister I trust. Charley will laugh her head off at me suspecting Striker of anything.

Wait! My stupidity dazzles me. I thump the table with my fist. Charley and Striker could be in this together. *No! No! No!* I don't want to believe that. I like Charley. She's awesome, and Striker's a good guy. He's my friend, the best person in the world to have on my side.

I stand and shove my chair up to the table. Have I allowed myself to be isolated on this island with no hope of escape? Is Charley bringing a cop here who wants to help me or to kill me?

I race out of the cabin and run down to the shoreline, shielding my eyes from the slant of the setting sun with my hand. *A boat.* I need a damn boat. If I could find one, I could escape and row out of these backwaters to the river and find help. Who would help me? I can't think of anyone. I'll have to call Dad. *No! Hell no!*

Besides, after peering up and down the shoreline—there is no boat—I realize it would be stupid for someone to leave a boat here to rot away. Even if I were lucky enough to find a canoe that didn't leak, one with an oar, how could I paddle out of this backwater maze? Each tree-lined shore and turn looks like another. I'm stuck here. Helpless. Alone.

The sun is just sinking halfway behind the trees, casting long, cool shadows over the water. I must have at least two hours of daylight left. Plenty of time for Charley to find Striker and return. Sweat trickles down my forehead, burning my eyes. Rubbing them, I trudge back to the cabin, fetch a can of pop from the cooler, and slouch down at the table.

A gun. If I had a gun, I could protect myself from anything that might happen. I search every room, look under beds and mattresses, and rummage in closets and drawers. A cabin for duck hunters, but there are no shotguns and shells. *Damn!* But in a kitchen drawer, I find a hunting knife in a sheath, a knife with a shiny six-inch blade. Sitting at the table again, I lay the sheath aside and run my finger along the knife's edge. It's sharp, razor sharp.

What can I do with a knife? Hide it. Catch Striker off guard. Ambush him. Jump him from behind the moment he enters the cabin. What if I'm wrong about Striker? *I have to be wrong.*

Searching through every drawer in the cabin again, I find what I'm looking for: a roll of black duct tape. I crawl under the oak table and secure the knife to the underside. Then I sit in a chair at the table, facing the kitchen with my back to the wall. With my right hand, I practice feeling for the knife until my hand lands on the handle every time. I don't know if I have the courage to use a knife or not, but at least I have one if I need it.

I lean back in my chair. I guzzle half my can of orange pop; it fizzles down my dry throat into my belly. A cool breeze blows in through the screened windows. I pray Charley makes it back before dark. I'd hate to wait for her and Striker until tomorrow morning.

What is Striker thinking? If he's guilty—I can't believe that— he'll be tremendously pleased when he realizes Charley is delivering me to him like a caged animal. Did he really take a personal day to visit a sick mother in Chicago? Would he kill Megan to hide an affair? Would he try to kill me because he feared Megan told me he's Stephanie's lover? Would hiding an affair be worth two murders and the risk of a lifetime in prison? *Hell no.*

I have to be wrong about Striker. My searching for a boat, my looking for a gun but settling for a knife was stupid! *Totally stupid!* When Charley and Striker show up later, we'll put our heads together and solve this mystery.

I finish off my can of pop. Another possibility jumps into my mind. Bobby McGinnis, Riley's brother, the guy who sent me black roses in the first place, could have followed me to River Valley. Maybe he's living here, and he killed Megan in revenge for my having killed his sister. When the frame didn't work, he tried to kill me by running me over. When he failed, he sent me a black rose to freak me out. He'll try to kill me again.

That has to be the answer! Wait until I tell Charley and Striker. Won't they be surprised?

I scratch the back of my head. How did Bobby steal my worn-out sneakers? How did he get the combination or the master key? How did he know I'd be pedaling my bike to Westlake on a road where he could knock my ass off with his car? How did he find out where I live so he could deposit the shoes on my front porch? How did he know the cops would be at my house to gather my clothes as evidence, including my shoes?

Only Striker—with Stephanie's help—could have known all those details.

My shoulders slump. Exhaustion drops over me like a blanket. I touch the bump on my forehead and the scar on my cheek. What's next? A bullet hole through my chest? The top of my head throbs a bit more with dull pain. Too much thinking. The events of the day have wasted me, mentally and physically.

I feel lonely, empty, and lost. My life is truly cursed. There's no way I can avoid disaster, no way I can find redemption and happiness. Not when my life is cursed. How do you survive a curse? *You don't give up!*

My eyelids feel gritty. My bones feel weary. But I don't dare sleep; I don't want to dream. I lay my head in the crook of my arm on the table. I won't go to sleep though. I wish I had my phone so I could call Charley. I have to get up and find the matches to light the lanterns. I don't want darkness to find me alone in this cabin. I saw matches in one of the cupboards.

I remember the thick blackness when I lay trapped upside down in the gnarled metal of my wrecked car the night Riley died. I remember pain gouging my ribs as I screamed her name. *Riley! Riley! Riley!* I begged her to answer. I remember my blood trickling down my throat and into my mouth, warm and sweet. The cops cut me loose with the Jaws of Life.

Now I slouch in a chair, cursed, my head buried in the crook of my arm on a battered table in a cabin on an island in the Mississippi River. Blackness closes in, my eyelids drop as if they're weighted with lead, and I fall asleep.

THIRTY-EIGHT

JOHN HAWK
CHARLOTTE COTTON

CLUNK! INSTANTLY AWAKE, STILL AT the table, I jerk my head from the crook of my arm and blink. The cabin is a black cavern. Fear coils around my body like a snake. My heart races. Did I hear a noise? Or did I dream the sound?

I remain crouched at the table, shifting my eyes from left to right. Because of the heavy tree cover above the cabin, neither moonlight nor starlight shines through the cabin windows. A chilly breeze ripples through the open windows and carries the sound of crickets. My scalp tingles. The air reeks with danger and the scent of locust tree blossoms.

I croak, "Charley?" I feel for the knife under the table—still there.

What time is it? I hear footsteps at the top of the stairs outside. The cabin door squeaks open. A flashlight beam zigzags around in the kitchen.

"John?" Charley's voice.

Stabbing the darkness, the flashlight beam hits me in the face, blinding me. I turn quickly away.

"What are you doing there, sitting in the dark?" she asks.

"I fell asleep at the table." My heartbeat spikes, leaving me nearly breathless. "Don't shine the light in my eyes."

"You all right? You sound funny."

"I'm fine."

"I'll find some matches and light a lantern." Charley and the flashlight disappear.

"Why are you here so late?" I call after her. "Are you alone?"

"I'm here," Striker announces softly from somewhere in the darkness. "Charley said she could find this place in the dark, and I thought we should talk as soon as possible." The floor creaks as Striker steps toward me. "How you feeling?"

Panic swarms me, but I hide it, stopping my legs from jiggling underneath the table and calming my breathing. "Fine."

"Can't see you in the dark. Banged up?"

I swallow. "A little bit."

Striker stands across from me. "You're lucky to be alive after getting hit by a car. Running from the hospital wasn't smart though." Striker's voice is still soft.

"Couldn't help it."

"Makes you look like you've got something to hide. Makes you look guilty."

"I didn't have a choice."

"Charley says you've got ideas about who murdered Megan."

I chew my bottom lip. Should I confront Striker with what I suspect and accuse him, or should I play it cool, test him to see where he stands—on my side or not? Really, before I accuse Striker of anything, I need to get off this damn island safely. I don't like it here. I feel trapped.

"Who do you think killed her?" Striker asks.

I shrug. "A few hunches are all I've got."

A cupboard door slams in the kitchen. "Matches!" Charley says.

I hear the rasp of a match and see a burst of light as Charley lights a lantern.

"Charley says you talked to Stephanie Jones."

I nod slowly. "For a minute or two on the phone."

Charley carries the lantern into the room. Standing on a chair and holding the lantern over her head—like the Statue of Liberty— she hangs it above the table from a coat hanger wired to a bent nail pounded into a rafter. The bright glow lights the center of the room but glares in my eyes. I think of standing to avoid its glare, but then I'll be out of reach of the knife. I shift in my chair.

Striker wears jeans and a hooded, zip-up sweatshirt. I can't tell if he's carrying a gun under the sweatshirt or not. Probably.

"What did you and Stephanie talk about?" he asks.

"Um… I just told her I was sorry about what happened to Megan. Let's get off this island. Then we'll talk."

Charley plunks down in a chair. The cop remains standing. That's when she butts in, and things turn to shit.

"John!" I shake my head at him. I can't figure out why he's being so cautious. Why isn't he spelling out our theory about Stephanie and her lover for Striker like I did? "I told you," I tell Striker, "that we know Stephanie Jones has a lover. Megan surprised them together and probably scared the crap out of them. We think the lover killed Megan to keep her mouth shut and tried to frame John so the murder would appear to be solved."

"We don't know that for sure," John says.

"Yes, we *do!*" I say, slamming a fist on the table. "What's wrong with you?"

"Charley—" John starts.

"When framing John didn't work, the killer tried to run him over on his bike and make it look like an accident." I hate cutting John off, but what else can I do? "Are you following me? This makes sense, doesn't it? Someone killed Megan then tried to kill John."

Striker nods.

John says, "It's all guesswork. Let's get the hell off this island. We can talk later."

But I keep explaining. "When the hit-and-run failed, Stephanie delivered a black rose to John at the hospital to keep him frightened and to keep his mouth shut till the killer could strike again. The way I see it, we've got to corner Stephanie Jones and make her talk."

"We could be wrong," John says and cuts me a look as though he wants me to shut my big fat mouth. Then he looks at Striker. "I mean, why would a guy kill Megan just because he's having an affair with her stepmother? Maybe it was a one-time hookup. A guy wouldn't kill just to hide an affair, would he?"

"People kill for less," Striker says.

I clamp my hands on my hips. "Why are you backing down? Stephanie asked you to meet her at the park. She's the *only* one who could've set you up."

Slowly, John sits straight and slides his hands off the table to his lap. He's acting way weird. What's going on? I can't figure him out.

"Did you see the car that hit you?" Striker asks, watching John carefully.

The cop pulls out a chair, and its leg hits something and sends it skidding across the floor—an empty knife sheath. Striker glances at it then stares at John. Striker sits in the chair, across the table from John, and repeats the question.

"Didn't see the car clearly," John says. "It happened too quick. I think my getting hit was an accident. Why don't we get in the boat and get the hell off this island? I think I left the hospital too soon."

An accident? I make a face and roll my eyes. Then a curious thought zaps me. *Does John know something I don't know? Has he figured something out? Something he hasn't been able to tell me? Maybe I really do need to keep my mouth shut.*

The cop asks, "Why'd you run away from the hospital?"

"Bump on the head from the accident. Guess I wasn't thinking clearly. Let's go back across the river. This place creeps me out."

"Who's trying to kill you?" Striker asks softly.

John shrugs then darts a look at me, as though he's telling me once again to shut up. I've finally got the message. Took me long enough.

"John's right," I say. "Let's ditch this place. We could be in for some nasty weather."

It's like Striker doesn't hear me. His eyes drill John through the bright glow of the Coleman lantern. The cop slides his chair closer to the table. I swear John is sweating, beads popping out on his forehead.

"Who?" Striker repeats.

"I don't know," John says. "Maybe Riley's brother. He hates me because of her death. He wants revenge. His name's Bobby Lee McGinnis."

"Can't be," Striker says. "The kid's in the Army. Boot camp. We talked to his parents."

That shuts John up. He looks as if he's going to bite off his bottom lip.

"Who do you really think killed Megan?" Striker asks.

"I don't know," John says.

I'm getting all panicky. I heave out a big breath and swallow. I thought we were all working together—a team. Apparently not. I'm tempted to ask what the fuck is going on, but I keep my trap shut.

"I think you do know," Striker says. "You're a clever kid. You *think* you know exactly who did it, don't you?"

The blood drains from John's face. In a single fluid motion—*I can't believe it!*—John slams his chair backward, jumps up, and points a knife straight at Striker's chest. Striker doesn't flinch, but I'm freaking out! *Holy shit!*

"He's the one," John says, his chest heaving. "He's Stephanie's lover. He killed Megan, and he tried to run me over. Ask him where he was the night Megan died."

"Is this true?" I wail.

Striker's face is stone. "Don't do anything stupid, either of you." His voice takes on a low, menacing tone that's so cold, goose bumps pop out all over my flesh. "Under the table, there's a gun in my hand. It's pointed at Charley's belly. You make one more stupid move with that knife, and the bitch is dead."

John blinks and backs up an inch.

I stare at Striker in horror. "A gun?" Fear heaves in my stomach.

Striker tells John, "Don't try me. Lay the knife on the table. Carefully."

John's really trembling now.

"You think I came here without a gun?" Striker says. "You think I didn't know you had a knife? The sheath's on the floor. Lay the knife on the table—slowly—then raise your hands."

John eyes Striker as though he's trying to decide if he should lunge over the top of the table and bury the knife in the cop's heart.

"If you try anything, she dies. Lay the knife on the table. Slowly. Carefully," the cop repeats.

Still trembling, John drops the knife on the table. It clatters, the blade gleaming in the lantern light. As if by magic, Striker pulls from under the table a snub-nosed revolver with a shiny silver barrel. His lips curl as he points the gun at John. I bolt up and face Striker.

"He's the murderer!" John says.

Striker stands, kicking his chair away from the table, and flicks the gun at me. "Sit down!"

I sag back into my chair. My breath comes in short, angry spurts, my heart thrashing. "I can't believe this is happening."

Waving the gun at John, Striker says, "Keep your hands in the air. Walk slowly around the table toward me."

John follows Striker's commands, looking wobbly, as if his knees are made of rubber. When John faces Striker, a cold glint flashes in the cop's eyes. "Turn around, hands behind your back." He looks at me then back at John. "Either of you does something stupid, you're both dead."

Striker pulls handcuffs from his sweatshirt pocket. With one hand, while he pokes John in the back with his gun, he clicks the cuffs around John's wrists.

Anger and humiliation choke me. "He actually did it?" My voice is shaky.

John turns and nods. "He planned everything down to the last detail."

His weapon leveled at John's gut, Striker smiles. "I got lucky. I searched your locker for anything I could leave at the scene, and I found shoes. Perfect."

"Clever," John says.

Striker says, "What juror would believe they were stolen from your locker when there was so much other evidence?"

"Right," John says. "My footprints had to be there along with the bra, panties, and Megan's body."

"Then came the rain," Striker says. "The river flooded, and nearly everything washed away."

Bitter tears smart in my eyes. The truth sinks into my brain, and I realize I've made a horrendous mistake. "You really did kill Megan just to hide an affair?"

"Shut up!" Striker flicks the gun at my nose.

I flip him off. "She died because you're horny. You bastard!"

"Shut up! You're going to haul us back across the river—or you're going to watch John die from a slug in his belly."

My lungs quit. No inhaling. No exhaling. Nothing. I feel something deep in my chest caving in. I stand. Slowly, with great effort, I breathe again, and that's when I realize my legs are quaking. But not from fear—from anger. *I. Am. Pissed.*

Every muscle in my body throbs. "If you shoot John, you'll drown in the Mississippi River. I'll dump you out of the boat and run your ass over. I guarantee it."

THIRTY-NINE

JOHN HAWK

WHILE THE OUTBOARD MOTOR HUMS, Charley guides the boat through the night. She steers it around an endless stream of sharp bends and narrow channels. Handcuffed and facing Charley, I hunch in the center of the boat, wishing I could grip its sides to steady myself.

Striker and Charley wear life jackets. I don't, though there is one for me in the boat. Striker said I didn't need one. I think he just didn't want to risk uncuffing and recuffing me so I could slip into a jacket. I might have found an opening to overpower him. Besides, he really doesn't care if I drown or not. If I drown, I'll be one less person he'll have to shoot later.

He's seated in the bow. I feel his gun aimed at my back, right between my shoulder blades. I shift to watch his flashlight beam darting to the shorelines. I shift again, throw my head back, and breathe deeply. The night sky has clouded over, blocking the moon and revealing only a scattering of stars. The air smells of rain. Lightning dances above the trees in the distance, and far away, thunder booms. A storm is bearing down on us.

With her Cubs hat perched on her head, Charley stretches her neck left, then right. Sometimes she half stands to peer around me and Striker into the darkness. I think it will be a major miracle if she guides us out of this jungle at night.

"You really know where you're going?" I ask her.

"Been catfishing in the dark a million times." She leans forward and touches my knee. "I'm sorry about opening my mouth back there. I had no idea what was happening."

"Not your fault. I should've figured things out sooner."

"Knock off the chatter," Striker says.

What will happen after we escape the backwaters and reach the Mississippi? Will Striker shoot Charley and me and dump our bodies into the river? I don't think so. A bullet lodged in a retrieved body might be traceable to Striker's gun. Besides, two friends of Megan's found in the river with bullet holes in them would raise too many unanswered questions. Striker will probably make our deaths look like a murder-suicide.

I shiver with fear. The stars have disappeared. The sky is black. The tree line is black. The water is black. I sit in a tiny boat, about to cross a river, with a gun pointed at my head and my hands handcuffed behind my back. Without a life jacket, if I fall into the river, I'll drown for sure in a second or two. A flash of yellow-white lightning stabs the sky. I flinch, and thunder rumbles.

"Faster," Striker growls at Charley.

Charley ignores him. Striker might kill Charley and me when we get to the mouth of Credit Island Harbor. Then he'll dump our weighted bodies into an abandoned quarry somewhere. Everyone will think I killed Megan then ran away with her best friend. That might be better than the murder-suicide scenario.

I wonder if I can gather enough strength in my legs to stand and heave myself at Striker, tumbling both of us over the side of the boat into the river. I'm going to die anyway. Why not take Striker with me?

Even if the boat capsizes, Charley will survive. She's wearing a life jacket, and she can probably swim like a minnow. But Striker will survive too. Charley will be left alone to face him in the river while I sink to the bottom. He'll overpower her and drown her.

Another bolt of lightning splits the sky. Thunder rocks the boat. I slump forward a little. I need a better plan.

"You all right?" Charley calls to me.

"Fine."

"Faster!" Striker yells. "Don't worry about him. Faster!"

"And hit a stump or half-submerged log and capsize us? Can you swim, Striker, or do you walk on water?"

"I can swim," Striker says. "Don't worry about that, but lightning hitting an aluminum boat with me in it isn't my idea of a party."

Charley laughs. "I think it's hilarious. We can *all* die! Fried fish!"

"Shut up!"

I wonder if I can rile Striker enough to make him stand. Maybe I can rock the boat and tip the cop into the water. Then Charley and I can speed away.

I turn halfway around, crank my head, and face Striker. "Megan caught you and Stephanie in bed, didn't she?"

"I knew she wouldn't keep her mouth shut long. She always talked too much."

"And I was the perfect guy to frame."

"I followed when you left the dance. Everything was perfect."

"Except for the rain and the flood," I said.

"You've lived a charmed life, John Hawk. Until now."

Charmed life? Me? That idea strikes me as insanely funny, but I don't laugh. "Did you run me over? Or was it Stephanie?"

"I did. Nothing will save you this time."

"Was strangling Megan easy?" I ask. "Did she struggle? Plead for her life? Did killing her make you feel like a brave cop? Did you do her first or after?"

"Shut the fuck up!"

I see the blow coming. I turn around and try to duck, but Striker cracks me in the back of the head with his gun. I slump sideways, unable to hold myself up. A sharp pain throbs in my head again.

"Are you crazy?" Charley screams at Striker. She kills the motor, jumps up, and catches me to keep me from tumbling into the water. "Help me! He'll fall in."

"Let him!"

"With your handcuffs on him? You want him found drowned in these backwaters like that?"

Striker grabs the neck of my T-shirt and yanks me up.

"You hit him once more," Charley says, "and you'll never get across this river. I promise you that. Guaranteed!"

My eyes focus again as the rain comes, and Charley restarts the motor. She eases the boat out of the backwaters into the Mississippi River. Striker still holds me up by the shoulder with his free hand. The cop is strong. His grip feels like steel.

I twist and jerk my shoulder. "I'm all right."

Striker releases me with a shove. "Not for long."

The ride along the river shoreline is bumpy, and the swirling wind blows sheets of rain at us. The cold rain chills me but clears my mind. My body seems to ache everywhere, my head worst of all. Behind us, the mournful wail of a barge horn pierces the night.

Charley is following the Illinois side of the channel. I imagine when the time's right, she'll cut across for the Iowa side and the harbor. As the rain beats on me, I lower my head and hunch my shoulders. I plant my feet firmly on the bottom of the boat, hoping for better balance.

Charley faces the pelting rain, the bill of her cap shielding her eyes. She drives the boat much slower than she did in the afternoon, when we raced toward Cotton's Island. Head still down, shoulders hunched, I feel the boat slowly swing to my left. Charley is making her run across the river. How much time do she and I have to live? Raising my head, I turn to see how far we are from the Iowa shore. Striker faces me, his gun still pointed at me.

"Turn around," he snarls. "There's nothing to see."

"You going to shoot me in the back?"

"Maybe."

Lights dot the Iowa shore, blinking in the rain. I guess them to be a half-mile away.

"Turn around!" Striker says again.

"On shore, why don't you uncuff me, toss the gun, and we'll go one-on-one? See what happens."

"If you don't turn around and shut up, you're dead *now!*"

"John, stop it!" Charley says.

I turn around, and that's when the motor coughs, sputters, and dies. Right there in the middle of the river—the wind, rain, and waves pounding our boat like hell—our motor conks out. Dead. Like we'll soon be, Charley and me.

FORTY

JOHN HAWK

STRIKER YELLS FROM THE BOW of the boat, "What the hell's going on?"

"We ran out of gas!" Charley half-stands and pulls at the motor's starter cord.

When I hear that, my heart double-pumps and somersaults into my stomach. "No gas? You're kidding?"

The boat swirls sideways in the swift current, catches a choppy swell, rides it, slips off, and tips. It nearly dumps us before climbing the next swell. I brace my feet harder and lock my knees, trying desperately to keep my balance and stay in my seat.

"Start the motor!" Striker barks.

I swivel my head around to see if Striker is standing. As the boat rocks, I might be able to rock it even more and spill the cop overboard. If I fall in and drown—which I surely would—I'll be happy if he drowns too. But Striker remains seated, his left hand clutching the side of the boat, his gun pointed at me, though he's unable to hold it steady as the boat rocks over each swell.

"You're not out of gas!" Striker thunders at Charley. "Start this thing, or you're both dead!"

"Kill us and you'll drown!" Charley hollers. "They'll find our bodies in St. Louis. Take John's cuffs off! Let him row."

"Do it!" I cry.

"No way!" Striker's voice rings loud and clear above the storm.

"Don't be stupid!" Charley yells. "We *are* out of gas. Let him row! It's our only chance."

I turn and watch Striker glance at the Iowa shoreline, which is slipping farther and farther away. Then the cop peers up and down the river. The windswept rain beats on the aluminum boat like a thousand hammers. Angry swells toss our little boat higher. Lightning cracks overhead. Thunder explodes.

"If we hit anything," Charley yells, "a log, a buoy, a wing dam, we'll capsize. We can't swim ashore from the channel. The current's too strong. Even with life jackets on, it'll suck you under. Let him row!"

"She knows what she's talking about!" I shout. "Do you want to drown?"

"Fine!" Charley hollers at Striker. "*You* row!"

"Turn around!" Striker growls at me.

I turn. I can't believe it when I feel Striker fumble the handcuff key into the locks, releasing the cuffs.

"This gun is pointed straight at your head! Remember that! Row!" he yells.

I rub my wrists then reach for the oars, already in the oarlocks on each side of the boat. My shoulders are numb, my arms stiff, but I welcome the challenge of battling the river. I've never rowed a boat though.

"Aim that way!" Charley shouts, pointing over my right shoulder.

"Where?"

"Head for the shoreline at an angle with the current! It's our best chance."

I lean forward, dig the oars into the water, and pull back with all my might.

"Even strokes!" Charley shouts. "Don't pull harder with your right arm."

I stroke again… again… and again…

"Not bad," Charley says. "Don't dip the blades so deep in the water. Longer, smoother strokes. Get into a rhythm."

I continue to row, getting a feel for what Charley is telling me. I smooth out my stroke.

"That's it!" she says. "That's it! You're doing fine! How do you feel?"

"Wet!"

Charley laughs.

"Shut up!" Striker bellows.

"Or what?" Charley yells back. "You'll kill us?"

I feel myself gaining a rhythm. My heart beats smoothly. My breathing is deep and regular, as if I'm pumping uphill on my bike. The power of the current surprises me. It's a tireless opponent. I row, and I row, and I row some more. My palms start to burn. My arms and shoulders ache.

Is the boat moving? Or is it just bobbing about in the same place?

With each stroke, I clench my teeth. I look over my right shoulder at the land. I focus on a shoreline light brighter than the others. If I'm making progress, the light should gradually become brighter. But the irony is horrible. The closer I row us to shore, the closer Charley and I are to death.

"Are we going anywhere?" I yell at Charley.

"You're doing great! You're out of the channel. It's not far to the harbor mouth. How do you feel?"

"Still wet."

"Keep rowing!" Striker yells. "And shut up!"

I shift my feet to get a kink out of my right thigh and realize for the first time that the water in the bottom of the boat is nearly up to my ankles. Has the boat sprung a leak? Or has that much water crashed in over the sides, plus the rain?

Breaking my newly found rowing rhythm, I look down to see if what my feet and ankles tell me is true. My heart skips. As I row, the boat feels heavier, as if I'm dragging the river bottom with me, and the oars feel like hunks of lead. Frowning, I peer at Charley. She shakes her head.

That's when Striker also realizes the water in the bottom of the boat is getting deeper. "This boat is filling with water! We're sinking!"

I hear Striker's words over the top of my head, and I know the cop is standing. *Standing!*

A fork of lightning cracks across the sky.

"We're sinking!" Striker cries again.

Grabbing the sides of the boat, Charley tries to rock it violently to toss Striker into the river. No need for rocking, not now. I clutch my right oar with both hands, lift it, and without looking, swing it around viciously. The blow catches Striker on the right shoulder, and his gun fires into the storm. His arms flailing, he tries to keep his balance, but he staggers backward. I whack him again. The cop grasps at the oar, but I hang on, and the next swell rocks the boat enough to send Striker tumbling overboard.

"*NOOOooo!*" The river drowns the cop's scream.

"I got him!" I cry in amazement. I stand, trying to peer into the black water to see if Striker will bob to the surface. If he does, I'll crack him again with the oar. I'll smash him as many times as I have to. But the river seems to have sucked him under and swallowed him.

"Sit down!" Charley yells.

"He fell in! I can't see him!"

"Sit down or *you'll* fall in! Row!"

I plop down. "Are we going to sink?"

"Row! If he surfaces, we don't want him to grab the boat." Charley clenches a fist and shakes it. "What a move with that oar!"

I stab the oarlock into the slot on the side of the boat. "Are we going to sink?"

"Hell no! I pulled the plug. I'll put it back."

FORTY-ONE

JOHN HAWK
CHARLOTTE COTTON

I GRAB THE OTHER OAR AND row. "The plug?"

"The drain plug," Charley says. "I put it back in while you were watching for Striker to surface."

"What the hell are you saying?" I stroke hard with the oars.

"The drain plug. It's back here on the floor by the transom. I pulled it hoping Striker would see the water in the boat, panic, and I could rock him overboard."

"That's what I wanted to do, rock him overboard."

"But you belted him with an oar. *We did it!*" she cries. "Row harder!"

Forgetting the pain in my arms and shoulders, I pull on the oars with all my might. Through the wind and rain, my eyes search the surface of the choppy water for a bobbing head, a waving hand, but the blackness of the night and the river make it impossible to see anything. Striker fell into the river with hardly a sound, except for his gun going off and his lone word, *No!*

Has he drowned? Gulping a deep breath, I pull even harder and quicker on the oars. Her back to me, Charley seems to be messing with the motor.

What if Striker drowns and the police find his body? Will they believe Charley's and my story about what happened? Garske won't. I could be a suspect in what the police will think is another murder, and I'll be in worse trouble than I already am. *A cop killer! The curse continues.*

The thought of being a cop killer launches a spasm of fear through me. Though I hate Striker, I hope he survives. "Could Striker swim ashore from where he fell in?"

She turns in her seat to face me. "Depends on how well he can swim—he's got a life jacket on. If he doesn't panic. If he doesn't fight the current. If he doesn't get caught in a whirlpool."

I smell gas. "That's a lot of *ifs*. But he could make it, right?"

"Right. We're close enough to shore."

I tilt my head. "Do I smell gas?" I sniff hard through the rain. "Charley, answer me! Do I smell gas?"

"You can stop rowing as soon as I start the motor. Then sit in the bow," I yell.

"What?" John heaves back on the oars. "Aren't we out of gas?"

"I pulled the gas line. That's why the motor conked out. Had to get you out of those cuffs somehow."

"And you pulled the plug—?"

"Like I said, I let the boat fill with a little water, hoping Striker would panic and I could rock him overboard."

John throws his head back and laughs, the rain smacking him in the face. "What a work of art you are, Charley Cotton."

That's a compliment, I hope. I can't remember ever having felt so proud of myself. "Remember that the next time you try to ditch me because you think I'm a delicate flower. Keep rowing! I haven't got this thing started yet."

"All right."

Half standing, I pull the starter cord twice—*C'mon, baby!*—and the motor leaps to life. John eases the oars into the boat. In water over his ankles, he crawls to the bow. I'll bet he can't wait until he feels the safety of land under his feet.

What's next?

FORTY-TWO

CHARLOTTE COTTON

JOHN AND I ARE HUNCHED over and shivering in the Joneses' three-car attached garage. It has two doors, a doublewide and a regular-sized. Each door has a narrow, head-high window. John stands by one window; I stand by the other. We're about eight feet apart. The light inside is murky. Every now and then, John and I peer out the window we're guarding.

A yard light perched on a telephone pole covers the winding drive with a pale yellow glow. Rain streaks through the light and drums on the garage roof. The place smells faintly of gasoline and decomposing grass, probably from a lawnmower shoved in some corner.

"Maybe we should've called the police," I say, feeling very nervous.

"You think Garske will believe our story? 'Striker killed Megan. He tried to kill us. He fell into the river.' No way. We're going to wait to talk to whoever comes home. Dr. Jones, Stephanie, or both. I don't care."

I don't agree with John, but… I sort of see his point.

After we docked the boat, thankful to be on land and alive and hugging like mad, we ran to the Catfish Hut parking lot and let the air out of Striker's tires. Striker had insisted that he drive his own car, so we'd both parked in the lot and hurried down the lane to the river. If Striker survived his tumble into the water, John and I hoped the flat tires would leave him stranded, but he could probably call someone for help. Like Stephanie.

After letting the air out of Striker's tires, John and I drove by the Joneses' house. We saw no lights on inside or cars in the drive, except Megan's, parked off to the side. We decided to hide Old Blue in a cemetery lane a half-mile down the road, walk back, and wait outside. Rain, cold, and the need for a good hiding spot forced us into the garage. John broke a window in the door in the back of the garage and reached in to unlock it.

"We've got to scare Stephanie into telling everything she knows," he says, rubbing his wet hair back with his hands. "Make her believe it's the only way she can save her ass. She's a co-conspirator to murder, but she might save herself if she tells the truth. Something like that."

"If she thinks Striker's dead, she won't say anything." I peek out my window then look at John. In the dim light, I can barely see him. It's like I'm talking to a shadow. "Why would she talk? She'll protect herself by keeping her mouth shut."

"We won't tell her he's dead. We don't know that he is. We'll say he tried to kill us, and we got away. We know she's having an affair with him."

I smile. "Just watch her face when we say that."

"We'll say we know Striker killed Megan and he implicated her."

"It might work," I say, nodding.

"We'll say she'd better tell what she knows, or she'll take the blame alone." John peeks out his window.

"I still wish we'd have called the police and taken our chances with them."

"I wish I knew where everyone is. What time do you think it is?"

I shrug. I pull my wet hoodie away from my chest, but that doesn't make me feel more comfortable or warmer. "Midnight maybe. We've been waiting probably an hour."

"Plenty of time for Striker to swim ashore down river, call for help, and get back here." John sighs. "His cell phone's probably waterproof."

I nod. "If he's alive, he's got to figure we're here."

"He'll probably show up with Garske and say he was trying to take me in after I ran away from the hospital and that I tried to drown him. I'm stupid."

The thought of seeing those two again chills me even more, and I shiver. "If Striker and Garske show up, we're getting out of here and heading for the police station, right? We'll talk to different cops."

John's head swings my way, and he shrugs. His wet hair is slicked back as though he just got out of a shower. For a second, I picture him naked, and heat explodes in my face. *Stop that!*

"I haven't had much luck with the police," he says. "Ever."

I blow out a big breath, calming myself. We're silent, both of us watching through our windows for any kind of movement outside.

John sort of coughs. "Um... Charley?" His head swings my way again. "I... I need to tell you something." He leaves his window and shambles to where I'm standing. He clasps my hands.

What's going on? Like always, his touch is electric. My heart nearly flies out of my chest, and my knees feel as though they might cave in. "Tell me what?"

"Promise you won't get pissed."

"What?" Now that he's close to me, I see his face in the dimness. I can't imagine what he's going to say.

His forehead is broad but marred by that bump. He licks his lips. "Back there at the cabin, just after you left and I figured out Striker might be a part of all this, I... I mean, this is so stupid. I really feel guilty. Seriously." His head hangs for a moment.

"What?"

"I mean, you risked your life to save us. You were so damned brave and smart. I've got to tell you this..."

My head tilts. "What, John?"

"I thought maybe you were part of it—the plan to kill me."

I step back, dropping his hands. "You didn't. I can't believe that. Did you really?"

"I did. I'm sorry."

I scowl at him. "That really does half piss me off."

"I was paranoid."

"You *actually* thought I was bringing Striker to kill you?"

"Yeah," he says sheepishly. "I thought that for a second. Just a second. I mean, I didn't know what I was thinking. I was so confused."

How can I be pissed? "I almost did get us killed by being so stupid and opening my mouth when you were trying to keep it shut."

He glances out my window then back at me. He's standing so close to me, I feel his warm breath on my forehead. My heart's pounding, and I'm wondering if he's going to move closer.

"Please don't be pissed," he says.

"I'm not, really. I probably would've thought the same thing." I breathe deeply and tell myself to concentrate on the danger we're in. Concentrate on what just happened to us on the river and what might happen next. Not on… other things. "Where'd you get that knife?"

"Found it in a cupboard. I taped it under the table." John looks out the window again. "I don't know if I could've stabbed him or not."

I stiffen. "I could've, once I knew what he'd done and for such a bullshit reason. How'd you finally figure out it was Striker?"

"My shoes," John says, shuffling his feet on the concrete floor. "It was all so simple. Yet so complicated." John touches my shoulder.

My heart leaps.

"You were great out there in the river," he says. "You saved us both. Otherwise, we'd be dead. Like Cole said—*dead meat.*"

Wrapping his arms around me and surprising me out of my skin, he gives me a giant hug. Despite our wet clothes and the chilly garage, I feel that wonderful warmth spread through my entire body. Me—Charley Cotton—snuggled into John Hawk's arms. Locked in an embrace.

"Thanks." My voice sounds husky, which isn't surprising because of the gigantic lump lodged in my throat. Still wrapped in his arms and wishing my heart would slow down before I have a heart attack, I hold my breath. I wonder what John will do next, what *I'll* do. I feel blazing circles on my cheeks. *Kiss me* rips through my mind. Again. *Get a grip, Charley!*

John releases me. "Look!" he whispers hoarsely. "Here comes someone."

A car shoots into the driveway, its headlights bouncing as their beams sweep over the garage door. We duck.

"Whose car?" John asks.

"I can't tell." Not with the lights in my eyes.

"It's someone in a hurry. If the garage door opener kicks in, we're out the back door."

Hunched down, listening, I stare at the door-opening mechanism bolted to the rafters and listen for its first hum. John stares too. It remains silent. The car lights blink out, casting the garage into near darkness again. The engine stops. John pops up. I pop up and stare through the window with him. The car door swings open then slams shut. A tall slender figure carrying a suitcase dashes from the car to the house.

"Stephanie," I say.

"Good! Let's catch her just as she gets in the house."

FORTY-THREE

CHARLOTTE COTTON

A s the front door of the house closes behind Stephanie, John grabs the door handle, twists, and stiff-arms the door open. I'm right behind him. The house is dark.

Stephanie gives a start and says, "Kevin?" When she realizes the person behind her is John—not her lover—she screams, "What do you want?"

John grips her shoulders. Trembling, she drops the suitcase.

"Don't scream," John says. "Nobody's going to hurt you."

She gasps. "John Hawk?"

"And Charley Cotton," I say. "We want to talk to you."

"We need some light," John says.

Stephanie picks up the suitcase, and we follow her down the hallway to the living room. She flicks a wall switch that lights a floor lamp next to a sofa. Her hand flies to her mouth when she sees how drenched we are, how ragged we must look.

"Surprised?" I ask. "Are we supposed to be dead—because Striker killed us?"

"We need to talk to you," John says, jabbing a finger in her face.

"I want you both out of this house!" Stephanie says, jerking back. "Now!"

"Or what?" John's eyes narrow. "You'll call the cops? Officer Striker, maybe?"

Her face is blank.

"You set me up so Striker could run me over on my bike." John points at his forehead. "See this knot? Your lover nearly killed me. But that's what both of you wanted, isn't it? What's another body?"

Stephanie tosses her blond hair. "You're crazy!"

"And thanks for the black rose you delivered at the hospital," John adds.

"You don't know what you're talking about."

"Yes, we do," I say, hands jammed onto my hips. "We know lots of things."

"Striker's your lover." John steps closer to her, backing her into the center of the room. "Megan knew, and he killed her to keep her mouth shut."

"You don't know *anything!*" Stephanie whips a hand through the air. "If you're smart, you'll get out of here *now!*"

"And let you go free?" I say, shaking my head fiercely. "An accomplice to the murder of my best friend? No way."

Stephanie's fists clench. "I had nothing to do with Megan's death."

"A jury will never believe that," John says. "Striker will probably say it was your idea."

Pointing toward the hallway, Stephanie screams, "Get out of here *now!*"

"We'll wait for Dr. Jones," John says calmly. "He'll find what we have to say interesting."

"Where is he?" I ask.

Stephanie glances at the clock on the fireplace mantel. It's nearly twelve thirty. "I don't know where he is."

I eye the suitcase. "What's in there?"

Stephanie clutches the suitcase handle with both hands. The blue veins in the back of her hands bulge.

Oh my God! I recognize that suitcase. "Hey! That's the suitcase Striker lugged out of the trunk of his car when he got home. Said it was filled with personal items he brought from Chicago. He took them up to his apartment before I took him across the river."

"Let's have a look," John says, reaching for the suitcase.

Stephanie swings it behind her with her right hand. Her other hand darts out, palm out, fingers spread wide. "Stay away! Neither of you know what you're getting into."

In the darkness behind Stephanie, I glimpse a shadowy figure approaching from the hallway.

"Nice to see all of you!" the shadow says.

"Kevin?" Stephanie says with a gasp and drops the suitcase.

"Who else?"

I cringe at the sound of his painfully familiar voice.

"Kevin?" Stephanie whirls.

Striker steps out of the darkness and into the glow of the living-room light. He has a gun with a long blue barrel pointed at John. Striker's eyes are bright and wide, his stare burrowing into John. His sweatshirt, jeans, and sneakers are wet and muddy from the river. His eyes blaze at John. "Did you think I'd drown?"

John swallows. I swallow. Striker waves the weapon, indicating for John and me to move into the center of the living room, the coffee table and sofa behind us.

Stephanie steps toward him, her arms outstretched and quivering. "Kevin, darling, I'm so glad—"

"Shut up!"

"Darling!"

"*Shut up!* What time do you expect Frank?"

She glances at the mantel clock again. "I don't know..."

"When, dammit?"

"An hour maybe." Stephanie takes another step.

Striker does a quarter turn and points the gun at her belly. "Getting a little greedy, weren't you, love?"

"Kevin, listen to me—"

"Going to keep the product for yourself?"

"Darling, I didn't want anyone to find—" She struggles for a word. "I mean... in case something had happened to you..."

Striker's face looks as hard as stone.

Stephanie says, "You said you were going down to the river with her." She gives me a hateful look. "You were supposed to be back in an hour or two, but you weren't."

Striker grunts.

"Darling, please believe me," Stephanie says.

"What's in the suitcase?" John asks.

"Money?" I ask.

Striker angles the gun at me, glaring with cold blue eyes. I feel a thud in my chest.

"You don't know how happy I was," he says, "when I parked in the cemetery next to that blue piece of junk of yours. I knew you were both here, and I wouldn't have to track you down. Thank you."

Now I understand why Megan hadn't seen a car the afternoon she discovered Stephanie and Striker together. He probably always hid his car in the cemetery and sneaked up a back way. I have a suspicion of what might be in that black suitcase that seems so valuable.

Wringing her hands, Stephanie looks at John and me. "What are we going to do with them?"

"Drugs?" I say. "Isn't that what killers carry in big black suitcases? Or drug money?"

"Shut the fuck up!" Striker shouts.

"Is that why Megan had to die? She knew you were doing drugs?" I ask.

Throwing his head back, Striker laughs. "Stupid people *do* drugs. Smart people *sell* them."

John's face is tight. "That's why Megan died? She knew you were dealing drugs?"

John looks as if he's measuring the distance between Striker and himself. It's about twelve feet. A lump of fear hardens in my throat. *Holy crap!* He's not thinking about rushing the cop, is he? *Don't do it! Don't!*

"If Megan told her old man about Stephanie and me—our little arrangement—it would've ruined everything," Striker says.

Stephanie's eyes flare. "You're talking too much!"

"No harm!" Striker snaps the gun at me then at John. "They're dead."

His words freeze my insides.

Striker's chest expands as if he expects a good report card—first honors for his achievements. "I drive the drugs in from Chicago myself. Where would you guess I hide them when I get to town?"

"Kevin… don't!"

"I have no idea," John says.

I say, "Where?"

"School," Striker boasts. "A high school whose principal says it's drug free. Perfect."

"That's a lie," I say and shake my head. "Dr. Jones would've found out."

"He must be part of it," John says. "They've blackmailed him because he gambles and loses."

"I don't believe it. That can*not* be true."

A wry smile twitches Striker's lips. "Megan's old man, sweetheart, is a big-time loser. The people he owes don't fool around with gamblers who can't pay their debts. Especially big ones."

"So what?" I say.

"So I dole out money to him so he doesn't get his head shot off, and he provides me a safe place to store my merchandise. And I get to bang his wife."

"Kevin!" Stephanie screams. "Stop!"

"I still don't believe it." But the big picture focuses in my mind. The answer to the mystery of Megan's death all at once seems so clear and simple that my brain spins with the impact as if someone had punched me in the face. My turn to glare. "Megan died so you could protect your drug operation?"

"You're a very bright girl. Too bright for your own good." Striker points the gun at John. "Too bad you got mixed up with this loser."

"He's not a loser."

"He turned you into a loser too." Striker steps closer to John then nods at me. The cop's face breaks into an evil grin. "She dies first."

"Screw you!" My voice shakes. I feel cold, as though I'm dead already.

John's chest heaves. "You'll never get away with this."

"Kevin, don't shoot them here. Please…" Stephanie looks at him with burning eyes.

"You're going to watch her die," Striker tells John, jerking the gun at me.

"Kevin, sweetheart, please… somewhere else…"

Striker ignores Stephanie and tells John, "Then you're next." He raises the weapon and aims it at my forehead.

I come unraveled. My skin shrinks with fear, and a chill seeps in at the base of my brain. Trembling, I'm in total panic mode. In high-definition clarity, I see John and myself lying dead on the floor.

Holy shit! Oh God! Good-bye, world! I love you, Mom and Dad!

FORTY-FOUR

JOHN HAWK

I HOLD MY BREATH AND CLENCH my fists. I'm ready to hurl myself at Striker and rip the gun out of his hand—the only move I can think of. But it would be a stupid thing to do. He'll shoot me dead in an instant. But maybe in the confusion, Charley could escape. *I'll have saved at least one girl.*

"Get Frank's gun!" Striker tells Stephanie.

Her head snaps around. "What?"

"Frank's gun, get it."

"Why?"

A muscle in Striker's jaw clenches. "*Get it!*"

Stephanie flees the room, and Striker backs up a pace. I feel my forehead bursting with sweat. I can't imagine why the cop needs another gun.

"Your gun doesn't work?" Charley asks.

"Try me," Striker says, his voice low and deadly.

I grab Charley's hand. It's sweaty and cold. "Be quiet."

"Smart," Striker says.

A trickle of sweat runs down the small of my back.

Trembling, Stephanie returns, balancing a black revolver in her palm. "Here." She holds the gun out for Striker.

"Shoot them," he says. "Shoot the girl first."

Stephanie's eyes fly wide open, and her jaw drops as if it's come unhinged. "What?"

"They're intruders breaking and entering. You were frightened. You thought they were going to kill you. You knew the boy had killed your stepdaughter. Shoot the girl first."

"Where does it show we broke in?" Charley says.

I say, "What were we going to kill her with?"

"Kill them!" Striker points at Charley then at me. "I'll take care of the rest."

"He wants you to be a murderer too," I tell Stephanie, trying to meet her eyes, but she isn't looking at me.

She stares wide-eyed at Striker.

Striker glares at her. "I've invested my life—everything I have—in this operation. Are you with me or not? Prove it." His voice hardens. "Kill them!"

"Then he'll kill you," I say.

Charley says, "He'll make it look as if we all killed each other."

"He'll be free." I flail a hand in desperation. "No one will know *he* killed Megan."

"*Kill them!*"

Stephanie's shoulders quake. Her eyes look haunted, and anguish fills her voice. "I'm with you. I've already *proven* that—you *know* I have. I love you! Think of what I've already done for you."

"Shut up!"

"He wants us dead," I tell Stephanie, "but he wants you to do it with your husband's gun at your house! Doesn't that tell you something about him?"

"Give me the damn gun!" Striker shouts.

Stephanie pulls back.

"Give me—" Striker pivots to grab the gun from Stephanie.

In a millisecond, I rocket twelve feet across the room and drive my shoulder into Striker. I cut the cop down before he can wheel and fire. My charge sends Striker crashing into Stephanie's legs, and the cop's gun fires at the ceiling. Screaming, Stephanie topples backward. A groan rolls out of Striker as he hits the floor, his gun still in his hand. We tumble across the floor. I lock my hands around his right wrist, trying to squeeze the gun loose.

"Not dead yet!" My breath is raspy.

"You will be!"

Out of the corner of my eye, I see Stephanie fleeing the room.

"Get her!" I cry.

With the strength of steel in his hands and arms, the cop tries to angle the gun at my head. The gun fires again, its roar blasting past my ear and rattling my brain, filling my nostrils with the smell of gunpowder. I can't hear anything after the blast.

Still hanging on to the cop's wrist, I smash his gun hand against the coffee table's pointed corner. Striker's mouth opens in pain, and the weapon flies out of his fist. I wrestle him across the floor. I scissor my legs around his waist. My right arm cross-facing him, I lock my left hand around my right wrist and snuggle my forearm under Striker's chin, against his Adam's apple. I have him in a stranglehold.

His wet clothes and red hair smell of the black river.

Images flash through my brain: Striker strangling Megan. Striker pointing a gun at Charley's head. At my head.

I wrench my right forearm up against the cop's windpipe. With my left hand still locked on my right wrist, I squeeze harder. Striker drives his right elbow into my rib cage. Each blow is a hammer in my ribs, beating the air out of me and filling my body with bolts of pain.

Gritting my teeth, I strain harder on Striker's neck. His chest heaves as he struggles for breath. The rib shots stop. The cop claws at my hands, digging skin and flesh away with his nails. I slam my eyes closed, concentrate, and squeeze harder. My blood pounds in my ears from the effort. As the buzzing clears from my ears, I hear a sucking in Striker's throat that sounds like water emptying down a drain.

A faint, frantic voice in the back of my brain screams, *"You're killing him, John! Let him go! He's blue!"*

The voice seems far away.

"John—!"

My eyes flip open. The voice isn't coming from the back of my brain. It's coming from Charley.

She stands over me, trembling, a gun in her hand pointed off to her left. I don't know why until I realize Stephanie's crouched in a chair, bawling.

"John, please let him go. You're killing him!" Charley says.

My chest heaving so bad it hurts, I release Striker with a shove and scoot away from him on my butt. He really is nearly blue, but he's alive and breathing—a gurgling sound. As Striker feebly claws at his throat, Charley hands me a gun and says she's calling the cops. Pointing the weapon at Striker's head, I sit on the floor and lean my back against the sofa. I wonder if I'll ever catch my breath. My ribs burn. My head hurts. Soon I hear the wail of sirens. Police officers swarm into the room with guns drawn. After an all-clear, paramedics rush in.

Striker hasn't moved an inch. He's pale white, still breathing, his fingers motionless at his throat.

I wanted to kill him, but I'm glad I didn't.

FORTY-FIVE

CHARLOTTE COTTON
JOHN HAWK

A T THREE A.M., JOHN AND I sit on the front porch steps of the Joneses' house. He says that's where Megan asked him to the prom. Now she's gone. It's still too difficult to believe. I bite my bottom lip hard to stop tears from threatening my eyes.

For the past two hours, the house and yard have been a beehive of cops and paramedics. Officers raced in and out of the house collecting guns, digging in the wall and ceiling for bullets, asking questions, taking notes, and talking on their cell phones. Sirens screamed. Red lights flashed. Two ambulances hauled Stephanie and Striker to the hospital.

The rain has stopped. A few stars peek through the clouds, though the moon remains hidden. The light over the drive gives us a bit of light to see by. The night air smells cool and fresh, promising a bright day.

"I wish Garske and his crew would hurry up inside," John says. "I want to go home. A cop let me use a phone in the house to call my sister, but she's probably still freaked."

"My parents couldn't believe me when I called and told them what had happened. And I got only half the story out. They're pissed at me." I don't tell John that just a few days ago, they told me to stay away from him. Now we're involved in a drug-trafficking scheme, a murder, and a shootout, and I'm crushing on the guy my folks warned me about. *Brilliant!*

Two cops leave the house. One tromps past us on the steps, nodding without a word.

The second cop stops at the bottom step and turns. "You guys did us a big favor. We couldn't figure out who the hell was flooding this town with drugs. Thanks."

John and I smile at each other, and I tell the cop, "No problem."

After the cops climb into their cruisers and slam the doors, they back out and speed off down the road, the cars' red taillights winking then dying in the distance.

Garske's cruiser is the only one left in the drive. Through its open window, I hear the police radio squawk.

John sighs heavily. "I hope I can go home and get a good night's sleep. Maybe turn out the lights. Maybe no nightmares. I might even call my dad."

I look at him. "What do you mean 'turn out the lights... no nightmares?'"

He tells me about his being frightened of the dark and about his nightmares, all because of his accident with Riley. He says I'm the only person except his sister who knows. I sit hunched over with my arms wrapped around my knees. John's story chills me.

"That's horrible," I say. "Nighttime in the cabin must've scared you to death."

"That, and coming back across the river in the dark. Striker's pointing a gun at you, at me." John massages his temples with his fingers then works on the back of his neck.

"Here, I'll do that," I say, surprising myself. I scoot around and kneel behind him. I knead my fingers up and down his neck, along his shoulders. I feel strength there, and knots of tension.

Gradually he relaxes. "That feels so good."

"The kids at school owe you an apology."

"I don't care about apologies." John rotates his shoulders. "I still don't understand exactly what happened between you and Stephanie."

"It's simple. As soon as you landed on Striker, Stephanie ran for the back door. She dropped her gun."

"She probably didn't know how to use it."

"Well, I did. I grabbed it and ran after her. I flicked on the backyard light. I yelled at her to stop, but she didn't. I didn't want to shoot her and maybe kill her—well, I did and I didn't. So I shot a tree near her. She screamed and tumbled to the ground. She twisted her ankle—maybe broke it—and fell, dislocating her shoulder. I think I scared the shit out of her."

In the dim light, I watch a smile creep across John's face. "Oh wow!"

"Marching her back to the house after that was easy—especially with a gun pointed at her head."

"She say anything?"

"She was totally freaking out, crying and moaning about the pain and saying none of this was her fault. I forced her to sit in a chair in the living room, kept the gun on her, and stopped you from killing Striker."

"I'm glad you did."

"Then while you were watching Striker, I marched Stephanie into the kitchen and called the cops from a phone on the wall." I work my fingers high on John's neck, underneath his hair. "Still feel good?"

"Like I never want you to stop."

My heart somersaults. *Oh my!*

As my fingers probe deeper and deeper into John's neck and shoulder muscles, his head slumps forward.

"You feeling any better?" I ask.

"A million times better."

As her strong, slender fingers continue their magic on my neck and shoulders, Charley and I glide into silence.

Twisting my head from side to side, I say, "I hate Striker, but he said something tonight that I'll never forget."

"What?"

"Something that makes me think maybe I'll be all right."

"What did he say?" she asks.

"'You've lived a charmed life, John Hawk.'" I shrug. "I've always thought my life was filled with rotten breaks: my mom running away, Riley's death, and Megan's. Things never turn out good for me. My life is cursed, and I have this scar on my face to remind me every day."

"Nobody's life is cursed. That scar proves you're a survivor."

"I am a survivor. I mean, I could've been, like, killed three or four times in my life. In a car, on a bike, in a boat, right here at Megan's house, but I'm still alive."

The front door opens and closes behind us. Charley stands, but I remain seated. Garske and Regan tramp down the porch steps. While Regan strolls over to the squad car and climbs in, Garske stands in front of us on the lawn.

"Do we have to tell it all again?" Charley asks him.

Garske shakes his head. "That takes care of everything. Evidence, reports, statements. Everything." He slips a notebook into his breast pocket. "I'll want to talk to both of you tomorrow though."

"You mean later today?" I say.

Garske nods. "Later today." He clears his throat. "Just got off the phone with the desk sergeant. Thought you'd like to know we picked up Jones on his way home from the casino. Got him at the station."

"What's his story?" Charley says.

"He's ready to spill everything. I'm sure he wants his wife and Striker to pay for his daughter's death."

"Good," Charley says. "They should."

"We'll most likely be able to bust Striker's Chicago drug connection and shut down the whole pipeline."

"What about Stephanie and Striker?" Charley says.

"They're demanding to talk to lawyers."

I say, "How did Striker get to Dr. Jones's house?"

Charley says, "The last time we saw him, he had disappeared in the Mississippi River. We thought maybe he'd drowned, but we let the air out of his tires just in case."

"He swam ashore, called one of his mules, and borrowed a car. We found it parked in the cemetery out back." Garske toes the wet grass and looks almost sheepish, his head down. Then he looks at me. "Sorry about the bad time I gave you, boy. With your reputation, you were always the most logical suspect. We figured you raped her, she fought, and you accidentally killed her in the struggle. Then you stripped her, left her, and fled with her clothes—most of them, anyway—or slipped her body into the harbor. Easy to do since the water was so high.”

“That bit about Megan being strangled by someone with the hands of a weightlifter? A wrestler? What was that all about?”

Garske looks sheepish again. “Just testing you. Seeing what you had to say.”

“You mean lying to me?”

“Testing you. Had to do that. Part of the job.”

Biting my bottom lip, I look away, disgusted.

Megan says, “You guys never suspected Striker of running drugs?”

Garske cracks his knuckles. “Well, Striker was quiet, kept to himself, did a good job, and was well liked. What more can you ask from anybody?”

“I thought he was a good guy,” Charley says.

“Me too,” I say.

“Cops are trained to spot typical vehicles, drivers, and passengers that haul drugs on the highways,” Garske says. “Striker knew that. In his little blue Honda sedan, he didn’t fit the profile. Even if he was stopped for a traffic violation, all he had to do was flash his badge, and they’d let him go.”

“He was running a perfect operation,” I say. “Right under everybody’s nose.”

Garske takes a big breath and heaves a giant sigh. “A single mom raised him, and she did a decent job. Can’t blame her for how he turned out. He graduated first in his class from the Police Academy. Worked for the Chicago PD for a bit and came to us highly recommended.”

Charley makes a face. “But he was a crooked cop.”

“He was a high-IQ guy who thought he could beat the system. He learned how drug dealers handled things in Chicago. He got greedy— it happens a lot—and set up his own operation right here in River Valley.” Garske releases another big sigh and nods. “This community owes both of you. You’re heroes.”

“I don’t feel like a hero,” Charley says softly. “Not when I think of what happened to Megan. Why do bad things happen to good people? I can’t figure that out.”

"My wife's in a wheelchair," Garske says. "Hit-and-run driver. No reason why that stuff happens. You live with it. Bad times test you and make you a better person, I guess. They give you a chance to see what you're made of. Prove yourself."

I look at Garske. Is he talking to me? I don't think so. His brows hang heavy over his eyes, and he's looking at the ground as if he's talking to himself. But what he says strikes me.

"How about we go home?" Charley says, sitting straight.

"Sure. You both need a ride?"

"My truck's down the road."

"You mind riding in a squad car again, John?" Garske asks.

My eyes meet Garske's in the darkness. It's the first time he's called me anything but boy, and despite his harassing me, trying like hell to nail me for a crime I didn't commit, and lying to me, I'm appreciative.

"John can go with me," Charley offers.

Getting up slowly, my bones weary, I stand next to Charley. I love her kinky auburn hair and freckles and the sweet, subtle curves of her body. She's one terrific girl. Having her on my side is a piece of luck I couldn't have done without.

A smile nudges the corners of her mouth when I say, "I'll go with Charley."

FORTY-SIX

CHARLOTTE COTTON

IT MUST BE AT LEAST four thirty a.m. when I ease Old Blue to a stop in front of John's house. Lights shine in nearly every window. We hardly spoke on the way. We were both too zonked and baffled, our heads spinning with every minute detail.

The moon's disappeared, but the clouds have drifted away. Stars sparkle like silver sprinkles scattered on black velvet. With my truck's windows down, the breeze inside Old Blue is cool and fresh. I'm alone with John Hawk—a guy Megan liked. A guy I like so much that every time my heart gets a chance, it screams *Kiss me!* What the hell's wrong with me?

What would Megan say? *Go for it, Charley!* Would she say that?

John turns to me. The streetlight in front of the house bathes his face in a soft glow. His scar is clearly visible through his stubble, and so is the soft smile playing around his lips.

Heat rushes through me. *Kiss me! Kiss me senseless! Shut up, you idiot!*

He says, "All those lights on in the house—my sister's waiting for me, probably out of her freaking mind. Maybe Donnie too. I've got to go."

I'm prepared for him to leap out of my truck and bolt for the house.

But he leans toward me. "So this is good night... or good morning."

Without thinking, I lean in too. When his soft lips lock with mine, my eyes close, and a wave of delicious shock rolls over me. My heart hammers, and my breath sticks in my lungs. The kiss lasts only a second or two—maybe five. It's simply a sweet, passionate pressing of melting lips. When our mouths part, I'm so amazed that I nearly forget to open my eyes. But I do, and at the same time, I gulp a breath of air.

"See you later," John says, reaching for his door handle. "I'll call first."

I'm still not breathing correctly. "Okay."

I give him my number. With that, John quietly but quickly closes Old Blue's door and races to the front porch.

I'm limp. I'm not sure I can drive home. I hear Megan yelling, *Way to go, Charley! You fox!*

FORTY-SEVEN

JOHN HAWK

WHEN I STAGGER INTO THE brightly lit house, cigarette smoke stuns me. I cough and pound my chest. Anne must have smoked a pack or more while waiting for me to get home.

She bolts from a chair at the kitchen table, stabs out her cigarette in an ashtray, and screams, "What the hell's going on!"

Luckily, Donnie's not in the room. I assume he's asleep. Anne's so pissed at me and her face is so red that I think she's going to pound on me with her clenched fists. But she grabs me and hugs me fiercely, like she's never, ever hugged me before.

Then she snarls, "You asshole!"

I don't think she means that, but if she does, I understand why. I've put her through a wringer.

I told her part of the story when I called from Dr. Jones's house. Now, after I get her to sit and calm down, I tell her the rest. She interrupts so often, asking so many questions, that it's nearly sunrise before I finish my tale. It evidently fascinates her, because she doesn't reach for another cigarette from the pack lying on the table.

At the end, she says, "God, after all that, you're alive. I can't believe it." She jabs me with her flashing brown eyes.

I don't give her a chance to say a word. "I know, I've got to call Dad. I'll do it first thing after a bit of sleep. I promise. If you'll give up cigarettes."

She stares at me, obviously startled. She bites her bottom lip. She glances at the pack and frowns. She shakes one cigarette out and leaves it on the table. Pack in hand, she pushes up from the table, goes to the sink, turns on the faucet, and runs cold water into the cellophane. Tired as I am, my eyes leap wide open. She crushes the pack and tosses it into the garbage under the sink.

She wipes her hand on a towel as she turns to me. "You've got a deal. After I smoke one more."

I jump into a hot shower. *Oh, that's good. Best ever!* I fall into bed. Though every muscle and bone in my body is aching, I can't sleep. My mind churns with vivid, jumbled, living-color scenes of all that's happened.

At eight in the morning, I'm sitting at the kitchen table in my jockey shorts, landline phone pressed to my ear with my right hand. My left elbow is planted on the table, my palm holding up my head as if it's the weight of the world. My mouth is desert dry. I should have gulped a glass of cold water before I called Dad.

"S-say that again!" he sputters.

"I helped nail two drug dealers in town. They're murderers too."

I'm smart enough to lead off with the good stuff so Dad won't be as pissed when I tell him another girl I dated died—was murdered—and I was the only real suspect. But a cop killed her. He and the dead girl's stepmom were the drug dealers. The dead girl's father is the principal at my school, and he was hiding the drugs there. He's addicted to gambling. Another girl I just met saved my ass from drowning in the river. I nearly killed the cop.

My story apparently ties Dad's mind into so many knots, he can't figure it out at first—and he's a lawyer. But when he sees the clear picture, he yells, "I knew you couldn't stay out of trouble. I knew it. You, your sister—what the hell's wrong with everyone? Your mom too—I don't know where the hell she is. Wasn't Anne watching you? What the hell!"

Ignoring that, I stick with the good stuff. "The cops say Charley— she's the girl who saved me—and I are heroes, Dad. There'll probably be a trial. Charley and I will be witnesses, and it'll all be in the papers.

We're heroes." I don't feel like a hero at all, but I can't emphasize that enough for Dad's sake. "We've stopped more drugs from creeping into River Valley and solved the murder of a girl I dated."

Dad's silent for a beat, apparently thinking it all over. "Yeah, well, that's good. You're alive and a hero. That's all good."

That *is* good. For the first time since I began screwing up after Mom ditched us, Dad sounds as though maybe he's cool with me. A feeling of well-being hits me and sinks deep into my mind and my body and my soul. I'm lucky, I'm alive—and I'm curse-free.

After I say good-bye, hang up, and fall into bed again, sleep overwhelms me.

FORTY-EIGHT

CHARLOITE COTTON

IT'S BEEN OVER THREE WEEKS since Megan's death, and today, with 248 other River Valley High cheering, cap-throwing seniors, John and I graduated from high school. We agreed that if we don't think about Megan's death, it's the happiest day of our lives. Of course, Riley invades John's memory all the time. He can't think about Megan's death without thinking about hers too. He's dealing with a lot but seems to be holding up well. I admire him.

It's almost midnight. John and I are sitting on my folks' dock behind the Catfish Hut, our feet dangling over the Mississippi River. An oblong moon drifting in a cloudless sky casts a silver streak across the river. Huge, unblinking stars help light the night.

John and I are pumped tonight because we've just had an awesome day. My parents threw a graduation party for John and me at the restaurant. We used the party room. It took me a week to convince John it was all right for him to share my party. He'd said he didn't want people to think he was sponging.

Lots of kids from school showed up, and tons of my relatives. I met John's sister and his little nephew Donnie. What a blond cutie he is! I promised to take him fishing.

John tells me how proud he is of Anne. She's quitting smoking. John's dad, Anthony Hawk, showed up for John's graduation and went to the party, totally surprising all of us. He bore gifts: a laptop and a printer. The man is drop-dead gorgeous, like John. He shook John's hand, embraced him, and patted his back. He called John a hero, the bravest kid he knows.

I pegged John's dad from the get-go. He values achievement. He heaps praise on his offspring when the kid does well—treats him like an all-American boy, promises him the world. But let the kid fail, and dad bails and distances himself from the screw-up. *Not my kid, man. Don't know who he belongs to.*

I don't tell John that. He's got it figured out.

He says, "I'm excited about Dad showing up and about the gifts and all, but I'm not sure this means we'll have a closer relationship. I'm bound to screw up again, and he'll be totally pissed once more."

"Who says you'll screw up?"

John shrugs and smiles a little. "Life's really unpredictable."

I shoulder-bump him—my shoulder against his bicep—and smile back. "I'll probably have to keep you in sight all the time."

Striker, Stephanie, and Dr. Jones are being held without bond. The word is the state's case against those three will be tough to beat.

Here's something that'll blow your mind—the real story of Stephanie and Striker.

Our local newspaper revealed they went to high school together in Chicago. After graduation, Stephanie worked as a dance instructor in Florida and Arizona—where there're lots of old guys with big money. Four years ago, she showed up at the *Rhythm* City as a blackjack dealer. Dr. Jones spotted her, latched on to her, and married her. Two years later, Striker began his career at River Valley PD.

This part's not in the newspaper. Everyone in town thinks Stephanie and Striker dated in high school. They lost track of each other, and they hooked up again in River Valley. A lucky coincidence for them, but not so much for everyone else involved. Striker shared his drug-running ambitions with Stephanie, and they targeted Dr. Jones, her husband, as an easy mark for blackmailing. Sounds good to me. We'll find out at the trial.

If that's not surprising, this will really blow your mind.

Are you ready?

After the prom, Dr. Jones took Stephanie home. She said she was too beat to help chaperone the after-prom party. Just like we thought, Striker followed John and Megan to Credit Island after the prom. He figured Megan would head for Credit Island, but he had to make sure. He also needed to see where she parked. Then he hid in his car in the cemetery by Megan's house, waiting for her to come home. When he saw her driving by at four in the morning, he called Stephanie on his cell phone.

When Megan walked through the front door, Stephanie cracked her on the head with a silver candleholder from the fireplace mantel and knocked her out. The coroner said that blow didn't kill Megan. Stephanie jumped on her and smothered her with a pillow. I hate how Garske told John that Megan died of strangulation. The cop figured it was an easy way to scare him into confessing to the crime—a crime he didn't commit.

Just thinking about how Megan died makes me want to cry.

Anyway, Striker showed up. He and Stephanie stripped the body, and Striker delivered it back to Credit Island, along with Megan's bra and panties. He kept the rest of Megan's clothes and threw them, along with the pillow, into a dumpster in Chicago. Stephanie scoured the candleholder and placed it back on the mantel.

So it turns out, Striker didn't kill Megan. Stephanie Jones did. All of us had it wrong.

Killing Megan, though, had apparently unnerved Stephanie—*I would think so!*—and that was why she couldn't finish off John and me, especially in the same room where she'd killed Megan. No matter how hard Striker tried to force her to kill John and me, she simply couldn't do it. She probably couldn't stand the thought of two more ghosts haunting her in that house. When the cops searched Striker's apartment, they found digital scales, packing materials for drugs, and thirty-six thousand dollars in cash. He had it made. Too bad he wasn't as smart as John and me.

I went with John to the funeral. I've never seen so many kids crying. Lots of kids patted John on the back, people he didn't know. I never liked Cole Wainwright—still don't—but I'll give him credit. After the service, he shook John's hand, and they both mumbled, "Sorry." I don't think they'll become best friends though.

"What are you thinking about?" John says as we sit on the dock in the moon-and-star-lit darkness, our feet dangling over the water.

"About the stuff that's happened. I can't get it out of my mind. None of it. No matter how hard I try. I feel guilty all the time, like it's clawing at me. I wish I could've done something to change things in Megan's life."

"You could've talked her out of going to the prom with me," John says flatly.

I stare at him and realize he's struggling with the same thought I am: *what could I have done differently to save Megan?*

John puffs out a breath. "I'm guilty too. I took her to the prom. I knew better, but I did it anyway. But I'm innocent—I didn't harm her. Still, if I'd said no like I should have… like I wanted to…" Tilting his head back, John gazes at the moon and stars shining over the river.

I bang a fist on the dock. A thought just leaped into my brain. "But you know what?"

"What?"

I say, "With what Megan knew about Stephanie and Striker, they couldn't let her live. No matter what either one of us did, she had to go. We should try to remember that."

John nods. "I hadn't thought of that, but you're right. We should."

I pull my legs up and sit cross-legged. "I still wonder if there'll ever be a day when I wake up and don't run it through my mind over and over and think about it like we're doing now."

"Eventually," he says.

"You think so?"

"That's the way it is with my memory of Riley. She's still in my mind, clear as ever. I'll never forget her, but I don't think about her every single day, five or six times a day, anymore. That's probably the way it should be." He leans back on his hands. "Want to hear something else?"

"What?"

"I haven't had nightmares lately."

"You're kidding?"

"Last night, I slept in the dark with no night light."

"Good for you." I smile at him. "Are you finally convinced your life isn't cursed? Good things can happen. You can *make* them happen if you give yourself a chance."

"I have. I really have."

His eyes lock on mine, and I kiss him. Talk about good things happening. It seems as though we're having a hard time keeping our lips apart these days, and every time our lips meet, electricity rushes through my veins and all my body parts heat up.

"It's probably midnight," I say. "I'd better take you home. Busy day tomorrow."

"You don't have to pick me up in the morning. I'll ride my bike. Seriously."

We've had this argument about three times today. John's going to Eastern Junior College tomorrow to talk to a counselor about enrolling this fall. They have a program in law enforcement, and John's decided he wants to be a cop. A good one, he says. One who will make a difference.

They also have a program in chef's training I'd like to look into. Since I've been old enough to help in my folks' place, I've wanted to be a chef. Maybe I'll have my own place or take over from Mom and Dad and make improvements in the menu. But John thinks I'm just saying that so I can do him another favor by giving him a ride. Just like sharing this party with him.

"I don't know why you're being so stubborn about this, John."

"I can't depend on you for a ride all the time."

"But we're going to the same place—Eastern JC."

He looks at me. "You're serious about being a chef?"

"I've been telling you that all day."

"You're not just making that up?"

"Hell, no."

He gives a little nod. "All right. Pick me up at nine."

Finally.

We push ourselves up from the dock and stand in the moonlight, kissing again. Crickets chirp, and the river laps at the dock posts, making little splashing sounds. I catch a whiff of John's cologne. Then we stroll toward the parking lot, our shadows wandering in front of us.

"I've been thinking about something," I tell John. "You want to drive out to Scott County Park after we finish at Eastern?"

"Sure? But why?"

"You have a swim suit?"

"No."

"We'll stop and get you one tomorrow morning."

He looks at me as though he's thinking, *What's with this girl?* "But why?"

"They have an Olympic-size pool at the park."

"So what?"

We're standing next to Old Blue in the Catfish Hut's parking lot, pole-mounted lights casting their pale glow around us.

"Well, look," I say. "If you're going to hang with me on this river and go fishing, and if a bad guy ever comes looking for you again, and if I have to take you across the river in the dark during a lightning and thunder storm—"

He laughs. "You think I should know how to swim."

I laugh too. "Right! Lessons start tomorrow. I'm the teacher."

He steps back and tilts his head. He's thinking about this really hard, wrinkles creasing his forehead. *Crap!* I can't imagine what he's going to say. I don't want him to get all pissy about his not being able to swim and my offering to help.

Finally he says, "All right. I'll let you teach me how to swim." His face breaking into a grin, he sidles up to me and slips an arm around my shoulder, the other around my waist. "But only if you let me teach you a few advanced wrestling moves."

His lips swoop down on mine, and I grapple in his arms. *Oh my!* A big hug, full body contact, and a hot kiss? I love wrestling John Hawk style.

ABOUT THE AUTHOR

After Jon Ripslinger retired as a public high school English teacher, he began a career as an author. He has published many young adult novels and truly enjoys writing books for teens. He has also published numerous short stories in *Woman's World* magazine.

Jon and his wife, Colette, live in Iowa. They are the proud parents of six children, and they have thirteen grandchildren and three great-grandchildren.

When not working writing, Jon enjoys the outdoors, especially fishing. He waits patiently for the next "big one" to strike.

ACKNOWLEDGMENTS

My thanks go first of all to Lynn McNamee, the owner of Red Adept Publishing, for offering me a contract for *The Weight of Guilt* and then guiding me though the process of publication. Next, my gratitude goes to super editors Michelle Rever and Cassie Cox. Their hard work and insightful editing have made this book better than I ever thought it could be. Thanks again, everyone!

www.ingramcontent.com/pod-product-compliance
Lightning Source LLC
Chambersburg PA
CBHW051305210726
48287CB00002B/687